I0544771

SAM CRESCENT

EVERNIGHT PUBLISHING ®

www.evernightpublishing.com

**Copyright© 2025**

**Sam Crescent**

Editor: Lisa Petrocelli

Cover Artist: Jay Aheer

ISBN: 978-0-3695-1118-8

**ALL RIGHTS RESERVED**

WARNING: The unauthorized reproduction or distribution of this copyrighted work is illegal. No part of this book may be used or reproduced electronically or in print without written permission, except in the case of brief quotations embodied in reviews.

This is a work of fiction. All names, characters, and places are fictitious. Any resemblance to actual events, locales, organizations, or persons, living or dead, is entirely coincidental.

# SAM CRESCENT

# A MONSTER IS COMING

## *Volkov Bratva, 4*

### Sam Crescent

### Copyright © 2024

### Prologue

*Niamh*

I always knew I was going to die. Never in my wildest dreams did I think it was going to be like this. Staring at the man I thought I'd fallen in love with while my father pointed the barrel of a gun at the back of my head, the last thing I want to do was cry. Tears were signs of weakness. Even though throughout my life there have been many times I've wanted to succumb to tears, I've always stopped myself. If it wasn't the memory of my mother, it certainly was the memory of my father.

I thought I'd gotten away from all of this, but that was the illusion. There is no getting away from the past.

The urge to scream was so strong, because of the pain in my body. It had been a long time since I took a beating like this. I didn't know what was worse—the fact that I hoped I'd get something out of this, or the pain of looking at the man I thought I loved. There was nothing good about any of this. There was only pain and suffering.

Anyone would think I'd be used to being lied to. Nope. It would seem I'm still a sucker for lies, for the falseness of people. Look at what trust and love did to people.

I was forced to my knees on a dirty floor. The scent of dirt, shit, and piss filled every one of my senses. I had to control the urge to vomit. The gag they'd tied across my mouth dug into either side, and I was pretty sure blood dripped from my nose. One of my eyes was swollen shut. I think that came from the first punch, courtesy of my father.

In the last twenty-four hours, I'd been hit, kicked, spat on, called every single curse name in the book. I was pretty sure my wrist was broken, possibly a few ribs, my heart, and if I was completely honest, my entire soul was a shattered mess on the floor.

There was simply no way back from this.

It didn't matter that the man before me held a gun, and it was unwavering. This was new, I was used to men being terrified of my father. Not Peter. No, he wasn't afraid of anyone.

According to my father, this man was a monster, and nearly rivaled that of his boss, Ivan Volkov.

I didn't know who Peter really was. I thought his name was Peter Shadows. I should have known it was a fake name. It was ironic, because I couldn't criticize him for using a different name. My own was indeed fake.

Niamh was real. I was not Niamh Long. No, I was Niamh Byrne, daughter of Finn Byrne, who happened to be the head of the Irish Mafia. I'd not kept up-to-date with all the lingo.

For as long as I could remember, I'd wanted out of this life. I'd wanted far away from it.

I'd tasted freedom for just a short time, but I knew what life away from death, pain, and chaos was like. One thing was certain: I would never have that taste again. Death was a guarantee for me. There was no way I would see tomorrow.

The saddest truth to date, after everything I'd learned, was I didn't *want* to see tomorrow. There was nothing worth living for.

# Chapter One

*Peter*

*Six Months Earlier*

I'd tried to come up with a million different reasons why Ivan didn't need to meet with me. Even though shit had seriously hit the fan, Ivan asking for me personally, and alone, was never good. The secret location also wasn't good. So far, I'd made it out into the middle of fucking nowhere. My soldiers hadn't been allowed to join me.

There wasn't even a chance for me to write a goodbye note. I didn't know if this was Ivan going off the deep end and killing his Brigadiers. My loyalty was without question. In the last few years, he did have a change of heart. At one point I was engaged to a horrible heiress slut, who I couldn't stand. It wasn't long after a meal with Slavik and his wife Aurora that all engagement and ties changed. This was a relief to me.

I couldn't stand the wife that had been chosen for me. She was a giant slut, which wasn't the problem. No, it was her nastiness and deep-seated evilness. I did happen to understand her, but I didn't like her. Fucking her had been easy. Sex always was, even if I didn't like the woman. Whenever Ivan needed information and it came from a woman, I was more than happy to provide. Sex was the easy part in helping Ivan become number one.

I'd do anything for that man. There was no limit, because I knew Ivan was a great man. Someone worthy of dying for.

The fog didn't help the horror about to unfold. It was no secret to me and Victor that Ivan was marrying off his Brigadiers. First Slavik, then Andrei, and the last one to fall was Ive.

There was only Victor and myself left. For the sixth Brigadier, the title was up for grabs with two people known as The Butcher and The Beast. You'd think it was two men, but Ivan had surprised me by revealing The Butcher was indeed a woman. I still didn't know her name, but I had seen her. The Beast, a man, also lived up to his reputation. Either one would prove to be one hell of a Brigadier, but I had no idea who Ivan would crown the victor.

Bringing my car to a stop, I already saw Ivan up ahead, standing at a gate overlooking the city.

He always liked the dramatics. Ivan considered himself an expert scene setter. He knew exactly how he liked things to play out. So far, I don't think anything had gone against his plan.

Again, the man knew what he was doing. Nothing had failed him, which was why the Volkov Bratva hadn't been torn apart. There were many times we could have crumbled, and Ivan kept it together. Even during that time when I thought he was dead. That seemed like a lifetime ago, but was probably only a few years, possibly more. So much shit had happened.

Ivan had known it was coming. No one could be in power for long without someone trying to take it away. I didn't know if Slavik, Andrei, Ive, and Victor remembered our warnings. That the job of a Brigadier wouldn't come without a steep cost.

Either way, I remembered, which is why I haven't given up. I wouldn't.

Parking the car, I unbuckled my seat belt and climbed out of the car. Buttoning up the two buttons of my jacket, I moved to step beside Ivan, overlooking the city.

For several seconds he didn't say a word. Together, we stood in perfect silence. There was no reason to draw too much attention. I had a horrible feeling about what will happen, and I'd rather wait for it.

Marriage wasn't something I cared for.

"You know, many years ago I used to think the fog that encompassed the city was some kind of supernatural warning. A call to a warriors' fight." Ivan turned toward me. "I was five years old. It was what made that fear worthy. Something out there was bigger than me. Bigger than all of us."

I didn't know Ivan at five years old. I'd heard rumors about him. Again, I didn't know the truth, and the last thing I wanted to do was speculate. All I knew was Ivan was rejected by his father, cast aside, and should have been killed.

Ivan was invincible. I believed that now more than ever. Nothing was going to stop him. Nothing and no one.

"Nothing to say?" Ivan asked.

"Never thought of the fog. Didn't really get the chance to see it growing up. Now, I know what it is."

Ivan nodded. "You took your time getting here."

"You asked me to come alone, and with the threats rising, my soldiers don't take too kindly to the thought of my untimely passing."

"They're going to need to get used to it. I need you to do something for me. There's a woman—"

There it was. A job. A woman.

I should have known.

"Shouldn't you use Victor? Or either The Beast or The Butcher? Aren't they eating out of your pocket?"

Ivan threw back his head and laughed. "It is good

you think I could get them to eat out of my pocket, but trust me, you're very wrong."

I doubted that. If anyone could get either or both The Beast and The Butcher, it would be Ivan. So far, keeping them both in the same place for a long time had been trying. Ivan had succeeded.

"This situation requires a delicate hand."

Now I nearly fell over myself laughing. There is no way I'd been described as having a delicate hand. Far from it. I was the one who could cause utter destruction.

"I need you to go to a small town, Pickle Quest. There you will find a woman going by the name of Niamh Long," Ivan said.

He opened his jacket and presented me with a file. Taking it meant I agreed to what was about to happen. Pickle Quest—I'd never even fucking heard of the town. Flicking open the file, I stared at a single picture of a woman. At first, I didn't care to look at it. She looked fucking bland and boring, but then I noticed something else. This picture wasn't taken when the woman was looking her best.

She had a split lip, blackening around the eye, and there even appeared to be sign of a cut disappearing into the hairline. What struck me hard was the look in the woman's eyes. She'd taken a beating, but it hadn't hit her soul. There was fire in her eyes. A desire to fight back. To get the hell away from what was hurting her.

"Who is this woman?" Peter asked.

"I told you, Niamh Long."

"And you expect me to believe you're interested in helping a total stranger?"

Ivan chuckled. "You're right. This needs to have a delicate handle. Niamh is her actual name, but her last name is different. You might have heard of a Byrne."

And then it all came clicking into place.

"This is Finn Byrne's daughter."

"If you want to get technical, she's his bastard daughter. Slept with a few whores during his time. It would seem he got his favorite pregnant, and, well, Niamh, is the subject of that ... union."

"Someone know who she is?" I asked.

"Oh, that handiwork was done by her father," Ivan said.

This made me look up from the picture. Now I was a little taken aback. Don't get me wrong, I've never met Finn personally, but rumor suggested he was very much devoted to family. Even if she wasn't born in wedlock, Finn had a lot of kids like that.

"You want me to infiltrate the Irish mob?" I asked. This might be a little hard for me to do.

I understood delicate. I also knew I had a way of going from place to place without being detected. Going into the Irish mob would be more difficult, and possibly even be a guaranteed death sentence.

There was no doubt about it. Not that I minded. If Ivan needed something, he wouldn't choose death unless he didn't have a choice.

"No, Niamh has run away."

Now this did surprise me.

"For the past year, she has evaded her father, as well as many other ... possible problems he might have. It's simple, Niamh is in Pickle Quest. You need to go and get her."

"What kind of fucked-up name is Pickle Quest?" This had to be some kind of joke.

"They're famous for their pickles," Ivan said. "Trust me, they are delicious. Back on point, I need you to go, locate Niamh, and make her fall in love with you."

This wasn't the kind of mission I thought he would have in mind. Far from it.

"Is this a joke?"

"You'd know if I was joking."

Thinking about it, Ivan was his usual self. There was no playfulness to him, no underlying mischief. Ivan usually found fun and humor in most things, but whatever it was about Niamh, he was not playing around.

I closed the file and looked at Ivan.

"What do you need me to do?" I asked.

"Plain and simply put, you need to put a baby inside her, marry her, and bring her back here, before she figures out it's all a lie," Ivan said. "For now, Finn is not preoccupied with finding his daughter. There will come a time when he realizes that mistake. Until then, we're going to fix it."

I glanced down at the closed file and then handed it back to Ivan. I already had all the information I needed.

"Get her pregnant?"

"Yes, I think it is safe to assume that if you succeed at this, Niamh Byrne will become your wife."

Ivan didn't say anything more and was about to head to his car.

"Do you not want Victor to do this? He is next in line."

I didn't know if Ivan's laughter was designed to freak me the fuck out, or to be genuine humor.

"Next in line?"

"For you to marry off," I said.

"There's no order, Peter. Besides, Victor is already busy, and it is you I need help with. You're the only one who will be able to lie to her without having a single care in the world, because I asked you to."

"What about my territory?" I asked.

"I have already taken care of it."

I was tempted to ask him if this was his way of getting me out of the picture, but I also didn't want to know.

Ivan had his reasons.

Finn Byrne was a dangerous man. I didn't even know the son of a bitch had a daughter. The very thought of a woman born to that man was a terrifying thought, and not one I relished.

There was no way this Niamh Byrne, or Long, or whatever the fuck her name was, would be a good woman.

I saw danger and I didn't know why Ivan was playing this game. This woman was pure trouble, and it wasn't going to end well, not at all. Not for any of us. I didn't like this. I couldn't stand it.

Running a hand down my face, I watch as Ivan winked at me. Gone was the serious man, even though he always lurked beneath.

"You better get started. There's an email with all the details you're going to need," Ivan said. "Time is of the essence."

I didn't like this and part of me knew Ivan was doing this to fuck with me. I didn't know why.

Whoever this Niamh Byrne was, her life was about to be fucking ruined.

****

*Niamh*

Working as a waitress wasn't so hard. Over the years I'd come to realize that taking a job at the diner was the best form of defense. I didn't know why, but everyone, be it local, regular, or even a tourist, always ended up at the diner. This was the best form of protection, though not always on a personal level.

Both men and women were not nice, and both

could be positively cruel. Yes, I'd had my ass slapped. I'd been called a lot of rude words that I didn't think children of any age should hear. But I did get to see everyone who arrived in town, which made the diner another great source of protection, While I was making my judgment of people, I was also well hidden. It helped that I wasn't a pretty girl. I was the kind of woman most people glanced over without a second look. This helped me.

If anyone came to Pickle Quest at my father's request, I would have time to make my escape, and that was most important to me.

Running away from my father wasn't the best idea I ever had, but it was the only one that made any sense. Going to my mother was out of the question. My mom was completely in love with Finn, and, well, I was the one at fault for everything. She would gladly sell my ass to the Devil if it meant she'd get a chance to marry Finn.

She had me, and had tried to have more children, but Finn Byrne was a fussy bastard. It would seem he had a taste for women, but once they gave birth, if they didn't provide him with the right kind of child, then you were all but dead to him.

This should have meant I got to grow up without a father. No such fucking luck. Nope, as much as my mother became dead to him, he kept coming around to play with her. I'd often heard him refer to her as his fuck toy, which was totally gross. She loved it, though, relished every second with him. Finn Byrne was all she wanted.

To be honest, I think she wanted the title he had to offer. It had nothing else to do with Finn. She loved the idea of people being afraid of her. That was the draw for her, the drug. She got a small taste of it and from that moment on, nothing else could compare.

Just thinking about my mother brought back all the anger and frustration I had spent a long time trying to repress. There was a time I worried about the way I felt for my mother. I feared I would turn into the very type of person I hated. The guilt would threaten to completely consume me, but now, I saw the truth.

It had taken me a long time to accept that it's perfectly fine to not like my parents. Not that it has always been easy to accept. For the longest time, all I ever wanted was to have a family like the ones depicted on billboards, or in cliché movies. Like the dad that wanted to spend time with me and see his little girl grow up, or the mom that didn't mind baking cookies or making spaghetti sauce from scratch.

That was the life I craved.

I never got it.

In fact, the last time I saw my father, I ended up with a split lip, a black eye, and a cut that bled into my hairline. This wasn't the first time I'd gotten on my dad's last nerve. What did I do? I wasn't pretty enough. He decided I looked too damn ugly, and he wanted to teach me a lesson.

There was a time when he also tried to rip my hair out. Yeah, that sucked. He wanted a blonde-haired, blue-eyed beauty. What he got was a brown-haired, brown-eyed ugly. That's what he called me.

Running away was either a stroke of genius, or completely stupid. I hadn't made up my mind yet which it was. With no one following me, I was happy to think of it as a genius move, but if he ever came for me, then I'd know I was a fucking idiot.

At least Pickle Quest was nice. Don't get me wrong, none of the locals were very accepting of a stranger. I'd been in town four months, and still, people didn't like to make small talk with me. Not that I minded. I wasn't good at small talk, or any kind of talk. It was easier not to get close to anyone. This meant I didn't have to fabricate any lies. I decided to keep to the basics. I was Niamh Long, twenty-five years old, and my parents were both dead. A tragic car accident. Graduated high school and since then, jumped from job to job as I traveled. Basic, easy to remember, and it doesn't give anyone the chance to ask questions.

So far, it had worked for me. It was terrifying. I didn't know if my father was ever going to come after me. I'd not stolen from him or my mom. Even before I left, I had been sneaking around, doing odd jobs, building some savings. The plan had always been to leave. Knowing who my father was, and what he was capable of, meant the only solid plan I had in my life was to run like hell.

That was all I wanted to do.

To be free.

Freedom wasn't quite as fun as I thought it would be. There was always that fear. The fear of my father finding where I was and ruining it. This is why I didn't even bother to try and make friends. I was guessing that was why the good locals of Pickle Quest hadn't tried to run me out of town.

I was a single woman, working hard, and not getting into anyone's business. This was all I wanted.

Plastering on a fake smile, I put down the latest steak-and-fries order. Three guys—I think they were ranchers—always came in and ordered the largest steaks the diner had to offer. The first day I worked here, I got their order wrong, and they made my life so damn hard that day. The next time, I got their order right, I expected the same kind of treatment, yet they left me alone.

This had been our pattern. They came in, ordered the biggest steak and fries, along with lots of coffee. I served them, they ate, and left.

When I first saw them, I thought they were going to cause a lot of trouble, but nope, just nice guys with a rough exterior.

My smile was pointless. With the last plate ordered, I spun around toward the door as I heard the bell dingle.

A guy I had never seen before stepped into the diner, cell phone in hand, along with a scowl on his face. My first instinct was to run. There was something about this guy that had every alarm bell going off inside my head.

I needed to run.

But he didn't even look around the diner. He didn't even see me noticing him, with how attentive he was to his cell phone. The only time he glanced up was to check for a seat, and I noticed he went toward the far corner of the diner and slid inside the small booth.

The diner wasn't too busy today, so he did have a choice. Lunchtime run had already gone, which meant we were on a steady slump till about five o'clock, when the dinner rush would start. So far, I'd not experienced anything too troubling.

This man, though… My alarm bells were ringing with his deep-black hair, and I think I'd spotted blue eyes, maybe. I hadn't really paid too much attention. He wore a white shirt, rolled up to his elbows, showcasing several tattoos, and that wasn't unusual either. A lot of the men in Pickle Quest loved to get inked. Even the three guys I served regularly had their arms heavily inked. The man in the corner was also dressed in jeans and what looked like boots. Work boots? I didn't know.

No one was serving that corner other than myself.

This was a risk. I promised myself that any question of doubt, and I'd be hightailing it right out of there. That was the super plan. Only, running away would mean defeat, for a guy that might have never come into the diner.

With my notepad and pen in hand, I made my way toward the mystery man. Squaring my shoulders, I was trying not to seem as tense as I felt. This was next to impossible. I felt so incredibly tense.

Standing in front of this man, I tried not to think or to feel, or to showcase fear. I had no idea if I was managing to achieve these things.

"Afternoon, what can I get you?" I asked.

He didn't even look up. His cell phone seemed to be interesting to him, which I was more than okay with. It allowed me to look at him closely to see if I recognized any distinguishing marks, like my father's insignia. Finn Byrne liked to use the insignia of a bull with horns dripping with blood. It was always a small symbol, but it was ugly as fuck. My dad always said that anyone willing to mark their body with such an ugly piece of shit would be loyal to him. There also had to be the initials, "FB." For generations my father and his father, and his father's father, had always been called Finn Byrne. This is why it was important to my father to marry the woman who had given him a son.

I had a brother out there. Actually, I had a lot of brothers and sisters. A woman finally giving birth to a son hadn't meant my father remained loyal to her. Nope. There were a lot of us Byrnes.

Seconds passed, maybe even minutes, as I stopped and waited for whatever he was going to order.

"What's good here"—he stopped to look up— "Niamh?"

Okay, first, I loved his deep, guttural voice. It was

kind of shocking, yet exciting at the same time. There was a slight accent there I couldn't quite place. It was so subtle, it was impossible to detect. Then the way he said my name ... wow.

"Uh, pretty much everything on the menu is good." I know because one of the perks of working here all day is they give you free lunch, so long as you try something on the menu. Over the last few months, I had tried pretty much everything.

The food was amazing. I knew why the diner was always so busy, and why a lot of people opted to come here to eat rather than cook at home.

Still, the guy hadn't said another word, so I knew he was waiting for the recommendation. Reaching out, I grabbed the menu and quickly scanned over the new recipes. "The chicken burger is great. The Mexican sub is amazing."

"I'll go with the chicken burger, extra fries, extra cheese," he said. "Also, chocolate milkshake, extra sauce."

Okay, it was wrong to be attracted to a guy I had only just seen for like five minutes, probably not even that.

Extra of everything, and a chocolate milkshake.

I quickly wrote down his order, kept a smile on my face, and then turned to leave. My nerves had started to get the better of me. I felt that twisting in my stomach, and that sick feeling I struggled to ignore.

Ringing up the new order, I told myself not to turn back and look, but I just couldn't help it. Turning back toward the corner of the room, the mystery man was still looking at his cell phone. He had absolutely no interest in me whatsoever.

I didn't know why all my senses were going off, but right now, I hated every one of them. This guy posed no threat to me. He didn't work for my father, and I needed to learn to stop freaking out. I'm the one that had nearly caused a scene. This was just a hot guy, traveling. I didn't know his name, who he was, or what he was doing, and it didn't matter to me either way.

We were two strangers who had found Pickle Quest, and that was how it was going to stay.

## Chapter Two

*Peter*

Niamh wasn't a total fucking idiot. That surprised me. The moment I entered the diner three days ago, I saw the way she tensed up. She sensed danger while I was close by. That was a good thing. She knew there were enemies out there, and at least she attempted to do something about it. Still, I didn't fucking like it either way.

Sticking to my cell phone was the easiest option. Also, glancing through emails was quite innocent. Pickle Quest didn't have a whole host of jobs, but there were some I didn't want—like trash collecting. I didn't have a problem with cleaning up trash, but that didn't give me the opportunity to get close to Niamh. According to the information Ivan had sent me, she had a library card, worked at the diner, and it would seem she had joined the local gym.

I wasn't working at a library on the off chance she'd turn the fuck up to bring back a book. Nor was I working in the diner, that would be too … suspicious. The new guy getting a job at the diner just wouldn't work.

Niamh wasn't stupid, which was also a benefit to her. I had a great deal of respect for her because of her nervousness.

No, the only way I was going to blend in and make this work was the fucking gym. I had no problem with working out, but I had to become a personal fucking trainer. Again, not a problem, but I had to hope Niamh arrived at the gym.

Getting the job on the day of my arrival into town had been easy. I'd already told Ivan my plans, and my resume was fucking ace. He'd also sent me a load of documents that gave me a few days to become acquainted with my new role. I'm a quick study, and since I had no problem working out, this was the easy part.

The guy who owned the gym, Carl Fields, wanted me to slowly get acquainted with everything—all the equipment, the rooms—and to assess each room before taking on a client.

This is what I'd been doing the last three days. The gym opened at five-thirty in the morning, and didn't close until eight at night. I didn't have a problem with the long hours. It worked with my plan to blend in. According to Ivan, no details had gone out about Niamh being missing. I didn't expect there to be.

Finn Byrne wasn't going to announce to the world that his bastard daughter was missing. I got the message loud and clear from Ivan. Just because a notice hadn't gone out, and there were no alerts didn't mean someone wasn't out looking for her now. So, I had to be careful.

I also needed to protect Niamh while also winning her heart. It shouldn't be too hard to win her over. I expected this to be easy. Niamh was curious about me. I detected a bit of fear as well, but that was expected. She didn't know who I was or what I was doing there.

After dealing with the Finn Byrnes of the world, I knew I was going to blow her mind.

Walking around the gym at six that morning, I saw a couple of women who'd appeared. I knew I was on their radar and if needed, I had plenty of women to keep me company while I worked on winning over Niamh.

For a split-second I wondered if gaining her attention would come from flirting with someone else.

I stepped into the swimming pool area and stopped, because the very woman I'd been thinking about was sitting at the edge of the pool.

The door closed behind me, but it was silent and Niamh was so lost in her own little world, that she didn't even look up to see what had caused the noise. She kept staring down at the water below her.

I watched as she moved her feet through the water. Her lips moved, but I didn't know what she said. Pulling her feet from the water, I watched as she squared her shoulders and then moved to the corner of the pool. She gripped the metal rail leading into the water, and slowly began to climb in.

It was then I realized what the problem was. Niamh was terrified.

She got into the water and still held onto the steps. She took several deep breaths, and I saw the fear in her eyes, and she let go of the rail and began to sink into the water. There was no one around.

I didn't even know why she had opted to go in the swimming pool if it scared her so freaking much. I didn't like it, though. She looked so small, so fragile. Stepping toward the pool edge where she was gripping the handle for dear life, I crouched down.

"You know, if you can't swim, you'd be better served learning by going to the top of the pool," I said.

"Thanks, but I'm not afraid."

"You've nearly bent the handlebar," I said.

This did get her attention. The handlebar was fine. There was no way she was going to break that, but she did loosen her grip a little.

"If you can swim, then you want to tell me what the problem is?" I asked.

"Nothing."

"You're not afraid?"

"No, I'm not afraid."

"Most people who come to swim don't look like they're afraid of the water wrapping around them and dragging them down," I said.

"Why would you say something like that?" Niamh glanced down into the water.

The deep end was always a darker color and this made me smile, because you couldn't see the bottom of the pool. I sighed, got to my feet, and then climbed in, fully clothed.

"What are you doing?" she asked.

I ignored her. I had a feeling that getting close to Niamh would not be smooth sailing, as I anticipated. Unlike some of the women I'd caught the eye of, Niamh didn't like the thought of me getting too close.

Climbing into the water, I put my hand over hers, and this caused her to let go of the handle rail. It wasn't exactly my intention to cause this.

She sunk beneath the water and on instinct, I grabbed the strap of her bathing suit, hauling her up to her feet, and keeping her head above the water. I paddled my feet and kept hold of the rail.

"You can't swim," I said.

"I can, and it's not like it's so hard." She frowned.

The last thing I wanted to do was argue with her, so I let go of her suit and she sunk beneath the water. She screamed, so I grabbed her suit again and lifted her up.

"What the hell?" she asked, pushing her hair out of her face, but I noticed she didn't shove at me to let her go.

"Do you want to keep arguing with me?" I asked.

"No, I don't want to argue with you. This was a

big mistake, and right now I need to go home."

"Or, you can swallow your pride and ask me to help you."

"What?"

I didn't know if it was wrong to find her entertaining, but I did.

"You can say, 'Peter, I don't know how to swim, can you help me?'" I tempted to mock her and do it in a female voice, but instead, I decided I was already embarrassing her, and the last thing I wanted to do was make her uncomfortable.

She frowned and I saw her gaze past my shoulder. She wasn't so stupid after all. Niamh was already planning her escape because she didn't have a clue who I was, and she was starting to think like a survivor.

"Who is Peter?" she asked.

"Me, my name is Peter."

"Is that your real name?"

This made me smile. "Yes, it does happen to be my real name."

She nodded after a few seconds.

I waited.

She looked at the water, then at me, before her gaze went behind me. There she went with her deep breathing, and I waited patiently.

Holding onto the strap of her suit, I couldn't help but notice how … full her tits were. This was a surprise to me, because I didn't plan to notice Niamh. I'd do exactly as Ivan said. Put a baby in her womb, make her mine. I didn't need to be attracted to her to achieve that. I could get my dick hard and ready for her when the time came. For now, there would be no fucking until I worked on winning her over.

"Peter, will you teach me how to swim?" she

asked.

This surprised me. I expected her to be a dick over this, and stubborn.

Offering her a smile, I let go of the handle rail. I'd never taught anyone how to swim, but it wasn't exactly hard.

My father liked the hard and rough way of training. He had no qualms about throwing his kid into the deep end and forcing him to learn to swim. He did this to me many times. There was no room in the Orlov family for a weak man. He wanted strong men, and if any of his sons, or daughters for that matter, were to drown, then so be it.

I lost a sister and a brother to that method. He didn't shed a tear. Now that I think about it, neither did my mother. I nearly died that day, and during every task he gave me.

He was a cruel man.

Leaving Niamh to fight was not an option. I now gripped onto both straps of her swimsuit. As much as I'd have loved to stay in the deep end of the pool, Niamh had to learn to swim.

"What are you doing?" she asked, almost in a state of panic.

"I'm going to teach you how to swim, but you're going to be doing it my way. Kick your feet out and stop fighting me. I'm not going to hurt you." Not unless Ivan demanded it.

Right now, Niamh was on the "safe and protected" list. If that were to change, I'd have no qualms about doing what needed to be done. If Ivan wanted her dead, she'd be dead.

Niamh surprised me by doing exactly as I asked, and she kicked her feet out. I know she struggled as I moved backward, swimming toward the shallow end.

My feet hit the edge of the pool, and now I was able to stand and simply walk back. Once we got to the center of the pool, I let Niamh go, and she got to her feet and stood. The water came to our chests, but it was safe enough for both of us.

"Thank you," Niamh said.

"Do you think that is the end of your lesson?" I asked.

"I … I … just thank you."

"Why did you go to the deep end of the pool if you didn't know what you were doing?" I asked.

Niamh shrugged and at the same time tucked some of her hair behind her ear. "I don't know. I figured it would all come to me on instinct. I didn't exactly get a lot of time to learn to swim."

"Your parents didn't teach you?"

This made her laugh. "My parents didn't have time for me."

I saw how vague her answer was, and this made me smile. She was cautious. This was good. I didn't have to worry about her telling anyone her little secret. The fewer people who knew meant it would be easier to keep her safe. In the small town of Pickle Quest, strangers were easy to detect, and the easiest way to be left alone was to blend in.

This is why I had joined the gym. It didn't look like I was after anything in town, other than a job. I didn't need a job. I had a job—Brigadier to Ivan Volkov with my own territory to run. For now, until my mission was complete, I would be a gym employee in Pickle Quest.

Ivan had to be fucking laughing at all of this.

"So you thought about throwing yourself into the deep end in the hope of not drowning?"

"I didn't exactly think it through."

"Well, at least I was here, and now your lessons can start. Come on, it's time to get you ready to swim." I didn't know what the hell I was doing, but it wouldn't be hard. Unlike my brother and sister, I didn't die that day, and I had no choice but to figure it out.

****

*Niamh*

Taking lessons from the new guy in town wasn't exactly what I had in mind when I decided to stay away from him. It had been three days since he arrived in town, and I already knew he'd made an impression.

Several women, young and old, married and single, had spotted him as well. I heard them talking at the diner about the new guy who worked at the gym.

The moment I arrived in town, after getting the job at the diner, along with a library card, which I rarely used, I also decided to join the gym.

My parents had often criticized me about my size. It had been never ending, so I decided to change myself completely. So far, I'd been able to lose a couple of pounds. I also found them in the food served at the diner. I wanted to look so different that my parents would never recognize me. I knew it would take dedication and time.

Losing weight had never been my strong point. I'd been placed on so many diets. My mom, in trying to impress my father, had even attempted to starve me. That didn't work either. My weight was always a problem to them.

I thought swimming would help me the most. It was a lonely thing to do. I didn't need anyone else to watch me, or keep an eye on my progress, and it worked a lot of muscles by simply going back and forth. This sounded like an awesome plan. The only problem was I didn't know how to swim.

Since joining the gym, I had tried different machines and rooms to help me, but none of them worked.

This was supposed to be my solid solution. Now, the one guy I'd been determined to stay away from was the one person who insisted on helping me. This surprised me.

For the next two hours, he got me working on my stance, my posture, and working my body until it was at just the right angle. He wouldn't allow me to let go of the side of the pool.

By the end of the session, my arms hurt, and my legs felt like they'd done a marathon rather than kicked out repeatedly to the same rhythm.

Peter called time to the lesson, and helped me out of the pool.

My legs ached and I knew I wasn't going to have any trouble sleeping tonight. I was already so tired, but I had to get ready for my shift that started at nine.

"I want you back here tomorrow," Peter said.

"What?"

"You heard me."

"But … don't you think there needs to be a break in between?" I didn't know if I wanted to see him again. I wasn't even sure if I was coming back to the gym. The thought of being around this stranger terrified me. I didn't know who he was or why he'd come to Pickle Quest.

I couldn't start asking a lot of questions in case *he* wanted to start asking questions, and I didn't want to answer any of them.

"The only way you're going to learn is to keep practicing. Think of muscle memory," he said.

"And you're going to be the one to teach me?" I didn't want it to sound like I had a crush on him or anything. I didn't. I'd promised myself not to get close to anyone.

"Yes, I'll teach you, but it will have to be my method. No one else's."

I nibbled my lip. That didn't exactly sound promising. In fact, it was a little terrifying.

"I don't know how anyone else works here. I'm still new, and learning the ropes. I'm going to need to start taking clients soon. You'd be my first, and you'd be helping me out."

I highly doubted it. Peter was a sexy man, and she'd already seen a lot of women interested in him. All he'd need to do was click his fingers and she had no doubt women would flock to him.

But, she did need this help. It was all part of her plan, and what was the point in running away if she wouldn't learn to defend herself?

"Okay, then I will see you tomorrow, six o'clock," I said. I'd never been able to sleep in late.

In fact, I struggled to get to sleep, kind of out of fear. I didn't imagine it helped the fear when your mother or father could walk in and start hurting you at any time. Yes, I had that. My dad had come in once, he'd been super pissed. I think it was because of something my mother did. Again, I didn't know the whole story, but I was the one that got hit with the end of his belt. He even made sure to use the buckle. The pain had hurt so bad, and I still had the scars on my back, butt, and thighs to show for it. That hadn't been a good day.

Afterward, it was the first time my mother had shown me any kind of affection. She'd been the one to rile my father, but I'd taken the beating she should have.

I couldn't help but wonder about my messed-up

life.

"I've got to get ready for work," I said.

"Ah, you know what, I'll wait for you. I've been designated with getting coffee and breakfast this morning. The order has already been placed. I'll walk you to the diner."

*Great. Every time I tried to create a distance between myself and this man, he seemed determined to close it.*

"Yay," I said, and hoped he didn't detect the level of sarcasm I knew was dripping from my voice.

I left the pool area and went straight to the changing rooms. I pulled the key from around my ankle and opened my locker. The key was mine as I paid for my gym membership. Seeing as I was on the run from my family, I rented a small apartment, and any money I had I spent on essentials only. I only ever had enough belongings to pack in a small bag, so I could be on the road in less than thirty minutes. The gym membership was a luxury, but seeing as I didn't plan to buy ornaments, or anything like a TV or a car, there was no point in worrying about the expense. Also, this helped toward the bigger plan—getting into shape and changing what I looked like, so it would help me hide longer.

To me, it sounded like a genius plan. On paper, it probably made me sound like a nutjob, which I could handle. I was more than happy for people to be afraid of me.

"Oh my, did you see what he looked like? Those arms … I bet they can show a woman a time or two."

"Arms, come on, girl, we've got to talk about the man's hands. His arms don't matter, but it's all about the hands. He could touch me any day."

"What is his name?"

Several women had entered the changing room,

and I could imagine who they were talking about.

"I think it's Peter. I don't know his last name. That man does not need a last name. All he needs to do is help me forget what my last name is."

There was a chorus of laughter.

I finished getting changed and stepped out of the small cubicle.

The ladies stopped talking, but I didn't pay them any attention. When I left, the door closed on a round of giggles. I didn't want to know what they were giggling at.

Peter was standing at the main desk, cell phone in his hand, one leg crossed over the other. He'd also changed out of the clothes that were soaking wet. He was in a new set of sweatpants and another shirt with the gym's logo, which was an image of a treadmill with the initial, "CF." Carl Fields was the owner of the gym. I heard him talking in detail about how hard it was to think of a logo.

I think his date hadn't been quite so impressed with his idea of dinner conversation. It was kind of funny, but so boring.

"You're ready," he said, standing tall.

"What's your last name?" I asked, and immediately regretted it. One of my key rules was not to ask questions. The less I knew, the better. The less I wanted to know, it meant others wouldn't want to know my business either, and that was the way I wanted to keep it.

"Shadow. Peter Shadow," he said. "What's your last name, Niamh?"

I opened my mouth about to tell him. "Wait, how do you know my first name?"

"Well, besides the fact that it's on your uniform." He pointed toward my uniform. "It's a pretty name and

I've made sure to always remember a pretty girl's name."

This made me open my mouth and then close it. Never had I been called "pretty." He had to be lying.

Rather than smile, I felt myself frowning even more. "Niamh Long," I said. It wasn't my name.

It had taken me several nights, constantly repeating my name—Niamh Long, Niamh Long—until it became second nature to say that name. I wanted Niamh Byrne to die, and the only way to do that was to make sure she didn't exist.

Stepping around him, I wanted to slap myself silly. Breaking rules because of listening to a bunch of giggling women. It wasn't the first time I'd heard them drooling over a guy. When they had their fun with Peter *Shadow*, then they'd move on to whatever flavor they wanted next. I'd seen the way this went.

Even though I hadn't been in town long, I'd been there long enough to see the trend. They liked shiny new toys, and Peter was a prime toy.

We stepped out of the gym, and I liked the fact that it was only a short walk toward the diner, and it would be a lot faster by car. But anyone attempting to lose weight wouldn't use a car, right? I didn't like the thought of making small talk, that was when mistakes were made.

I wasn't trying to be rude. I just didn't want to make small talk with anyone. It was easier this way.

"You know, I'm starting to get the sense that I have done something to upset you," he said.

"That's impossible. I don't even know you, so you can't do anything to upset me."

"No? Then why does it feel like I have?"

I wanted to argue with him, but as we got to the diner, I stopped and turned toward him. "You don't have to lie to me. I'm not under any illusion about what I look like. You're going to teach me how to swim, and I'm going to keep letting you. Lying is not going to change that, unless you don't want to help me."

And with that, I spun on my heel and walked straight to work.

## Chapter Three

*Peter*

I should let it go.

All day long I couldn't help but see the hurt in Niamh's eyes, and I didn't know exactly what had put it there, but I did know it pissed me off. She looked so damn hurt.

I didn't know what I lied about.

I'm not usually so distracted and not when it came to female bullshit. Niamh had confused me. For the rest of the day, she played on my mind. Even when Carl was giving me a hearty slap on the back for getting more people to sign up at the gym. It didn't come as a surprise to me that more women wanted to know if I had planned to become a personal trainer.

All I knew was how to train myself. I knew nothing about being a personal trainer or doing that kind of shit. I'd read through the paperwork Ivan sent me, and it seemed pretty straightforward. My only problem was, my goal was to get Niamh, and the only way to do that was to blend in.

So, against my better judgment, I began to take on a few more potential clients. Carl had given me the files on every member who wanted a personal trainer. He had everyone fill out detailed applications to help us better understand their personal goals. It made a lot of sense, and seeing as Niamh was also my client, I had gotten hers as well. Sitting alone in one of the many offices, I glanced at Niamh's file. The lies of her name were there, but I noticed she didn't lie about anything else. Standard information was there, including where she currently lived. I knew this information. When it got to her goals, she had simply indicated she wanted to be half the weight she was now. That was all. It didn't tell me why she was pissed off.

By eight o'clock, I still wasn't any wiser. I did, however, have three women I now had to train. Each of them had an appointment tomorrow. I'd start my day with Niamh, which also meant I'd become the guaranteed coffee-and-breakfast collector for the staff. I could walk Niamh to work, get the food, come back, eat breakfast, then I had Colleen from ten until twelve. Then I had lunch break. Anna, from one to three, then from four until six, I had Caitlynn. Two of the three women were married.

I already had a rough idea of what I was going to do, but right now, I was more interested in dealing with Niamh and her lack of tact.

Tonight, the diner closed at nine. I didn't mind waiting.

Staring into the diner from my car, I watched as Niamh worked around the room. There were still several customers, and she kept the fake smile. Seconds passed, then minutes, and I expected boredom to sink in. Watching a woman work was not my idea of fun, and yet she worked that room so well. Every now and then, she'd tuck some of her long brown curls behind her ear.

She looked exhausted. This morning, I had worked her body, trying to do the whole muscle-memory trick. I didn't know if it would work, but it would be better than allowing her to drown.

My cell phone began to buzz, and I didn't even bother to look at the caller. There was only one person who would call me.

"Hello," I said.

"Settling in?"

"Yes."

"Have you put a baby inside her?"

"I know you think our sperm is magical, Volkov, but remember, it still takes time."

"So what you're telling me is you're losing your touch?"

Even though I couldn't see the bastard, I knew he was finding this humorous. I wasn't entertained, not even a little. This was a job. Nothing else.

"I'll get it done," I said.

"What is your progress?"

"I'm teaching her how to swim," I said. "That is my job."

Ivan laughed. I didn't find the humor in this.

"Do I even want to know?" Ivan asked.

"No."

Again, the laughter.

"Do you need me to come home? I could just grab her, we could lock her up in one of Ive's cages, and we could get what we want that way?" That sounded way more logical to me than getting a woman to fall in love with me so I could knock her up.

It wasn't a solid plan. This was Ivan's plan, and I knew he had a reason, but I didn't see how this was gong to work. Niamh was skittish, for good reason. I needed to break down those walls she'd built. This was going to take fucking time.

"Yes, that would be an easy plan, but it's not what I want, and seeing as I'm the boss, and I like to get what I want…"

"Then I better hang up and get the job done," I said.

"Time is ticking."

Ivan hung up before I did.

Staring at the phone, the urge to crush it was

strong, but that would cause more problems.

My only problem was a brown-haired stubborn woman who looked so freaking tired. Niamh was twenty-five years old, and as I looked at her, I couldn't help but remember the pictures Ivan had shown me. She'd been beaten, not too badly, but enough. I imagine having Finn Byrne as a father wasn't all it was cracked up to be.

Something told me that Niamh had been used to a few hits in her time. Also, I had seen the scars on her thighs, at the back, front, and some disappeared under the swimsuit she wore. Those were the kind of scars you got from the metal end of a belt. There was a lot more to Niamh than met the eye.

I know, because I had them myself. The ink helped hide them, but if I ran my fingers across that part of my skin, there were still raised scars.

The minutes ticked by, and I watched as the last customer left. Niamh didn't leave right away. She stayed behind, helped clean up, and then at nine-thirty, she stepped out of the diner.

I climbed out of my car, and she spotted me, even though she tried to pretend she couldn't see me.

"Anyone ever tell you that you're a terrible actress?" I asked.

Niamh sighed, glanced at me, and then took several steps toward me. "What do you want?" she asked.

I stared at her and knew I had to choose my words carefully. "This morning, you accused me of lying, and I didn't like it. Also, I don't know exactly what you accused me of. What did I lie about?"

Niamh tilted her head to the side and I watched as she licked her lips. Three women had licked their lips suggestively at me today. Niamh wasn't one of them. I doubted she even realized what she was doing, and I could tell she was just deep in thought.

"I, uh, I, when you called me pretty … you don't need to lie to me about stuff like that. I'm going to come and learn to swim, and you don't need to dress it up, or do any of that. I'm not a child. I know the truth."

This made me fold my arms across my chest. "You think I was treating you like a child?"

"Yes. You don't need to call me pretty or pretend or anything like that."

I smiled. "Okay, so to be clear, you don't like me saying you're pretty."

"I don't like you telling me lies," Niamh said.

I took a step toward her, then another. Much to my surprise, Niamh didn't back down. She stayed perfectly still. I don't know if that made her smart, or real fucking stupid. Possibly a mixture of both. I was taller than her and Niamh had no choice but to tilt her head back to look at me. From this angle, it felt like she was at my mercy, and in a way, she was. I didn't know how far I could push it. Should I touch her? Grip the back of her neck? Give her a warning?

Her lips were so close and so tempting, but I didn't close that distance between us.

"Between us, Niamh, I wasn't lying. In fact, I think you're very pretty, and I broke the rules of the gym today in saying so. I'm not supposed to say things like that to clients. But, when I see a beautiful woman, I'm not going to lie to her." The urge to kiss her was strong, but I had to play this game right.

Diving in with Niamh, she wouldn't trust it. She was messed up in the head, and I got it. It didn't take a genius to know who her father was, and to have been in her company for a couple of hours to recognize it. Also, it helped one messed-up head to recognize another.

I'd been forced to watch my brother and sister

drown. That was how messed up my father was. He wanted his children to see what happened to weaklings. Only the strong Orlov survived.

I had tried to dive into that pool to save my sister and brother. On each occasion I had been forced to take a swift punishment—a beating. It had been easy to take, especially because I'd been dealing with the grief of watching my siblings die.

My father had been evil.

He didn't care, and because they had died as weaklings, he wouldn't even mark their graves with the name Orlov. They had been buried, and a simple cross had been placed to show where they were. No other details. Like strangers.

Stepping back, I moved to the car and opened the passenger door. "Get in," I said.

"I'm not getting in a car with you. I don't even know you."

This made me smile. "Good, but you're going to get in the car, and I'm taking you home."

"You don't know where I live."

"Actually, I do."

This made her tense up.

"How?" she asked.

"You filled out all the details at the gym. I got to read your file today, seeing as you're my first client. I need to start taking on more clients. I saw your address, and it is not hard to remember. It's late. I'll take you home." I didn't want her walking the streets. She might have been okay to do this before I arrived, but I wouldn't allow her to do it now.

"You don't have to do that," she said.

Stubborn woman.

"You do realize it doesn't matter where you go, murderers and psychopaths are everywhere."

"Nothing bad happens in Pickle Quest. Trust me, it's a nice town."

It wasn't going to be nice for long, while Niamh and I stayed here. We were going to bring danger and chaos.

"I can pick your ass up and force your butt in my car if you'd like," I said.

She folded her arms and I waited, brows raised. If she wanted to test me, then I was more than happy to force her into my car.

I took a step toward her and she quickly held up her hands. "Okay, fine, it's okay. It's fine. I'll get in the car."

I suspected she was going to run away, but it would seem I didn't have the first clue as to how Niamh was going to react. She walked toward me, slid past, and sat in the passenger seat of my car. This was progress.

I put the child lock on the door and slammed it closed. I wasn't stupid, and of course, as I rounded the car, I watched her test the door handle. She was going to try and make her escape, just as I knew she would. It was good to know some of my instincts were right on point with Niamh.

Whistling to myself, I climbed into the driver's side of the car, and started up the engine. My machine purred to life, and I began to pull out of the parking space and head onto the road, in the direction of Niamh's apartment building.

I hadn't rented an apartment in a shitty part of town. There were some things I refused to do. Instead, I had purchased a house in not the best part of town, but a decent street that had kids playing out in their front yard. I would blend. There were several men who were bachelors living on the street. It was a nice family location, which was one of the reasons I got it. I would lie to Niamh and say I rented it from a friend.

There were some creature comforts I would take with me. During the whole drive, Niamh didn't speak at all, but I knew her game. She was trying to keep things as distant between us as possible. I could play that game. It would only be a matter of time before she talked to me.

\*\*\*\*

*Niamh*

*One Week Later*

I expected Peter to get bored.

Instead, the lessons at the gym were every day, except Sundays when the gym was closed. Not only were we now working on my swimming, Peter had also opted for different exercise strategies. I thought he was going to get me on the treadmill or doing weights, or other machine-based routines.

Instead, we had to do stretches, and work out muscles. Before we went to the pool, he got me on the mat, working on my core, doing some stretches and yoga poses. My body was not designed to do any of these, but he wouldn't take us straight to the pool.

One hour with close contact—him touching different parts of my body, showing me how to do each pose so I didn't hurt myself. Then we did an hour in the pool, followed by a thirty-minute cooldown session back on the mats.

Peter was always there.

Close to me.

Six days a week.

That wasn't all. I intended to keep my distance, which should have worked, but didn't. He would wait for me because Peter had volunteered to walk me to work. Yep, every day, Monday through Saturday. I also happened to have Sunday off work, not that I did a lot with my time.

Then, to top it all off, after work, Peter waited for me. He would drive me home. So far, for the past week, I had been able to keep silent. No small talk. No risk of giving away little secrets I wanted to stay hidden.

My only reprieve from all things Peter were the hours I worked, and when I went home to sleep. Unless my traitorous sleep ignored my request, and made me think about Peter.

I didn't like any of this.

I totally got that Peter was an attractive man, but I'd never been put in a position like this. I'd never been close to any man. Not even the men my father brought around. Sometimes he got my mother to entertain them. There were times I truly felt my father loved the power he held over my mother. The fact he could get her to do anything he wanted with a simple click of his fingers. It was a power play to him, one he thoroughly enjoyed, and annoyed me.

Ignoring the thoughts of my parents, I stretched my arms out in front of me, drawing my ass back and then flopped down on the mat, all too aware of Peter's hands at the base of my back.

"That's it," he said. "Slowly, remove the tension."

There was no way I was removing any kind of tension. My whole entire body was tense, my core was tense.

His fingers massaged areas I wasn't used to being touched, and as he pushed up the shirt I wore, I remembered the scars on my back. Quickly, I moved, pulled away from him, and spun around on the carpet.

"I've got to get to work," I said.

We'd already done a lot of stretches, and time in the pool. This was our cooldown session where I only had a shirt and the bathing suit to provide protection for myself. Not that I thought I was in any kind of danger from Peter.

All my life I'd been told I wasn't the kind of woman men wanted. There was no desire, no passion, no yearning, nothing. I was perfectly okay with that. I didn't know how long I would be in Pickle Quest. It wasn't that I had a solid plan. Far from it. The only plan I had was to keep moving. Not to get too comfortable in one place and not to build bridges, or even chance a relationship.

My father could use it against whoever decided to be in a relationship with me, and I would not let that happen. This was my problem, and I was going to deal with it in my way.

"I told you, you've got to cooldown. It's good for the muscles."

He went to reach for me, but I held my hand up. "Which I totally get, but I feel fine. No stiff muscles, no other worries or concerns." I started to chuckle, trying to distract him. This helped me scramble to my feet. "Thank you," I said.

I hesitated before heading toward the changing rooms, but I didn't even get a step before Peter grabbed my hand and pulled me close.

"What's the problem?" he asked.

"Nothing. There is no problem." We were very close, and for some odd reason, I didn't know if I liked it. I was trying not to freak out.

"Haven't I shown that you can trust me?" he asked.

I'd not really been assessing him on trust. Did I believe he was who he said he was? Part of me did. The one side of my brain that had to wonder why a hot guy would work at a gym in a small town. I'd made up all kinds of stories during my lunch break and slow periods at the diner, to help stave off boredom. None of them made any sense. I'd thought he could be an assassin, part of the Italian Mafia, part of the British Mafia—I didn't even know if there was a British Mafia—or a gang, maybe. Again, I wasn't exactly up to date on the kind of rival gangs my father had enemies in. He might not even be the enemy to my father. For all I know, this was his right-hand man.

Then, I'd decided he was a runaway like me. Or, he was just plain and simply a guy trying to find his place in the world. I was both—a runaway who was trying to find her place in the world without causing anyone to get hurt.

"Ugh, I really … I don't even know why I have to trust you, but work is calling." Also, I had a strange sensation as he held onto my hand. I … kind of liked it. I think. Again, I'm not sure. I'm not used to men touching me, unless it's my dad giving me a beating or a punishment for whatever bad stuff I'd been accused of, mainly by my mother. There went the sucky memories again.

It wasn't so bad, not all the time.

Not that I can remember a good time with my dad. He'd never been the kind of father I could get a hug from. He never kissed my boo-boo or told me everything was going to be okay. Never. Neither had my mother. Whenever I did get a cut or graze, I had to take care of it myself.

Peter let me go, and I nearly breathed a sigh of relief. I had to get away, as far away as soon as possible. This was scary.

I stepped into the changing rooms, going to my locker like I did every day. Grabbing my stuff, I snuck into the bathroom and changed into my waitress uniform. My hair was nearly dry from doing the cooldown stretches.

Opening the door, I almost jumped out of my skin. There was one of the women I noticed lurking around the gym the past few days, watching Peter.

"You know, he will never go for someone like you," she said.

Normally, I'm very good with names and faces, but I was drawing a blank with this woman.

"I have no idea what you're talking about," I said.

She took a step toward me and then pressed a long, thin finger against my chest.

"Back the fuck off him. He's not yours to have."

I was being threatened. This was now clear to me. The woman startled me because she had a wedding ring on her hand.

"Look, I don't know who you are, or why you're even doing this, but you've got this all wrong. Peter is helping me learn to swim and that is all." I wasn't here to cause problems. All I wanted was to be invisible.

She glared at me, and I quickly left the changing rooms, stepped out into the main entrance of the gym, only to come face-to-face with the problem.

Peter was growing a little fan base. Again, it wasn't hard to see. Being a waitress made me seen but not heard, and allowed me to listen in on all kinds of conversations. I was aware he'd taken on more clients, which brought me back to the trust issue.

I couldn't help but worry. The heavy brick in the pit of my stomach that caused me to freak out, also helped keep me on my toes.

"You're ready?" he asked.

No, no, no, I wasn't ready. This was not helping me. The idea of coming to the gym was to lose weight. To attempt to change what I looked like. I knew this wasn't going to be plastic surgery kind of changes, but it might help me become unrecognizable. Yeah, I even struggled not to mock myself at the very thought.

"Look, I think I should go alone today." As I made the suggestion, I was already walking toward the main doors in the hope of doing exactly that, only Peter had other plans.

What was it with this man constantly grabbing at me? This wasn't fair. He all but dragged me to his car. I wonder if I could still scream "stranger danger," and whether it would count. Not that I was going to do that.

Being dragged to a car by a guy I didn't know wasn't exactly knew to me. My dad had a tendency to do it often. He'd send one of his goons to pick me up. The first time it happened when I was a kid, I was so excited. My dad had come to get me. Well, not my dad, but someone who knew my dad, worked for him. Yeah, for some reason, that ended up with me getting my face slapped and locked in my bedroom for the weekend, with someone pushing only bars of candy beneath my door. By the time he left, the place was trashed, and Mom was crying. I did have an en-suite bathroom, so there were no worries about toilet breaks.

That happened often, which sucked big time.

It didn't take me long to figure out a way to escape. No one came to check on me, so finding a ladder and using all the courage I could, I'd climbed out of my bedroom window and made my escape.

Peter opened the car door, and like every other time, he put the child lock on. Every time I left his car, I might also remove the child lock, but I couldn't seem to completely get rid of it. Not going to happen. I didn't know the first thing about cars.

He slammed the door closed, and I couldn't help but wonder what had pissed him off. It wasn't me, or it shouldn't be me, because I didn't do anything wrong.

My stupid brain was working against me, and suddenly began to list the potential things I'd done wrong. First, insult him. Second, during our beginning warm-up, I might have accidently kicked him in the balls. Again, that hadn't been intentional. I'd not been trying to hurt him. In fact, what I had been trying to do was stretch, and his fingers touched my stomach, I flinched, and somehow managed to knee him in the balls.

He rounded the car, and then climbed into the passenger seat. Every other time, he started up the engine, and we'd drive off toward the diner. He didn't turn over the ignition. No sound of a purring car. We sat there in silence.

I wondered if his little stalker was at a window, her face pressed against the glass. I had to stifle a giggle at the thought of her face pressed against the glass, watching me, watching us.

There was no *us*.

"Do you want to tell me what the problem is?" Peter asked.

"Yeah, you're not listening to me. I've got to get to work, and we're just sitting here, staring."

"Something is bothering you," he said.

"Nothing is bothering me." I pushed some of the hair off my face. I didn't get a chance to put my hair in a proper ponytail, and strands were escaping. "Just a warning, though, there is a woman who I think might be stalking you. I don't know if you and she have anything going on, but she has told me to pretty much stay away from you. Also, I think she might have hinted at me having ideas when it came to you. I *don't* have ideas. In case you were wondering. I don't even think about it, so you don't have to worry about any of that because I don't have feelings for you."

I couldn't help but ramble.

Peter was looking at me, and it made me a little uneasy because I didn't know why. I didn't know what to say or do, so I continued to look ahead in the vain hope that I knew what I was doing.

"I'll handle Wendy," he said, turning over the ignition.

And just like that, it would seem the conversation was terminated. Not going to lie, I was a little disappointed, and I didn't even know why.

## Chapter Four

*Peter*

*One Month Later*

This was new for me.

I was not used to a woman being like … Niamh. I thought I was breaking her down insisting on the close contact, stretch exercises, but I didn't even think she registered what was happening. If she did, she was completely silent about it. Sometimes, she even hummed.

When I was in the pool with her again, there was nothing. No sign of arousal. It's like she's completely oblivious to me being a man. I didn't get it.

Driving up to the private location early Sunday morning, I put my car into "park," climbed out, and stared off into the forest. As a kid, I was forced to hunt in a forest. It was part of being an Orlov. According to my father, a real man can survive anything, all weather conditions, all woodland creatures. To survive meant power. It meant making the elements my bitch. Again, all according to my father, which was a load of bullshit.

I lost a sister with this new wave of testing. My father wanted strong children, not weaklings. My sister was killed by running away from what had scared her. We found her, fallen, blood seeping from her head. Death had already claimed her. She must have fallen. What I didn't know at the time was my father actually paid people to hunt for us. He wanted to test our strength. Sick fuck. I had killed anyone who came near me when it was my time in the woods.

Being the eldest son, he ran all tests through me,

and I never failed any of them. I wasn't allowed to fail. My need to survive always kept me one step ahead. I was willing to do whatever it took to live.

I despised the man I called a father. Hated the woman who claimed to be my mother. She did nothing to protect us. I saw a lot of death at a young age. It was only when I met Ivan Volkov that I realized my father wanted me dead. He wanted us all dead, and he was using his children as a means for entertainment.

Wanting strong men and women—fighters—was a lie. He really just wanted entertainment. He made a sick and twisted game of it. His friends were rich, wealthy, disgusting sons of bitches, who could watch and gamble on who would survive. Ivan was the one to show me what was happening. He opened my eyes to what my life had become.

I wasn't earning my father's respect or gaining my place at his side. No, I was the best player in his game. So I put him in his own game. I also took out a few of the men who sat back and watched, who bet money on my sisters and brothers losing their lives.

After I took out my father, I learned he had some kind of deal going with several foster homes. Not all the boys and girls who took part were family. No, he used unwanted children, those who were problems, who were easy to put on the runaway list, where no one would look for them. If they turned up dead, no one would care.

I didn't even know why I was thinking about this. I'd dealt with all of this years ago. I took care of the men and women who were involved, with Ivan by my side.

Maybe it was Niamh. Knowing the scars I detected told a story. She had lived her own kind of horror story, and she was constantly keeping me at arm's length.

Leaning against the hood of my car, I stared off

into the distance, not really paying much attention to my surrounding area.

Ivan had wanted a meeting, in person, but private. My home wasn't private enough, but I did have nosey neighbors. I'd already made multiple excuses to them declining dinner invitations, as well as game night invites. I was not here to make friends or to play that part. I had one mission in mind, and I'd already been at it for a month and a week, and nothing.

Niamh always showed up for training. She was never late, and she always made sure to keep an eye on the time. Not once had we run over, nor did she show any signs of being aroused by my closeness. No matter what I did, she seemed completely oblivious to my touch.

"Are you going to update me?"

I'd been so lost in my thoughts, I hadn't noticed that Ivan had approached from the side. This sent alarm bells off in my head. I hadn't been paying enough attention, and if Ivan was able to sneak up on me, there was no telling who else might do it.

"Where did you come from?"

There was no car, and Ivan didn't even have his cell phone. He stood, arms at his sides, looking like he could blend in as any ordinary man. Only, Ivan wasn't an ordinary man. He was a king. I didn't like that he was out here alone. There was no telling what our enemies could do.

"You shouldn't be alone out here," I said.

Ivan smiled. "I'm not alone."

I knew Ivan was more than capable of taking care of himself, and I accepted that, but we had a lot of enemies, new and old. The last few years should have taught him to be more careful.

"Is Slavik with you? Andrei? The Beast? The Butcher?"

He waved his hand in front of his face, and shook his head. "That is no concern of yours, Peter. Give me an update on what is happening with Niamh Long."

I stood up and ran fingers through my hair. "She's … learning to trust me."

Again, I had my doubts about that. She wasn't a foolish woman. She didn't trust easily, which told me her father had done a number on her. Even though she tried to blend in the town of Pickle Quest, she hadn't made any friends.

While she'd been working and during one of my lunch breaks, I'd already broken into her apartment and seen what I needed to see. Niamh was ready at a moment's notice to make a run for it.

I'd already put two and two together and figured out why she opted to work at the diner. This was her way of assessing a threat. The diner was at a prime location in town, where most tourists stopped, and anyone who was anyone went there.

I went because I knew she was there, and it was about breaking the ice. Also, when Niamh didn't realize I was watching her, I was. I saw how she assessed everyone. When she recognized the faces, she relaxed and went about her business. She took a step toward the exit in the back when she saw those she didn't recognize. Always prepared.

"Which means you're nowhere. Time is ticking and there's only a matter of time before her father realizes where she is."

"Is he even looking for her?" I asked.

Some parents didn't give a shit about their kids. Something told me that Finn Byrne didn't love his daughter. The thin and fading scars were evidence of that. Some of the times I touched Niamh, it was to get a feel for the depth of her scars, to figure out what caused them.

She had a belt used on her, of that I was certain. I also believed she had been slapped and punched. There were no telltale signs of the latter, but it didn't take a genius to work out what kind of man Finn Byrne was.

"Yes," Ivan said.

This surprised me.

He reached into his jacket pocked and pulled out a sheet of paper. I took it and glanced over it. The sun was starting to come up and I read the details.

"He's got a 'seek and obtain'?" I asked.

"Yes, bounty hunters will be looking for her," Ivan said.

"Bounty hunters?"

"Yes, this was not placed through law enforcement. Private firms. The Beast alerted me to the movement of Finn Byrne."

I didn't like this. If it had gone through law enforcement, I could have dealt with it differently. Even private assassins were easier. Bounty hunters were different, especially those who seek and obtain. They were a deadly bunch, and not known for having polite social skills. The only benefit for these kind of bounty hunters was they always worked alone.

This got me thinking.

"He doesn't want people to know she is missing," I said.

A seek-and-obtain bounty was a private call out. Glancing at the information, I was surprised Ivan had it, but then, The Beast being a bounty hunter and an assassin, it shouldn't surprise me.

Bounties were only given to the hunters. It was their job to keep it to themselves, and ninety-nine percent of the time they did. They kept that kind of information to themselves, mainly to get the job done. If enemies discovered their target was on the loose, all hell would ensue. There were some rules, at least within our world of war and chaos.

Now I had to be on the lookout for fucking bounty hunters, and they were not always easy to detect.

"Finn Byrne is making a move, or he plans to make a move very soon, in the hope of taking back territory."

This wasn't good news.

Finn Byrne hadn't been a problem to us in a long time. In fact, he made a point of assuring us that attacks on Ive's turf were not his.

Running a hand down my face, I looked toward Ivan.

"Can you reach out? Make a deal?" I asked. "Offer one of us for his daughter?"

Ivan smiled. "This is not a negotiation, Peter. You will do what I ask, and I'll take care of the rest."

"This is bullshit. You know I will be better suited taking care of my territory and helping you keep hold of Pavlov's." Just thinking about that traitorous fuck was enough to get my anger boiling.

I'd never liked Oleg Pavlov. He'd been one of the original sons from the Russian Bratva, but he attempted to fool Ivan into believing he was loyal to him and him alone. The truth was, he'd never been loyal to Ivan. He planned to bring him down, to tear down all that the Volkov Bratva had built.

Oleg Pavlov was dead, but his territory was still unstable, which is why Ivan had approached The Beast and The Butcher. Both would be more than capable of putting that territory back in line.

Slavik, Andrei, Ive, Victor, Ivan, and I had been dealing with the unruled territory. It was time to find another Brigadier. I just didn't think either The Beast or

The Butcher were likely candidates.

This got me thinking as I handed back the piece of paper to Ivan. "Byrne's going after Pavlov's territory, isn't he?"

Ivan neither confirmed nor denied it.

"Time is ticking, Peter. Get the job done."

I had never failed Ivan and I wasn't going to do so now. Niamh wasn't easily fooled, and she was also used to keeping people at arm's length. She didn't seem to be able to grasp flirting, or when I touched her inappropriately. I wanted to get her to make the first move, and simply respond, but that shit wasn't going to happen.

I couldn't allow this to go on much longer.

Ivan needed me. My territory needed me, and for whatever reason, Ivan wanted his plan to go this way. He'd never steered me wrong before, and I knew he wouldn't start now.

\*\*\*\*

*Niamh*

I was bored.

I'd gone to the library too late yesterday. I had no choice but to return the book I'd been reading, only I didn't have enough time to pick another.

The woman behind the counter had looked so disappointed as I walked through the main doors. I figured she wanted to leave for the day, so I dropped off without a glance around.

Now, it was nearly nine o'clock, and sleep was not coming to me. I didn't own a television and one didn't come with the apartment. I'd spent most of my Sunday cleaning my apartment. I didn't like living in mess.

My mother didn't have a problem, and the days my father would come to visit, and I got locked in my bedroom, the state of the house afterward was disgusting. Mom didn't care that alcohol and vomit were being rubbed into the carpet. Once, when I was cleaning up, I even had to dispose of used condoms.

Even though I loved tidiness and cleanliness, I hated cleaning. It was a necessary evil, and one I was less than happy to do.

Why was I thinking about my mother and those gross parties? They were not fond memories. They were the worst. I hated when my father arrived.

Pushing hair off my face, I rolled onto my back and stared up at the ceiling, watching the fan whirl around. Normally, it helped put me to sleep, but not today.

I took deep breaths and decided to start counting imaginary sheep about to jump over the fence, when there was a bang on my door.

Gasping, I sit up, gripping hold of the blanket I had placed over myself. It was kind of warm, summer was approaching, and I tried not to panic. Who could be knocking on my door at this hour? I didn't notice anything strange yesterday. Sundays are difficult as I never knew who had arrived in town. The diner was often closed, so I always hoped any potential problem didn't stick around and hated little towns.

Another large bang had me jumping out of bed. I didn't know who it could be making all the noise. I hated how my heart was racing, but I rushed toward the door. I didn't have a weapon on hand.

"Niamh, open up."

I frowned. That sounded like Peter.

It didn't surprise me that he was able to get to my

apartment through the supposed security on the main door. The apartments were so cheap that only one of the elevators worked, and according to several people living in this building, that elevator had stopped going to the top floors years ago. Everyone tended to take the stairs.

Opening the door, there was Peter at my door, and he looked drunk.

To stop him from touching me, I had no choice but to stand out of the way while he stumbled into my apartment. This is not what I wanted to deal with. Not on a Sunday night. I was quite happy to be bored.

"Peter?" I asked, and quickly closed the door behind him, locking it.

I knew I was going to have to start considering moving on. I'd been in one place for too long, not that I was an expert in running away and not being found, but something told me I had to keep moving. This was all dependent on whether my father gave a shit about what happened to me.

With the locks all placed—not that I was under any illusion of them working—I turned to find Peter had stumbled a little too close.

He squinted at me and I couldn't help but wonder if he even realized he'd made it to my apartment. There was alcohol on his breath. I wasn't even sure if it was on his breath, but he did reek of the stuff.

"Hello, Niamh," he said.

"Hi, Peter, enjoying the liquor?" I asked.

This made him laugh. It was such an odd sound, and that was when it suddenly occurred to me, I'd never heard Peter laugh. He was always so serious.

He held his fingers together and seemed to sway a little. His other hand went to my shoulder, and he held onto me, trying not to fall. "Little bit."

"You and I both know you've had more than a little bit." At least he wasn't banging at my door. I didn't want the cops being called, not that I'd seen them around these parts, even when fights did break out.

Peter didn't let me go, and I think he was using me to stay upright. I still forced a smile to my lips. Alcohol and men, I didn't like. I'd seen my mom drunk plenty of times. Sober she could be mean, but with beer or whatever drink she wanted, she turned cruel.

He held a finger against his lips. "It's a very important day. Don't tell anyone. This is the day my father died … a long time ago," Peter said.

Just because I didn't have any love for my parents, and if my parents did die, it would honestly be a relief to me. For a split-second, I wondered if I would be upset. Was it a built-in response to mourn your family, even parents you couldn't stand?

I didn't know the answer to that, and I was afraid of it. The last thing I wanted to do was miss my parents. I hated my parents. It would be cruel to miss people who treated you like shit.

"I'm so sorry," I said.

"I know. I shouldn't have been alone, but I can't remember your number, and I don't even know if you want my company." He still held onto me as he ran a hand down his face. "I know there are a lot of women who would like my company, but the only person I wanted to be around was you, Niamh." He smiled and I'm not going to lie, this man should attempt to smile more often.

He stopped looking like a killer, and transformed into a heartthrob. I didn't know if that was possible with all the ink and the deadly intent in his eyes. For several seconds I didn't know what to do or say. I could only stand still and wait.

"Does that shock you?" he asked.

"I think the alcohol is making you a little … strange," I said. There was no way I was going to believe it, although some of the things my mom said when drunk, she'd claim to be lies, but deep down I knew it was the truth. One time, my mother admitted that she had even considered killing me. She'd held a pillow in her hand, stared down at me as a baby, and wanted to kill me. I'd been a baby girl, not something of any value to her or Finn Byrne. She wanted the problem gone.

What had stopped her? My father showed up and showered her with attention, at least that's how the story went. Either way, she kept me and didn't do a great job in raising me. Or maybe she did an amazing job, and I just didn't see it. I don't know.

"Nah, alcohol is making me say the truth." He cupped my face. "Have I told you how much I look forward to our training sessions? Teaching you how to swim, and then helping you stretch your muscles?"

This was getting out of hand. Every other word was slurred, but not to the point where I couldn't understand him. I understood him just fine.

I didn't know if this was the right thing or not. It didn't seem right to me.

I watched him, worried, a little cautious about what to do.

"I bet you don't even think of me when I'm not there."

I didn't even realize there was a distance between us, until Peter closed it. There was a small gap of space between us, but all too soon it was gone. Like it had never existed in the first place.

I was still standing at the door, and if I attempted to step back, the door would stop me.

My heart raced.

I didn't know what was happening.

"I think about you, Niamh. I think about you all the time, and seeing as I am drunk, and this is not real, I can do this." He slammed his lips down on mine, and this shocked me. I was twenty-five years old, and I had never been kissed.

Being socially awkward and a little terrified around guys didn't make dating easier. My father being who he was, didn't help me with this problem either. Some of the guys who showed interest had only wanted to get closer to my dad. It sucked on every level.

Even though Finn Byrne didn't have his own territory, and he'd lost any real power, there were those who believed it wasn't his fault. They wanted him to be in charge once again.

I had lost interest in who had taken over his turf. I often doubted he deserved the adulation others showed him.

My first kiss, given to me by a drunk man, who would not remember this in the morning.

I didn't know what should happen first—if I pull should away, or if Peter would suddenly slump in my arms. I had no choice but to catch him and attempt to stop him from falling on the floor. He's falling asleep. Kissing me had sent him to sleep. I'm sure of it.

"Niamh," he said, speaking my name on some kind of groan.

"You're tired. You need to sleep."

I don't want him sleeping in my apartment, but it didn't seem right to kick him out on my doorstep.

So, with Peter's pathetic help, we got him to the sofa and he collapsed. Before he even hit the seat, I'm sure he was asleep. For several seconds, I stopped and stared at him, not sure what to do. Peter looked so vulnerable.

He had his boots on, and I was tempted to just leave him like that, even though my lips still tingled from our kiss. Instead, I sunk to my knees and removed his boots, putting them to one side.

I moved him to sit down. The sofa is not long enough for him, but the furniture came with the apartment. It had seen better days, but it would do for a bed. Once I had him into a slightly better position, I went back to my own bed, grabbed a blanket, and walked toward him. I didn't want him to freeze to death.

Now that he was settled and he looked okay, with my tingling lips, I made my way back to bed.

# Chapter Five

*Peter*

I wasn't drunk but I needed something to break the ice. I wasn't even upset about my father's passing. I'd been the one to fucking kill him, but I had to work with what I could.

I hadn't touched a drop of alcohol. All I did was use it as a mouthwash, spitting it onto the ground, and then dropped some on my clothes so I would smell of the stuff. It would take a lot more than a bottle of whiskey to make me lose sense of my faculties.

I needed a way to get into Niamh's apartment without raising suspicion in her. Once she put me to bed, I slept for a few hours. It had been a long time since I'd slept through the night. It was very rare for me to have a restful sleep.

It was five o'clock on Monday morning, I'd already put the kettle on, and checked the fridge to find only a few essentials. Enough for breakfast, and maybe a couple of meals. She'd already told me she ate at the diner for lunch. It was one of the perks of working there.

I also noticed she didn't have a lot of cutlery. There was enough for two people, I imagined because it was cheaper to buy in twos than to go singular.

I had set the small table in the kitchen when Niamh suddenly appeared. She was dressed in her gym clothes, and she held a small backpack. This is the bag I knew she carried at all times.

"Peter," she said.

"Niamh." I nod at her. "I would have made you breakfast, but I get the sense you're a cereal kind of girl."

Also, she didn't have any bacon or eggs in the fridge.

"Uh, yeah, I'm not a big breakfast person."

"And you like instant coffee," I said, holding up my mug.

She looked like she wanted to run away.

Kissing her last night had been the first step, but I had felt how tense she had gotten in my arms, which was why I slumped as if I was about to fall asleep.

"Yeah, I like instant. It's … cheap," she said, pressing her lips together. I saw how flushed her cheeks were and I couldn't help but wonder if she was thinking about me and that kiss last night. I hoped that was exactly what she was thinking about.

I knew I enjoyed the feel of her lips. They were soft and plump. In fact, glancing down the length of her body, which I knew she'd gotten completely covered, I couldn't help but wonder what it would be like to fuck her.

Ivan had given me the mission. I'd do what he said, but now, I had a feeling I would actually enjoy fucking this woman. She's pretty. Skittish, but pretty.

Over the past four weeks, I had come to love her eyes. That twinkle she couldn't quite disguise when she had figured something out, or she'd been able to do something. She was breathtaking.

I poured her a mug of coffee and placed it on the table where the milk, sugar, and cereal were waiting.

"How are you feeling?" she asked, pulling out her seat and sitting down.

"Fine."

"Fine? No hangover? No need for some magical cure to help ease your poor head?"

I shrugged. "I don't get hungover." Not exactly a lie. I don't drink enough to ever get hungover.

People took advantage of drunks, and I made sure

I was never put in a compromising position, so it would never happen to me.

"You know, a lot of people are going to hate you," she said, smiling. "So, if you don't get hungover, do you forget things?"

"I remember I kissed you last night."

She stopped pouring cereal out and glanced over at me. I stared right at her, and I watched her cheeks go flush.

"Oh," she said.

"Do you want to talk to me about that?"

"It's fine. It was a mistake and you were drunk and it is never going to happen again. We don't have to talk about it."

She was cute when she rambled.

"It wasn't a mistake."

She jerked the cereal up, and several pieces spilled out of the top, landing on the table, and a few ended up on the floor. I made her nervous.

"I, uh, I don't think we should talk about this."

"Talk about what? The fact that since I first saw you at the diner, I've been thinking about kissing you?" I asked.

"You shouldn't say those things."

"Don't you like the truth?"

She pushed her chair back and took a step away. I got to my feet, and it didn't take me long to close the distance she was trying to create. Nor was it hard to manipulate her movements and have her pressed up against the door of the fridge, with no way to escape.

If, for even a second, I thought she was afraid, I'd back away. I'm not here to scare her. I'm here to … well, arouse her. To get this party started.

I couldn't waste more time with bounty hunters on the loose, potentially tracking her down. Putting both of my hands on either side of her head, I stared into her eyes.

"Peter?"

"What's the matter? Are you afraid of me?"

"I ... no, I' m not afraid of you."

"Then what is wrong?"

"There are other women who want you, and they will do anything you want."

I close the distance between us, so that she could feel the hard ridge of my cock pressing against her stomach. "No other woman makes me feel like that." I had to stop playing the long game, and instead play the short game.

Ivan, for whatever reason, needed this woman pregnant. It was my job to get her pregnant, and training her, touching her, wasn't doing the trick. I could no longer attempt to flirt or take my time. I needed to get into her pants, fast.

"Peter?" she asked.

"Is there another guy?" I asked. "Is that why you don't want me? There is someone else you want."

"I don't know what to do with this. I've never been put in this position. I ... I..."

She was struggling and that was when I realized something. Niamh didn't have a clue what was happening right now. Even though her father was Finn Byrne, and I had been under the assumption she knew exactly what was going on—sex, fucking, making love, whatever word people wanted to call it—Niamh didn't have a clue. I was attempting to seduce a woman who'd never experienced it. Did Ivan even know this?

I didn't know the extent of the abuse she'd suffered at the hands of her father. All I could do was make assumptions.

Sinking my fingers into her hair, I decided to just go for it, and I took possession of her lips, kissing her hard. She gasped, and I used that to my advantage, plunging my tongue into her mouth, and hearing her moan. She tasted like mint toothpaste. She'd not even gotten to sip her coffee, and her cereal wasn't eaten.

Niamh smelled good, and she tasted good. I ran my other hand down her body, and knew she felt good as well.

My arousal wasn't forced. I wanted to be inside her. This was not going to be a hard task.

All too soon, Niamh pulled away and nibbled the corner of her lip. "I don't know what to do," she said.

I think it could be the most honest she had ever been with me.

"Normally, you kiss me back."

"I, uh, Peter, I … Pickle Quest is not my home. I don't intend to stay here too long."

"You're moving on?"

"Yes."

"When?"

"I don't know." She frowned. "I don't know, when it's the right time. I'm traveling, you know. Making enough to be able to move on."

Now that was a lie, but I wasn't going to call her out on it. Niamh wasn't leaving Pickle Quest alone.

"Then how about you and I have some fun while we're at it?" I asked.

She shook her head. "I can't have fun."

I wasn't going to be swayed. Winking at her, I pulled her in and kissed her again.

\*\*\*\*

*Niamh*

I didn't want to go to the pool that morning, but Peter was a giant pain in the ass, and wouldn't take no for an answer. He drove me to the gym and told me to hurry up. We did the usual warm-up, only this time as he helped me into certain positions, I wondered if he was doing it on purpose. His fingers seemed to linger, like he wanted to remind me of his hands on me this morning.

It was impossible to forget the kisses Peter had given me. The one last night and the few this morning. Even when we were alone at the gym, I couldn't help but wonder if he was going to kiss me again. He didn't.

But I couldn't stop thinking about it. That was all I could think about—him and kisses, and so much more.

This was totally inappropriate and insane, and so many different things all wrapped into one. I shouldn't be thinking or feeling this way. It was only a matter of time before I had to leave Pickle Quest, and I didn't really know Peter.

Getting into any kind of relationship came with serious consequences. My father would kill him. Not out of any parental concern, but because he was my dad. He would do anything to hurt me, especially if he thought I had feelings for Peter. Which I didn't.

I didn't know what love was, or how you were supposed to feel about a man. I didn't even love my parents. To me, love was a feeling that was meant to be strong. It was a feeling that had power over everything else. I wasn't stupid, I didn't think love would heal all wounds or any of that crap. I knew love had the *ability* to make pain heal.

I didn't know why I was thinking about this now. The lunch shift had already come and gone. Now was the lull, when I cleaned tables and filled empty containers. Customers didn't like when salt or pepper were out. I also had to replace mayonnaise.

Taking a deep breath, I glanced around the diner, checked to see the familiar faces, trying to make sure no one snuck up on me. I'd been tempted to phone my mother lately, to see if I could get an update. I know she'd lie for my father. If I called her, that might alert her to my presence. This was all insane.

This was the part of running away I didn't think about. The part of not knowing what he was doing. If he even cared what was happening. I didn't even know if my father was out looking for me. There was no way to get in touch. I hated this. All I wanted was to live my life as far away from him as humanly possible.

I wanted to be alone and be free. I didn't know if I would ever get that.

Being the bastard daughter, I thought I would have more freedom. I wasn't a good enough child for him, and yet there were times I did feel more trapped by being this person to him. What did he want with me? If I wasn't a good enough daughter, why bother to find me? I could spend days trying to figure something out, but the truth was, I think it was a power trip for him.

Why did Peter have to do this? I didn't like the challenges this caused.

That kiss shouldn't mean anything. I was a woman of twenty-five and yet, that was my first kiss. But it was just a kiss. People kissed each other all the time and it didn't have to mean anything. For all I knew, Peter was just using me to have his own fun, and that wasn't a problem. Or was it?

I was so confused now.

The lull picked up for the dinner rush, and I was pleased to not think about Peter. It would only be a matter of hours before he was waiting for me, or maybe he wouldn't be. Maybe one of the women who kept flirting with him at the gym would finally pique his interest.

I was not free now. I didn't have the freedom to kiss a random guy.

The minutes ticked by, and finally, the dinner rush came to an end, and all too soon, I finished helping with the cleanup, and then it was my time to leave.

The other waitresses were used to my lack of conversation. I didn't make friends easily as a kid, or as a grown-up. It was hard to make friends when you didn't know how your parents were going to react. My mother didn't like me bringing friends around. She always wanted to make sure her home was free and available to Finn at all times.

Seeing as he didn't do everything *legal*, that meant no friends. It probably didn't help matters that I was also socially awkward. Like with Peter. I didn't have a clue what I was doing.

He kissed me, and I pretty much stood there like a statue, not sure what to do next. He must be so embarrassed of me.

Stepping out into the night, I was not surprised to see him waiting for me. Like so many times before, he leaned against his car.

"You know, you don't have to wait for me. If you've got stuff to do, I'm happy to walk home on my own." I'd been doing it before he came around.

He released a sigh and stepped closer. "I know you're perfectly capable of taking care of yourself, but this time I'm not going to let you be." He pulled open the door to his car. "Come on. I'm taking you back to my place."

"Your place?" There was no way I was getting into that car. Maybe this is what it was all about. Luring me into a false sense of security, and when my guard was down, he would throw me into his prison cell. It made perfect sense to me. I was a little afraid. Who wouldn't be?

Peter closed the distance between us. I should learn to turn on my heel and run, but I have a problem. When under threat, I can't seem to make myself move. It was impossible.

Suddenly, he gripped the back of my neck, and before I even knew what was happening, his lips were close to mine. I couldn't think or form any words. I was at his mercy.

"Trust me."

And then he kissed me. At first, it started out soft, gentle, almost the merest breath of a whisper. Until he changed, and then I found myself putting my hands on his chest. Only, I wasn't pushing him away, but in fact fighting for him to get closer to me.

That was what I wanted—him, as close as possible, which made absolutely no sense.

\*\*\*\*

*The Beast*

I was used to wiping away blood from my hands. It was no different than wiping dust, or engine oil, dirt of any kind. The man that was now dead was part of Finn Byrne's clan. He'd been getting a little too close to Ivan Volkov's current problem.

Speaking of Ivan, he chose that moment to step inside the mess. We were currently working from an abandoned warehouse. I'd already called my cleaning crew and they were on the way over. Ivan needed to be gone before they arrived.

"What did you find out?" Ivan asked, not even

bothering to glance at the body.

I found this odd. Ivan was a mystery to me. On the one hand, he seemed to be the meddling sort, always sticking his nose where it didn't belong. Then there were times he seemed to always be one step ahead of everyone else, while also maintaining this rather blasé exterior.

"Not a whole lot. Some stuff we already knew. He's planning to start with your area six. Other than that, this guy didn't get too close to Finn Byrne." I thought it was clever of me to refer to all of Ivan's Brigadiers as areas. It didn't matter who was in control. Area six felt a lot quicker than, say, Oleg Pavlov's territory before he died, very wordy. Area six was much better. The same area I knew Ivan had offered to me and … The Butcher.

There was no way I was sharing any territory with that bitch. She was a fucking nightmare. It was bad enough having to deal with the same problem with her.

I liked to think of myself as finesse, while she … well, it was a complete and total nightmare and shit show. The Butcher didn't care about the mess she left behind, whereas I did.

"Makes sense," Ivan said.

See, I just told him that another bad guy intended to take over his turf, and he didn't seem to care. It wasn't like it was news to him. I doubt it was. The man had been in charge of the Volkov Bratva, and where the previous Bratva had a small territory, they hadn't thought big, like Ivan. He'd already made ten times the Bratva than his previous predecessor.

Like now, Ivan walked to take a seat in the corner of the room. He stared at the mess of the man that was now dead, and it was like he was staring into space. Death didn't bother him.

"The word has been put out. Finn Byrne is looking for his daughter. It now doesn't just extend to the bounty hunters. He's got men and women, anyone who wants the reward."

"How much is the reward?" Ivan asked.

I didn't know if Ivan was curious because he wanted the reward, or if he was just curious.

"A thousand."

Not going to lie, a thousand bucks to find someone's daughter wasn't exactly a great incentive. Finn Byrne was pretty much announcing to the whole world that even though he had a daughter and wanted her, she wasn't that important. To me, this meant she could end up back in her father's care a little more broken than when I found her.

"That it?" Ivan asked, and then laughed.

"Do you think he knows the danger he is putting his daughter in?" I asked. I wasn't sure exactly how much Ivan knew of Finn. As far as I was aware the two had never crossed paths, not personally.

Ivan may have pushed Finn Byrne out of his territory, but he'd been losing it long before Ivan came along.

"He knows," Ivan said.

Once again, he was this mystery man. I didn't know if he was upset or didn't give a fuck.

Tapping my fingers against my leg, I continued to stare at Ivan. He wasn't exactly known for small talk, and I wasn't used to having anyone look at my craftsmanship.

"Can I ask you a question?" I said. Even if Ivan said no, I was going to ask it. I was merely attempting to sound polite. Didn't mean I was going to be polite.

"What?" Ivan asked.

"What does this girl mean to you? I mean, she's no one. She's not important. Even her father hasn't put a high enough price tag on her head, and she also ran away, which tells me she is either a brat or knows what the hell she is doing."

Ivan smiled at me, and it wasn't a nice smile. This was the deadly side of Ivan. The one no one could read. "That's none of your business."

"Seeing as I'm here, cleaning up any problem Peter and Niamh might have, I figured I had a right to be in the know."

Silence filled the space between us. If it were anyone else, I'd have killed them. Ivan wasn't just anyone.

It took a lot for me to be afraid. Living my life, surviving day to day, the life I led, what I did for a living, I was used to basking in fear, and channeling it into my work. There was a price tag on my head, and so far, no one had been able to take me out. No one would either, that was how good I was. Also, the fear of what I'd do. Most people that put a hit out on me didn't last the week. So, even though there was a price on my head, it never lasted.

I didn't expect Ivan to answer, but when he started speaking I turned toward him.

"Let's just say, Niamh helped me at a time that I needed it."

I waited for more, but he didn't say another word. So now, I had more questions than answers. How the fuck did Niamh Byrne help someone like Ivan Volkov?

## Chapter Six

*Peter*

"Why are we here?"

I couldn't help but smile at the tone of her voice. She sounded so scared. I knew I'd startled her, but I was not going to spend another night sleeping on that fucking excuse for a sofa. Even though I'd only slept on it one night. It wasn't even the worst experience of my life. I'd slept in worse places over the years.

Niamh deserved better.

Her apartment was a piece of shit. I knew that, but it was the best of her situation. If Ivan wanted me to put a baby inside her, then she didn't know it yet, but she was going to be my wife. My wife would not live in a rundown apartment, keeping cockroaches at bay as a job. Not happening.

Pulling into the driveway of my home, I shut off the ignition and turned toward her.

"You're terrified."

"Nah, it's fine. You know, every single day a strange guy gives me a ride to his ... amazing home. This is your house?" she asked.

I laughed. "Yeah and no. I'm house-sitting for a friend. He's out of the country, away on some business, and he wanted me to keep an eye on the place. He sees it as some kind of investment."

Not a total lie. I'm away on business, and it is kind of an investment. This helped me to mingle with the crowds, which is what I wanted. I didn't want to raise questions.

This job that Ivan has given me is fucking shit.

Working as a damn gym instructor, fending off advances from both married and single women. Some men might think this was a dream job. Not me. It's shit. I like running my territory, even killing people is more entertaining than this.

The only good thing about what we're doing is I'll get to keep Niamh. This is not going to be easy. I'm already lying to her, just as she is lying to me. I accept it.

"It looks amazing," Niamh said.

From the brief information Ivan had given me, and knowing Niamh, I didn't believe she had the classic traditional home. Her mother lived in a small home paid for by Finn Byrne. I guessed he used that as a stopping point, doing deals, and potentially bringing danger to Niamh every chance he got.

If I ever met Finn Byrne, I was going to hurt him.

"Do you want to come and see inside? It's just for us to hang out," I said.

Actually, my plan was to get closer to her. I needed to bridge this gap that Niamh seemed determined to keep between us. The only way to do that was to make sure she didn't keep finding reasons to disappear on me. At my house, I made the rules.

Climbing out of the car, I rounded the vehicle. Niamh was already out, and she offered me such a sweet smile. We walked to my front door, and I unlocked it, stepped through, and activated the security codes as I closed the door. Now, there was no way for her to escape without me knowing. I threw the keys into the little dish on the cabinet a few feet from the door.

Niamh did a little circle as she looked at the space. To any prying eyes, it looked like a family home. There were no personal pictures or anything like that.

"This place is incredible," Niamh said.

"Yeah, the guy I'm helping said it was. He

wanted it to be a family home as well. He just hasn't found the wife for him."

Again, not all lies.

Actually, they were all lies, but there were some she didn't need to know.

I watched her as she stayed in one place and then clasped her hands together and offered me a smile. "So, I've seen your place, and I'm a little jealous, but I think it's time you take me back to my apartment."

I was not a movie star boyfriend. I didn't have a clue what to fucking say. All I had to do was click my fingers and women flock to me. I didn't even have to care about satisfying them. Sex was sex.

Ivan had seriously put me in the fucking deep end. I didn't know what to do with Niamh. She had shown no signs of finding me attractive. She was ready to run. That's all she wanted to do, and Ivan wanted me to trap her. How the fuck did a guy trap a woman? Wasn't it the other way around?

"You know, how about I get you a drink?" I asked, and I was already heading to the kitchen.

"I, uh, I don't drink."

"I can offer more than alcohol." Opening the fridge, I read off what I had. "Orange juice, soda, water, milk."

"Milk," she said.

"I get why you're nervous," I said, grabbing the milk and turning to her.

She tucked some of her hair behind her ear. She'd confined the full brown locks at the back of her head in a ponytail as I'd seen her do for the last few weeks. It never stopped her from having to tuck her hair back behind her ears. "You do?"

For a second, I didn't have a clue what she was talking about, and then I remembered we were actually talking. This was highly unusual when it came to women. I'd yet to meet a woman worth having a conversation with. Most of them were only interested in my dick, my wealth, or my title. I didn't mind that, but I was only ever interested in looking for a good time.

"Yeah, you're nervous because you're in my house, and I bet you're worried I'm some kind of thief, but trust me, I'm not."

I had no idea why Niamh suddenly began to laugh. It wasn't one of those forced fake laughs, or even the kind that was mocking or some shit. This was a full-on belly laugh. Like she found what I said fucking interesting, and I didn't have the first clue what she found so funny. The last word anyone would ever use to describe me was *funny*. I was the least funny person I knew.

None of this was entertaining.

I couldn't help but wonder if this was Ivan's way of playing a practical joke. He'd gotten me in Pickle Quest, trying to make this woman fall for me, so I could impregnate her—which sounded like a horrible alien movie—when in fact I was the one the joke was being played on, and Niamh had to get me to fall in love with her.

If that turned out to be the case, then the joke truly was on them, because I didn't do love or feelings. I never had. I was already aware of most of the rumors about me, how I had no feelings, no love, and I didn't care.

I can act all the parts, do what needed to be done, and say what needed to be said in all the right places, but that didn't mean for a second I felt any of it. Not a single thing.

I'd never understood love. I never would. Love was for the weak. I didn't even know why Ivan had gotten Slavik, Andrei, and now Ive to comply. Although, I didn't consider any of those bastards weak. No, they were still scary as fuck.

Now that I thought of it, they might be even scarier. I'm pretty sure I heard one of them suggest that now that they had more to lose, they were even more terrifying. I didn't know. I had never felt love.

I didn't have the first clue what love was.

"What's funny?" I asked, and I was struck by how beautiful she looked. This was the first time she didn't have her guard up.

She pushed some hair out of her face, and then laughed again. "I'm so sorry. It's not funny, it's not funny at all, and I have no reason to laugh, but I can't seem to stop myself."

I had a feeling I knew what she was laughing about, but I couldn't know that shit. She couldn't know that I knew she was a Byrne. There was a lot I wasn't supposed to know.

Seconds passed, finally minutes, and Niamh got herself under control. "I don't even know why I laughed. It's nothing."

"Laughing is good for the soul." I didn't know if that was true.

"Really?"

"Yeah."

"Do you spend a lot of time laughing?" she asked.

I had to stop, because the truth was, no, I didn't laugh a lot. Certainly not recently as I didn't have a lot to laugh about. Life was way too serious, and right now, being stuck in a fucking shit town, while I knew bad stuff was going on, was hard to do.

"No, not as much as I should." Laughter was for the weak.

I couldn't help but get a flash to those men all those years ago who found it funny to watch young children lose their lives in the sick games my father set up. It had all been a fucked-up game.

"Come on, I'll make us something to eat, and then I'll give you a tour." I didn't wait for her to argue with me. Instead, I grabbed her hand and walked to the kitchen. Only then did I let go of her hand, and it was strange as I still felt the tingle of her touch work its way up my arm.

I wanted to hold her hand again, to touch her to see if that was real or not.

Strange.

"Uh, you know, you don't have to feed me. You could just … take me back to my apartment."

I closed the fridge and turned toward her. I was not knowledgeable in all things romance. In the back of my mind, I couldn't help but remember that her father had put out a seek-and-find mission. I doubt that would end well for her. He clearly had no qualms about hurting his daughter. I'd seen the photographs of what he'd done to her last time.

Finn Byrne was not a good man. Not that I could claim to be a better one.

When it came to Niamh, my only job was to protect her and get her pregnant. I didn't know what Ivan hoped to achieve, starting our potential future on lies, but I trusted him more than I trusted anyone else.

"Look, I know you don't trust me, and I'm getting the vibe that you don't trust a whole lot of people, and I totally get it. Trust me, I do get it. I'm a strange guy. In fact, both of us are strangers in this town, but we're looking for something. Maybe we could find that something together."

"I don't plan to stick around." She nibbled her lip.

"I'm not looking for anything long term."

I wasn't looking for anything myself. My boss, however, was looking for the long term, and when Niamh was pregnant with my child, she wasn't going anywhere. I didn't for a second believe I'd be a good father, but I wouldn't abandon my kid.

"Then how about you and I test the waters? We see where this might lead?" I asked.

She looked doubtful and I knew I was so fucking bad at this.

"I … uh, I'm not good at this. It might have something to do with the fact that growing up, I never knew my mother. Never had a great father. He was a piece of shit, in all honesty. Liked using his fists and playing mind games and shit like that." Not a lie, but vague enough for her to not ask too many questions. "I … like you. I get that you may not like me now, but do you think there's a chance you could grow to like me?"

I didn't have a fucking clue what I was doing or saying. All I knew was if I didn't do as Ivan asked, there would be consequences.

Niamh opened her mouth, pressed her lips together, and then glanced down at the floor, before lifting her head. "I, uh, I kind of like you. I mean, there are a lot of women that like you."

"I don't give a flying fuck about them," I said.

They had tried to come on to me. Offered me money in exchange for favors. Even if Ivan hadn't given me this job, I still wouldn't have taken either of them up on their offer. I didn't offer up my body for money.

"You don't?"

"Do you see them in my place? Me offering them food?" I asked.

"No."

"Then I don't give a fuck about them, and I'm

with the one I want to be with."

****

*Niamh*

*"Then I don't give a fuck about them, and I'm with the one I want to be with."*

That shouldn't have sounded so romantic, and maybe I'd not known or been around a lot of romance to know what it is when I see it. Either way, Peter's words hit right in the chest.

I knew I was messed up, growing up with a mother who couldn't stand me, who openly admitted to wanting to kill me because I wasn't a boy. Hating me for not being beautiful, or having the right hair, or the right look. For hating my weight, and just for breathing. Also a father that hated me as well. Love was not something I was accustomed to.

I'd watched a lot of romance and family dramas, and sitcoms growing up. I loved them, and it was what I had craved for my own life. It was something I had promised myself—that when I grew up, I was going to have the family, the husband that loved me, and never was I going to allow my parents access to my child.

That didn't go according to plan.

Staying in Pickle Quest was a mistake. I knew that, but I really liked the small town. I did feel safe, and I felt I could build a life here. Maybe I was just living the fairy tale right now.

My father was going to come and look for me. He'd told me many times that I was a Byrne, as if it meant something. To me, it didn't. I hated the name.

Peter was the first man in my life to be nice to me. He wasn't after his own agenda. There was nothing he wanted, and he seemed to like my company. Also a bonus, he could cook. He'd pulled a couple of pieces of chicken out of the fridge, and thought he was going to cook us a stir-fry as he'd grabbed some mushrooms and bell peppers. The cheese he'd gotten as well, and then I watched him begin to work.

He started with slicing the chicken through the center to make thinner breasts. He moved around the kitchen, grabbed a few spices and herbs, and added them to the chicken, using his fingers to massage them into the breast. Even raw with the spices, it looked good.

Next, he got to work on the mushrooms, and by the time he was finished, the frying pan was steaming hot.

"You know how to cook," I said.

"I know how to feed myself. I wouldn't call myself a chef." This made me smile. It felt good to smile and laugh. I'm surprised he didn't push my ass into the car, and take me back to my apartment when I had that laughing fit.

My dad is a complete and total bastard, and I didn't consider Peter even in the same league as him. To think he was worried I thought he was a thief, was so funny. I knew evil, and Peter was not. All he'd shown me was kindness, and I liked that.

Yes, I was attracted to this man, and that terrified me. I didn't know if I wanted to be attracted to anyone, least of all someone I had lied to.

Peter could never know my last name. This was fleeting, and I found that a shame. I did like him.

Once the mushrooms were cooked, he put them into a bowl, and then he started to work his magic on some bell peppers. It was all smelling incredible. While I'd been lost in thought, he'd set up a grill plate, and it was already getting hot. With the bell peppers cooking, he added the chicken to the grill. The sizzle and smells were making my mouth water. This was next to impossible to control, and I couldn't help but wonder if he was doing this on purpose—driving me crazy, making me want the food so badly.

It all smelled good.

He turned the chicken and it was so thin, that it was nearly cooked, but it had such pretty grill marks. The mushrooms were added back into the peppers, and I watched as he portioned the veggies into four rectangles. It all became clear as he added a good amount of cheese to each pile, and then he opened up some rolls.

Peter took the chicken, sliced it, added it to the roll, then topped it off with the mushroom, bell pepper, and cheese concoction. He did this three more times, and then he was finished.

"Ready to eat."

I was starving. All I could do was nod my head.

He winked at me, and even that set my heart fluttering inside my chest. I followed him to his dining room table and sat down.

We had two sandwiches each, I was in heaven with that one bite. It was hot, and I had to remember to blow across the food, but it was so good. Even as my mouth was burning, it was watering for more.

"It good?" he asked.

"Yeah, so good." I took another large bite, and wow, my taste buds were tingling for all the right reasons. It was so good. In only a few bites, the first roll was gone, and I was already getting started on the second.

Halfway through, I realized Peter was watching me, and then I couldn't help but wonder if I had looked like a pig with all the shoveling of food.

"I'm sorry," I said, feeling my cheeks heat with

embarrassment.

"Don't be embarrassed. It's good to see you eat."

I highly doubted that.

Once I had finished the food, I licked my lips and tried not to glance around his home. It was a nice place and I certainly could see a family loving this home. I knew it was a place I would have loved as well.

It's the kind of place I imagined having—a driveway, a garden, a family room, a lovely kitchen. It was the family home of my many dreams. Most of which were never going to be a reality.

Forcing a smile to my lips, I tucked some of my hair behind my ear. I was about to ask him to take me home, but Peter started to talk.

"Would you like to stay the night?"

Okay, not talk, but straight up asked me to stay the night.

"Ugh, you mean … ugh…" I didn't know if I could say it. "Do you mean stay the night as in … sex?" That very word shouldn't make me embarrassed.

Peter had this sexy smile on his lips and I had noticed it plenty of times. Okay, not the smile—he rarely did that—but he did have sexy lips. Maybe I was starting to lose my mind. That was what made sense to me. I had to be losing something.

"Sex sounds like a lot of fun, but I'm guessing you're not ready for that."

"I'm a virgin," I said, blurting out that little home truth quicker than I expected to. I had no intention of telling anyone. Least of all Peter. Crap!

I pushed my chair out and I could feel my cheeks getting hotter with every passing second. This was insane. Why did I blurt out that nonsense? He didn't need to know I was a virgin, but the whole mention of sex and my mind was blown.

"You're a what?" Peter asked.

"I'm sorry. Can we rewind and forget this conversation, and maybe just go back to saying, hey, that food was really great, but I think it's time I walk home?" I don't think, I act, and start to walk toward the door.

I should have known there was not going to be an easy escape for me. I wasn't so lucky.

Peter spun me around and I expected him to bombard me with multiple questions. Instead, he slammed those sexy lips right on top of mine. The panic didn't leave, not immediately. It was still very much there, threatening to bubble up inside me and take complete control.

However, when he traced his tongue across my bottom lip, and then somehow ended up touching my tongue, all thought was lost. My hands were by my sides, and then I was touching him. I was tempted to push him away, but I was loving the feel of his lips so much, and I didn't want to push him away. I wanted him to keep kissing me.

At this point, I knew I was being selfish. Peter deserved a woman who wasn't running from her past.

He was the first to break the kiss.

"I was wondering if you would like to stay the night. Not for sex, but just the night. I could make up the spare bedroom if that would make you more comfortable."

At this point, I didn't for a second believe anything would make me feel comfortable. I was far from comfortable. But it was late, and I was so tired, and I didn't see a reason to run.

"Yes, I'd love to."

In that moment, I knew I wouldn't have minded the sex either.

How crazy could that be? I had never been with a man, and I was running away from my life, but I was quite happy with the thought of having sex with a complete and total stranger.

Who was I?

## Chapter Seven

*Peter*

"She's a fucking virgin!" I spun around and glared at Ivan.

I was surprised he'd been willing to see me so close to the last time. It made me wonder where he was staying, and if he was close by, why he wasn't trying to win over Niamh fucking Byrne. He didn't have another woman. There was no one waiting for him back home.

He was close to his other Brigadiers' wives, but that's because he liked them. It was no secret he seemed to gravitate toward broken women. Aurora, Adelaide, and Charlotte had come from messed-up backgrounds.

Ivan had been the one to save them.

Niamh fit the profile of the women he'd been matching to his men.

"And?" Ivan asked. "You do realize knocking up a virgin is the same as knocking up any other woman. There is no secret society or special lock."

I ran fingers through my hair and turned toward him. "Why?"

"Because I've told you to."

"You know I don't love her!" Not that it would matter.

Ivan smiled, but it was one of those smiles that didn't quite reach his eyes. "I don't need you to love her."

"What about the others?" I asked.

"Others?"

"Slavik, Andrei, fucking Ive. They all love their women. You made sure you chose right by them, and what, I don't get the same regard?" I asked. There was no point in pretending. The moment Niamh was pregnant with my kid, she was going to be my wife.

Ivan had chosen her for me.

She matched all the descriptions Ivan chose when it came to wives for his men. She was damaged but she also provided something to the Volkov Bratva with her name.

Not that I'd see Byrne and Ivan sitting down and enjoying civilized meetings. Far from it.

Ivan chuckled. "You think they were in love with their wives when I forced them to marry?"

I turned to look toward him. He hadn't moved from his perch on the hood of his car. Ivan was dressed in a suit, impeccably, without any wrinkles. Always calm, always in control. Nothing could knock that coolness.

"Don't..." I said, holding my hand up and shaking my head. "You're not going to play me for the fool."

"I'm not playing you for anything, but you might want to consider the fact that the others were not in love with their wives. All three of them hated being married. It was a job to them, but then, most marriages are jobs, right? Sacrifices."

I stopped and ran a hand down my face.

"Niamh doesn't deserve this."

"Three bounty hunters have been killed in the past twenty-four hours," Ivan said, making me tense up. "They're closing in and your opportunity to make this work is closing. I don't give a fuck what it takes, make her pregnant, and speed this shit up."

With that, Ivan didn't say another word. He climbed behind the wheel of the car, and took off, leaving me in our secret meeting spot. Running fingers through my hair, I blew out a breath. That didn't end how I wanted it to.

I'd never been with a virgin. Niamh deserved better than this.

Climbing behind my own wheel, I turned over the ignition and headed back into town. I'd already cancelled the day's appointments, even Niamh's. I didn't go home, instead, I parked my car in the only available parking space outside the diner, climbed out, and headed inside.

It was busy, close to lunchtime, and I made my way into the small booth at the back. This allowed me to check out the locals, as well as any potential bounty hunters making their way into Pickle Quest.

I didn't realize they were so close, but now that I was aware, I was more prepared. I'd already gotten used to the locals. There were one or two tourists that were part of a group. They had arrived yesterday and were exploring the town. They had a map, and I watched them talk and mingle together. No one had infiltrated their group.

There was no bounty hunter in the diner.

Niamh was also serving, dashing around like a madwoman, taking orders, speeding across to the kitchen, leaving tickets, picking up food. Keeping a smile on her face as she served.

The locals were kind but not too trusting. They were happy for her to serve them, but they were not willing to open their hearts to her. I couldn't help but wonder what it would take for them to accept her. There would be trouble wherever she went.

Finally, after what felt like an hour, Niamh was able to come to my table. "I'm so sorry. I've been trying to come and take your order. What can I get you?" she asked.

"How about you get me the same thing you're

having when this rush is over?" I asked.

"Uh … are you sure?"

"Yeah, I'm sure. I can wait." I needed to turn on the charm.

"Okay, I've just got to, you know, finish serving people, and then when it slows down, I can take my lunch break."

"Until then, I'll have a coffee."

She nodded and left. I watched her ass as she walked away. I loved the curve. The uniform wasn't flattering, but the way she moved, there was no hiding the body beneath. She was all temptation, and I was more than ready to take a bite.

Niamh was going to be mine, and it was time for me to start acting like it.

I was not going to act like a spoiled brat. I was going to do exactly what Ivan had told me to do, and that was to knock Niamh up, and then I'd deal with the fallout. There was no doubt in my mind Niamh was going to hate me. One day, she'd forgive me, because she'd know I did it for her.

No, I was doing this for Ivan, and his messed-up reasons. I was annoyed.

The time ticked by, and finally after an additional thirty minutes, Niamh came back to my table, carrying two plates, which looked to be overloaded burgers and fries. Not that I was complaining. They looked good.

The food at the diner wasn't bad. I had no complaints. Niamh sat down opposite me. Her hair was falling out of her ponytail, and she looked so incredibly tired. I picked up my burger, took a bite, and watched as she ate some fries. It suddenly occurred to me that I'd never cared for a woman's company. I'd taken women out on dates plenty of times, but that had been for one purpose—sex.

Glancing over at Niamh, I watched as she grabbed a napkin to dab away some mayonnaise she'd gotten on the corner of her mouth. Niamh wasn't trying to impress me. There were no fake giggles. She wasn't hanging off my every word. She was just being herself, which was a shocking reality to what I was used to. I found it refreshing that she wasn't faking anything with me.

Ivan's plan was pissing me off. I wasn't interested in the subterfuge, but at the same time, this was in fact a chance, one I didn't think was possible.

"How has your morning been?" Even though I suddenly saw this as a new opportunity, considering I was going to be married to this woman and having kids with her, small talk wasn't exactly my strong suit. It was very, very, very, very (possibly a few extra verys) bad, probably more awful. I didn't do small talk.

When your father at a young age trained you how to survive, small talk wasn't on the menu. Fighting your way out of every situation, doing what you could to survive—hunting, killing, maiming—anything to keep your heart beating. Not realizing you'd become entertainment for a group of spoiled men. It certainly didn't change a man's perspective.

Niamh smiled. "It's been pretty busy. I came in early and helped set up seeing as you cancelled our morning session."

"Yeah, about that, how do you feel about doing an evening one?"

"At the gym?" she asked.

"Yeah, I had some business to take care of, which was bullshit, and I'd like to be able to make that up to you. Do you think I can do that?" I asked. I had to figure out a way to get close to her.

I didn't have a clue how the gym would help, but

that did require close, physical contact, so there was a chance right there.

"Ugh, sure, I guess. I don't see why not."

Offering her my best smile, I took another bite of the burger. "This is good."

She chuckled, and I happened to like the sound. I wanted her to chuckle a lot more often, because there was going to come a time when she was going to need a reason to. I had no doubt these lies were going to mount up. It was just a matter of time.

**\*\*\*\***

*Niamh*

Being on the mat with Peter in the not-so-distant past didn't seem quite this hard. My bathing suit was beneath the large sweats I'd quickly thrown on. Being prepared to leave at a moment's notice meant I was ready for anything. A quick, late-night training session hadn't been a problem, not for me, Miss Prepared.

Peter's hands on my body, though, I was finding a little more distracting than usual. Were his hands always this large, and did they press in all the right places? Like right now, the tips of his fingers were so close to the apex of my thighs. I wasn't used to the contact, and it was driving me crazy. A little more than crazy.

I released a moan, and his hand gripped my thigh a little harder, which didn't help.

"Are you okay?" he asked.

"Ugh, yeah, I'm fine. I think we should be good to get into the pool." I sat up, needing to create some space, because right now I didn't have a clue what was happening.

I get that Peter and I kissed a couple of times, and I told him I was a virgin. That didn't mean anything. We'd not promised anything to each other, so I didn't have a clue why I was nearly freaking out. It made no sense.

We're just two consenting adults, in the gym, quite late, but not too late, alone. The owner of the gym, Carl Fields, had given Peter the keys. I didn't know how he'd managed to do it, but he'd earned Carl's respect, and, well, now he could use the gym whenever he wanted.

Peter was damn good at what he did. Even if it was only with his hands.

Crap, now I was thinking about what those hands could do to my naked body, and this wasn't good. Sitting up, I forced a smile to my lips.

"We don't want to be too late. The last thing we'd want is for Carl to think we're … you know … outstaying our welcome." I pulled away from his touches and quickly got to my feet, trying to create some distance.

Peter got to his feet smoothly. I felt all jerky, like my body wasn't quite my own. How did this happen? How did he get to look smooth and calm, and I felt all jittery? It was insane.

*Get over yourself. Right freaking now!*

I spun on my heel and made my way toward the swimming pool. It was not too far, and as we entered the pool area, I removed my shirt, followed by the loose sweats I'd thrown over my costume. A one-piece. I never wore a bikini. It would never happen. I was a one-piece girl all the way, and as per instructions, I went toward the small set of nozzles on the far wall, and sprayed myself with some water.

Before getting in the pool, one must step into the

shower first, and now I walked to the shallowest end and climbed into the water.

Now, over the past few weeks, Peter has been in and out of the pool with me. It wasn't always a guarantee that he'd be by my side, because according to him, I had to learn to stand on my own two feet when it came to matters of water safety. It was great.

I thought tonight wouldn't be any different, but it would seem I was wrong, because Peter didn't just step under the showers to spray himself with water. Nope, he had stripped down to just his boxer briefs, and was showing off his very impressive arrangement of ink. I'd known he was covered in tattoos, because he had told me. He'd been getting them from a young age. When I asked why, he'd just say he liked them, as if that made any sense.

I had thought about getting a tattoo a couple of times, but then always dismissed the notion. It would require me sitting with a stranger touching me, and of course the needle. Not happening. There were limits on what I could take. Strangers. Touches. Needles. It all sounded like a recipe for a horror movie to me.

He climbed into the pool, and how did someone make wading through water look sexy? I'd seen it in a couple of movies, but those walks were slowed down and made to appear … I don't know, natural. Peter didn't have any special effects. All he had was me for company, and no slow-motion machine, but he looked so good.

"Are you ready?"

It took me a second to understand what he was asking me. What was I ready for? And then, it dawned on me—ready to start swimming.

"Yeah." I had to stop and clear my throat, because it sounded like I had a frog caught in it. "Yes, of course. What's it going to be, Boss?" Now I was just speaking without any rational thought. *Please shoot me.*

I didn't want to embarrass myself, but that seemed to be the goal I was going for, which sucked big time. Big, big, big time.

"Show me what you've got, Coach."

Peter laughed. It was a nice sound. I had a feeling he didn't know how to laugh, not that it was any of my business.

"Do you have any family?" I immediately wanted to slap myself. My one rule was not to ask personal questions.

"No," he said. "It's why I'm here."

"Me neither." It wasn't a lie.

*Liar.*

It was a lie. My parents were alive and well when I went on the run.

Peter's hands went to my hips and he drew me close. "You're nervous," he said.

I didn't know if that was supposed to be a question, and I didn't feel comfortable answering it.

"Ugh, no, of course not, what do I have to be nervous about?"

He turned me around so my back was pressed against his chest. Both of his hands were at my hips, and I couldn't help but cringe wondering if I was having one of those days when they felt large or small. I was so confused right now.

Peter's lips brushed across my neck and I closed my eyes as pleasure seemed to rush through my body. Is this why people acted so irrationally when it came to someone they wanted to be with? Was this sex? Attraction? Flirting? I'd never experienced anything like it, and I felt so out of my depth.

"You have nothing to be nervous about," he said.

"I don't think this is part of a lesson, Peter," I

said. Did I have to remind him that we were at the pool? That he was supposed to be doing a job? I didn't want to remind him of anything. Not a damn thing.

My body felt on fire. My nipples were incredibly tight and my breasts felt so heavy. Between my thighs, I didn't know why, but I felt need for friction, pressure, something to relieve the tension coursing through my body. I needed it.

And I tensed up as one of Peter's hands began to travel up my body. It was such a slow process, and I couldn't help but moan as he got so close to my breast. His other hand stayed at my side, not moving.

I licked my lips, trying not to think or feel, or do anything that was going to mess up these feelings. I had no idea what was going to come next, or how I was supposed to react.

Then his lips were wreaking havoc with my body as well. Soft, light brushes against my neck. Sinking my teeth into my bottom lip, I tried to focus. I tried to think of anything that would keep me grounded, but all thought left my mind. All I could feel was Peter. He stood behind me still, his hands on my body, and as he cupped one of my breasts, his lips seemed to set fire to my body.

My neck felt so sensitive as he nibbled, right near my pulse. It was like that one bite forced me to submit my body. I had no control. My nipples tightened and he stroked them through the fabric of the suit. I didn't want him to stop. The pleasure was so good.

The hand at my hip didn't stay still. No, he slid down my body, going beneath the water line, and held my pussy within his palm.

"I know you're a virgin, Niamh. I know it's going to take time to get you ready, but I can be a patient man."

Here's the thing: I was not saving my virginity for anything. The men I'd been around had been total bastards. Most of them wanted to get to know my father, or be around my father when he came around. No one else showed any interest in me. It was always about getting close to my father. Never about me. This man was the first person to want me, for me. And I couldn't help but find that a heady combination—one I didn't want to let go, so when his hand sunk beneath the fabric of my bathing suit, I didn't fight him. I let him touch me, because the truth was, I'd run away and forced myself to live in even tighter confines than I had when I was near my mom or dad. They were still controlling me.

I knew I was afraid of my dad finding me and what would happen. I hoped he never did, but I didn't want to still be a virgin, chasing away the one guy who wanted me.

I spun around, breaking all contact Peter had with me, and I lifted my head, looked him in the eyes, and asked him to take me back to his place.

I was ready, because I didn't know what the future held, but what I did know was that right now I wanted to be with him. My father wasn't here, so who I was didn't matter. Peter wanted me for me, and I wanted to hold onto that with both hands and not let go.

# Chapter Eight

*Peter*

Standing in the bedroom, I wait for Niamh to arrive. She was in my bathroom. I'd followed her request exactly. Tonight, the plan had been to try and break down those walls she had built around herself. Ivan had given me time. I had to believe he had men or women in place to deal with whatever bounty hunter made their way to Pickle Quest. Also, it helped that no matter what, I was ready and alert for whoever the fuck made it into town.

I didn't know what had changed her mind. From the moment we hit the mats, she'd been tense, trying to create distance between us. Even at the pool, I knew I made her nervous. Those were the kind of senses she needed to start listening to. I wasn't a good man.

She was in the company of a bastard, and her body was telling her that, but she wasn't going to listen. Need had taken over. Need and curiosity, and possibly a whole lot of everything else.

I'd waited for this moment, but now, as I stood here waiting for her, I realized I wasn't exactly prepared for a fucking virgin. If Ivan was here, regardless of the respect I had for him, I believe I would have punched him, not just once either.

The door to the bathroom opened and Niamh stepped out. She wore a bathrobe, and her cheeks were a lovely shade of rosy red.

"I'm sorry. I didn't mean to take long."

She'd taken a shower. I'd already taken one, giving her time to get used to being at my home. I wore a towel around my waist. I would have suggested we take one together, but I knew we both needed time.

"You know, you don't have to do this if you don't want to," I said. Again, I didn't know why the fuck I was giving her the choice, when the truth was, neither of us had a lot of choice.

I needed to get her pregnant, and quickly. The bounty hunters would figure it out sooner or later, and one of them would get too close. I had a time limit.

"I want to do this," she said. "I'm nervous. I've never done anything like this. I'd never even kissed a guy until you."

Okay, that shouldn't make me so fucking happy, but it did. In fact, I felt myself getting harder by the second, and all I wanted to do was fuck her, to take her hard. No other man had touched her. Niamh was a virgin. She'd not even been kissed.

"No one else had ever kissed these lips?" I asked.

"No."

Cupping her face, I tilted her head back and stared at her lips. They were lovely and plump. Running a finger across those lips, I felt that temptation to kiss them again. I didn't ignore it, and slammed my lips down on hers, feeling her moan as I did so. I swallowed the sounds she made and growled against her lips, not wanting to stop. I loved the feel of her mouth against mine.

Sinking my fingers into her damp hair, I held her against me. With my other hand, I couldn't resist sliding down toward the curve of her ass, and gripping the flesh hard. I drew her against my body so we didn't have any space. I didn't want any distance. She felt amazing and I didn't want to let her go.

But, I couldn't just kiss her. I had got to get her ready. Even though Niamh being a virgin was a heady thing, I also knew this was going to hurt her. I had to be what I'd never been in my life—gentle. I didn't even know what gentle was. I'd hurt, murdered, done everything I could to win.

Right now, Ivan needed me to be this suave gentleman to win the woman, and I didn't fucking know how to do that. I only knew one thing, and that was I never failed.

He wanted a baby inside her, and that's exactly what there will be. I moved us toward the bed, giving her time to tell me no. I would never force her to do anything she didn't want to do.

She didn't stop me, so I reached for the belt of her robe, slid it open, and there she was, in all her naked glory. I loved her curvy body, the fullness of her tits, the roundness of her hips, her full, juicy thighs.

I tipped her back to the bed and swallowed all kinds of protest. Only, this time I didn't linger at her lips. I kissed down her neck, sucked on her pulse, which I'd come to see as a rather erogenous zone for her, not that I was complaining. It would help me arouse her.

Slowly, I trailed my lips down her body, going toward her tits. Pushing them together, I marveled at the size. She had gorgeous, red-tipped nipples, not too small, not too big, but a delightful mouthful, which I took full advantage of.

She released a moan.

My dick was getting harder by the second, and we are both wanting to plunge, balls-deep inside her virgin cunt.

I was in control. I was the man, and I would make sure Niamh was as ready as she could be before I took her.

Sucking on each rounded nipple, I loved how she writhed under me. I took my time, allowing her to get accustomed to my touch. She was not used to kindness, of that I was sure. I didn't even need to see the evidence of what her father had done to know she had suffered cruelty.

I fucking hated her father and if I ever encountered Finn Byrne, he was going to die. I looked forward to ending his existence, but it would not be a quick death. No, I intended to make it as slow and painful as possible. I couldn't wait to do it.

Niamh would know freedom.

Unless of course she ended up with my baby, then she would always be my wife, and I'd never let her go.

Kissing down her body, I wanted to spend a lot more time on her tits, but I needed to have a taste of her pussy. She whimpered as I passed her belly button, and then I spread her legs. I pulled away, just enough to stare at her pretty, virginal cunt. I couldn't stop thinking about the fact no other man had touched her. She was all mine.

I'd never been the kind of man to seek out a virgin. I was aware there was a market for them, but virginal women held no appeal for me. I'd always wanted a woman who knew what she was doing.

Niamh wasn't just some random woman. She was going to be the mother of my children, which already put her in a completely different category.

She would be protected.

She belonged to me.

She was mine.

Running the tips of my fingers up her inner thigh, I moved closer toward her pussy. I felt how tense she was, but she's not asking me to stop, which was a relief. If she needed me to stop, I would have done so.

I needed to put my sperm inside her. It was a driving force for me to take the lips of her sex and spread them open. This first time wasn't going to be good for her.

To virgins, this was painful, so all I could do was hope for the best, which is what I did. I go toward her clit, focusing on her pleasured nub. Sliding my tongue back and forth across her clit, I circled the bud and created a small pace.

Niamh gasped and her wriggles increased beneath me. I put my hands on her inner thighs, because there were a few times she tried to close those thighs on my face.

"Please," she said, whimpering.

I knew exactly what she wanted, and I didn't play around. I focused on that little nub, sending her higher and higher, until there was nowhere else for her to go. I sent her over the edge, quite quickly, bringing her to an orgasm that had her screaming my name as it echoed around the room. It was a heady sound, my name, as my tongue rode that wave, sending her over the edge and keeping control of the subtle aftershocks as I did. I only brought her down when she could no longer stand any more of the pleasure I gave her.

I knew in that moment I would gladly lick her pussy all day long. But, I didn't have all day. I didn't even have all night.

Moving her up the bed, I followed her, crawling between her spread thighs. I'd already lost the towel, and now there was nothing between us. I was not going to wear a condom.

With both of my hands resting either side of her head, I stared into her brown eyes. I saw the headiness of her orgasm, but also her nerves.

"We don't have to do this," I said.

I was not a gentleman. I didn't even consider myself a considerate man, and those words were like a nasty aftertaste on my tongue. They're the last things I wanted to fucking say to her. I wanted this. I wanted to feel her tight cunt wrapped around my cock. In that moment, I wasn't sure if this was because of Ivan's orders, or the fact I really wanted to feel her.

She put a hand on my chest, and I expected her to push me away, but she surprised me. Niamh smiled up at me.

"I'm ready."

I doubted it, but I also wasn't going to argue with a woman who knew what she wanted. I'd been bitten by that before way too many times, and I wasn't going to do it now.

Reaching between us, I slid the tip of my dick between her wet pussy, getting it nice and slick, and ready. With the help of my tongue and her orgasm, she was soaking wet.

I eased the tip down, feeling her entrance, and I stared into her brown eyes. They looked up at me with a mix of excitement and nerves. I knew in a second they were going to be filled with pain.

I didn't want to hurt her, so I warned her.

"I don't care," she said. "I want this. I want you. Please."

Fuck. It was that "please." And now, I knew I couldn't hold back.

Tensing up, I tore through the veil of her virginity, slid my dick balls-deep inside her, and finally sealed the deal that Ivan had sent me to do.

**\*\*\*\***

*Niamh*

*A Few Hours Later*

"How are you feeling?" Peter asked.

I couldn't help but chuckle.

We were laying in his bathtub. There were some soothing salts beneath the water, and Peter had not left my side. Well, not since he came back after taking care of the bottom sheet.

I had been a virgin. I wasn't a virgin anymore. I was a woman. At twenty-five years old, I knew I'd been a woman for quite some time, only now, I was *really* a woman. I couldn't help but frown. Did having sex make me a woman? I didn't know. My head was in a confused place.

"I'm fine."

I knew it was going to hurt, but I hadn't figured out how much it was going to hurt. The pain had taken a few minutes to subside, and I was pretty sure Peter had even tried to not finish. He'd wanted to take care of me, and to call the whole thing off.

Not happening. I was doing this for me.

I wanted Peter, and even though I knew there was a chance this wasn't going to last, I at least wanted my first time to be my choice. Not my father's or my mother's, or anyone else's. This was *my* choice. And I chose Peter. Sweet, kind, charming Peter.

"Are you sure? I could warm up the water. I've got a few friends who might know a doctor."

This made me laugh. "It's fine. I'm fine. Please, don't worry." I tilted my head to the side and offered him a smile. "I do feel okay, I promise."

He stroked a finger down my cheek. "I … hurting you … I didn't want to."

"I know," I said. I did believe him. "There won't be any more pain now."

"I know, because we're not doing it again."

I chuckled and moved out of his arms. The bathtub was pretty large and I was able to straddle his waist. As I did this, I was careful because I didn't want the water going all over the place. I happened to like Peter's home. I'd never dream of trashing the place.

I didn't even know where I'd gotten the confidence to spin around, smile at him, and slowly ease down onto his lap. His cock was still flaccid. He really, really, didn't like hurting me.

How could I not be charmed by this man? I'd never known someone so gentle, so caring. I hadn't grown up in my father's home, but his presence lingered no matter where I was.

I cupped his face, staring into his blue eyes. They were so bright and beautiful, I knew I'd gladly look into his eyes all day and night.

"We're never having sex again?" I asked.

"No."

"What if I would like it?"

"I'm not going to hurt you."

I kiss him. "You won't hurt me, that is a promise."

I was not even trying to have sex with him again right now, but I needed him to know that I was fine.

His hands slid up my back, going toward my neck and between my thighs. I felt an answering pulse of his cock as he started to thicken. He was getting aroused, and this surprised me.

Breaking the kiss, I stared into his eyes. "Are you so sure about not wanting to?" I asked.

"I won't hurt you."

"What if I want to feel you again?" I asked. "Without the pain."

Peter grabbed my arms and I let out a yelp, not in pain, but in shock as he spun me around, pressing my back toward his chest, and banded an arm around me. The sheer strength and force of him took me completely by surprise. I was at his mercy, not that I minded.

He was in control.

I couldn't move.

I was not afraid.

I loved the power he had just shown, which was a rather strange feeling to have.

"Not tonight," Peter said.

"But—"

"No, I am not going to take you again tonight. It's going to be a couple of days before you feel my cock inside you."

I was pretty sure he gritted his teeth as he spoke. I'd never been so forward with anyone in my life.

Peter ran a hand down my body, and I stopped wriggling as his hand moved between my thighs.

"But that doesn't mean I cannot make you feel good in another way," he said.

He pressed a finger between my slit, stroked across my clit, and then delved down toward my entrance.

I gasped as he slid a single finger inside me. There wasn't any pain, but I was still getting accustomed to the feel of someone inside me.

This was a different kind of feeling. He pulled the finger out of me and I couldn't help but whimper because I didn't want him to stop. Peter chuckled, and then eased it back inside me.

"I'm not going to stop, but I am going to play."

Sinking my teeth into my bottom lip, I tried to contain the noises I wanted to make.

The pleasure Peter was causing my body was a heady thing. He drew that finger up and began to stroke my clit. I felt an orgasm already starting to build, which he took away from me by thrusting back inside me.

He changed it up, adding a second finger, and now he was fucking me with both, and then stroking my clit. Each time he touched my nub, I felt myself getting closer to an orgasm, only for him to stop before I went right over that peak. I wanted to scream at him, but again he had control over my body.

I didn't know how long we ended up like this, where he teased and pushed my body from one extreme to another, but then it was like he knew I couldn't take much more, and he thrust me over the edge, sending me hurtling into another shocking orgasm that took my breath away. I was sure I screamed his name a time or two, or even more.

## Chapter Nine

*Peter*

*A Few Months Later*

Sliding my blade into the neck of the man who'd wandered into Pickle Quest, I had recognized him immediately. He'd tried the whole damaged car trick to gain information. For his unlucky day, I was the guy he got to ask for directions, and then of course, he asked me if I knew of a Niamh Byrne.

This guy had to have been an amateur. I was not a trained bounty hunter, but I knew a thing or two about killing people, and you didn't go in all guns blazing, nor did you start by asking a whole heap of questions. That just didn't happen.

Killing this bastard had been easy, way too easy, but if one had finally arrived, it was only a matter of time before more did.

Once the man was dead, which didn't take very long, I stuffed him into the trunk of the car, climbed behind the wheel, and drove. I'd already put the call to Ivan that I was going to need a clean-up crew, and gave him the location to come and pick up the car and the dead body.

It took me less than ten minutes to arrive to the spot, and I climbed out, slammed the door, and felt the rage consume me. Danger was getting close to Niamh.

If I hadn't been on my way back to the gym after dropping her off at the diner, he'd have found someone else to give him Niamh's location. One of the locals wouldn't have thought twice about laughing off the inaccuracy of her last name, and saying they didn't know a Niamh Byrne, but they did know a Niamh Long.

This is why you had to change your first fucking name.

I didn't have to wait long for Ivan to arrive, but I was surprised he wasn't alone. The fucking Butcher was there, at the front of the car with him. Since when did they become such close pals? I was pissed off.

"What the fuck?" I asked, the moment Ivan got out of the car.

"Don't get your panties in a twist," The Butcher said.

She wore a hat, a pair of jeans, and a blouse, making her appear like an ordinary woman, when I knew she had a lot more kills under her belt. She was a professional killer. No one knew her story. In all honesty, this was the first time I had truly met her.

No one knew her name. She was a butcher. Her and The Beast's identity had remained a mystery. I'd tried to find more information about the two, but there was nothing.

They killed and took care of business, and they were rivals, that was all. However, time to time, they would partner up to deal with whatever problem had arisen. Is that what was happening now? Ivan needed both to take over section six.

"He in the trunk?" The Butcher asked.

"Yes." I waved my hand at her.

"You're going to need to get yourself cleaned up," she said. "Everything you need is with Ivan."

I had blood on my hands as well as my shirt.

I turned toward Ivan who held out a duffel bag.

"Here you go, son," Ivan said.

I wasn't in the mood for Ivan's playful mood.

"We need to take Niamh in," I said. I was done

playing this game.

The Butcher went to the back of the car and opened the trunk. "Nice," she said. "You did this?"

"Do you see me with a fucking partner?" I asked, irritated.

Niamh was back in town, and I had to get back to her.

"Have you gotten her pregnant yet?" Ivan asked.

I had intended to wait to see if that first time we were together would take care of it, but it hadn't. Also, it would seem Niamh had a little more power over me than I realized. There were only so many times I could deny her, but the moment she looked at me with those eyes, almost pleading, and said "please," I couldn't say fucking no. I'd never had a woman say please, or even beg me.

Niamh wasn't trying to take from me. It was the strangest feeling, kind of heady as well. Niamh wanted me for me. There was no second play. But, she wanted the lie.

The Peter who was a personal trainer, who worked at a gym, who was helping a friend, and on paper, looked to be a nice guy.

I was not.

It's all a lie, as the dead body in the trunk of the car could attest. It wasn't even my greatest work. Death didn't bother me. Nor did torture. I'd experienced my fair share on both counts, being tortured and torturing. I'd become quite good at it as well. Kind of like an unknown art, one I did enjoy exploring.

"No, but did you see how close that fucker had gotten?"

"To the trunk of his car?" Ivan asked.

"For fuck's sake, if I had been one moment later, he'd have already gotten to Niamh."

"We're taking care of the rest. This sneaky little bastard was already on my radar. If it makes you feel any better, he never takes his target on the first try. He tends to wait, kind of like a hunt. He'd have watched her, and trust me, he's not subtle about it. You'd have gotten to him," The Butcher said.

"And that is supposed to make me feel fucking good?" I was losing my temper.

The Butcher shrugged her shoulders and then got to work dealing with it.

I turned my attention back to Ivan who was waiting for my dirty clothes.

We were going to do this outside in the secluded open. I knew it didn't make sense. It was a secluded spot out in the open.

There were wipes, and a change of clothes, and some other shit. I was angry as I wiped my hands, cleaning off the blood.

The Butcher, the sick fuck she was, hummed to herself.

"You know you're going to push too far," I said, looking at Ivan. "It has already been a couple of months with the bounty hunters. One finally made it into town."

"So you better get back to town and do as I instructed." Ivan glanced down at his wristwatch. "Time is ticking."

I'd never wanted to punch Ivan more than I did in that moment. I liked Ivan. More often, I understood his reasoning but when it came to this situation, I was at a fucking loss. I didn't get it.

The other women for the other Brigadiers were in different positions. They weren't lied to, manipulated, or forced to carry a child. Niamh was being put in those positions.

I was changed and Ivan took my dirty clothes

along with the duffel bag.

"You know, maybe you should start asking why this is bothering you," Ivan said.

I glared at him. "I know exactly why it's bothering me, and so do you."

Ivan laughed. "No, no, there is something more to this and you know it, but we can play the pretend game if that makes you feel a little better."

None of this made me feel any better.

"This is not a game."

"Oh, but it is. You see, our very life and existence are a game. Once you realize that, maybe it will be time for you to play."

I wasn't a child.

"Some of us get bad rough hands," Ivan said. "Some of us get shittier-than-shit rough hands. Rarely is there a silver lining. Then there are some that don't deserve the … crap they've been dealt, and even though day in day out, they are worn down, stomped down so much that for most people that would make them a shell of their former self, there are a rare few that lose the spark that makes them different. It makes them good. Then there are some that persevere no matter what life throws them, one shit hand after another, and all you can do is travel that bouncy ride to the bitter end."

I had no fucking clue what he was talking about. I got it. Everyone got dealt different hands. Some of us had it shittier than others.

"Death is the final chapter in every person's life, Peter. Birth and death, the journey is what we all make it." He glanced past my shoulder and I turned to find The Beast arriving in another car. "Here is your ride. Get the job done."

And with that, I was dismissed like a fucking child.

I didn't even know what the fuck Ivan was talking about and now I was even more angry than when I had arrived.

Niamh might be pregnant. She had missed her last menstrual cycle, and I should know. I'd documented when she was last on hers, and it was over five weeks ago.

The last person I wanted to ride with was The Beast, but I needed to get back to town, and riding in a dead man's car was not an option. Clearly, Ivan wasn't going to drive me into town.

Slamming the door closed, I couldn't help but wonder why Niamh was so different. I was made aware of Ivan's constant meddling in the other Brigadiers' lives. He was a constant presence, talking with their wives, getting close to them. Being more like a friend and possible brother to them.

Yet, Ivan was nowhere to be seen when it came to Niamh.

Why not?

Why was he keeping his distance while at the same time protecting her?

This made no sense to me. The Beast didn't talk.

I wasn't about to ask him questions. Ivan might trust these two killers, but I wasn't going to trust them with anything, not until they had earned it, and right now, they hadn't earned jack shit.

The Beast pulled up on the sign outside of town, and parked the car. I was about to reach for the door handle when The Beast finally spoke.

"Can Ivan Volkov be trusted?" The Beast asked.

I turned toward the man.

The Beast was as big a mystery as The Butcher. Only, The Beast was tall and looked like he could kill anyone. The Butcher, on the other hand, didn't look quite so capable, although I had heard she'd gutted many men and had even removed limbs, penises, and plenty other horror stories, all of which I didn't want to think about in that moment.

"Yes."

"You're not even going to ask me why I've asked?" The Beast asked.

"No, I'm not interested in knowing why you're curious."

"Ivan Volkov is a … mystery."

I shrugged. "There is no mystery. Ivan Volkov is a loyal man. He's scary as fuck, and the shit he can do, well, don't get on his bad side, it doesn't end well for you. Of course, there is also that pesky rumor that he's immortal and he can't die." He might have faked his own death once. "Ivan has his own ways of dealing with stuff. We don't always know why he does the things he does, or his reasoning, but when he's ready for you to know, it will be revealed to you. It always is."

Which is why I knew I had to wait. Ivan had his reasoning for not coming to see Niamh, for not meddling. One day, I would find out the truth, and when that happened, all would be revealed.

****

*Niamh*

I should have left town. Each day I planned to tell Peter that it is time for me to move on, we'd start kissing, and then I'd forget what I meant to say.

Then of course, the kissing lead to, well, more kissing, which lead to us being naked, and then sex. I liked sex. The first time had been incredibly painful. I'd even expected the pain. The second time had been much better, and now I'd lost count of how good it was.

Several of the women in town couldn't stand me. They didn't like that I'd won Peter Shadows and they hadn't. They hadn't stopped trying, though. Peter told me regularly of some of their antics, but he was already well-prepared for them. I could imagine that pissed them all off.

Stepping out of the diner at a little past eight, I turned to find Peter leaning up against his car, a smile on his lips.

When we first met, he rarely smiled, but now, as I stepped toward him, he opened his arms. He embraced me and I felt … safe. This is another reason I hadn't left. For the first time in my life, I felt safe. I was in Peter's arms. Nothing bad could happen. But I knew I was a fool. My father would kill this man without a second thought, and I didn't want to be responsible for killing him.

I liked him and I was a little afraid I might even be falling in love with him. Which had to be crazy. I'd read the stories of love at first sight and all those other tales of meeting "the one," at the perfect moment. They sounded like the perfect dream, only to me that was the fantasy, because of my father.

Yet, we'd known each other a few months, and I had developed feelings for Peter. Was it love? I didn't know, because I didn't know what love was supposed to feel like. I'd never known love.

"I've been waiting for that all day."

I smiled. "Me too. Did you have a good day?"

"It's getting better."

He moved away from the car and opened the passenger side. I slid in, and Peter surprised me by reaching in and securing my seat belt. I smiled at him as he closed the door. He seemed a little distracted tonight.

"Bad day at the gym?" I asked.

"You could say that."

He was being vague.

I couldn't help but wonder if one of the women had tried to come on to him again. A couple of the women had tried to tell him he was making a mistake in dating me. Kind of rude, but they had their opinions, I had mine.

He clearly didn't want to talk, so I stayed silent as he drove us back to his place. I'd only been back to my apartment to change clothes, toss out the spoiled food, pay the rent, and that was pretty much it.

Peter insisted on us being at his place. I got the feeling he didn't like my apartment, but he'd also not asked me to move in. I was grateful he hadn't asked me, because I would have had to say no.

Strange, I just realized that in my twenty-five years, Peter was my first-ever boyfriend, and I felt that hit of guilt, because I was already lying to him. This was not a relationship.

I needed to leave. I'd already stayed longer than I should have.

Pickle Quest was a nice town, but the only reason I stayed was for Peter, and that was a bad reason. My father could be out looking for me. So far, I'd not seen anyone who might be working for my father. That could all change, though. I had to leave to protect Peter. If someone started asking questions, Peter could get hurt.

We arrived at his place and he parked the car. I turned toward him, about to tell him I'd be leaving soon.

Peter started to talk. "I'd like you to move in with me."

Okay, now that was a surprise. I was a little taken aback, seeing as that was what I was just thinking about. But I had to leave.

"Move in with you?" I asked.

He pointed toward the house. "I've been wanting to ask you for a couple of weeks now, but, I didn't want to scare you away. I kind of like having you around."

This made me smile, although this was now the last thing I wanted to tell him.

"I, uh, I'd love to but … Peter, I'm going to have to leave soon," I said. The moment I said those words, I knew I didn't mean them. I didn't want to leave him, and once again, I couldn't help but hate my dad.

"I know. You've said before that you don't intend to stay in Pickle Quest, but how about, until you leave, we kind of see where this goes? You never know, when you've got to leave, I might just go with you."

This surprised me. "You'd come with me?"

"Yeah, why not? Nothing is keeping me here. I know my friend can get another person to take care of this house. It'll be fun."

I reached across and kissed him.

He'd be willing to give all of this up for me. It seemed crazy. I couldn't let him do it. If he came with me, that was the guarantee of a target on his head. I didn't need to leave right away. Moving in with him, trying this out, could be fun. Dangerous, but also fun.

"I would love to move in with you," I said, and it was strange how good that felt to say.

Even though I was terrified of my father finding me and of the consequences of anyone learning who I was, this was something I wanted to do.

I'd run away from my father to have my own life. To live how I wanted, and stop being afraid of whenever there was a knock on the door, yet, I'd been living my life like I expected that knock. I didn't even know if my father was around, if he was close, if he even cared what I was doing.

Peter pulled away, opened his car door, and I saw that look in his eye. I'm no expert when it comes to men, but I knew what that look meant, and I didn't hesitate to remove my seat belt, and join him out on his front driveway.

Within minutes we were inside his home, and it didn't take us long to start tearing each other's clothes off. In our desperation to get naked, we didn't make it upstairs, and much to my surprise, we were in his sitting room. The curtains were already drawn closed and he pressed me over the long edge of the sofa. He spread my legs and I couldn't contain my moan of pleasure as he cupped me between the thighs. One of his fingers slid knuckle-deep inside me, and I cried out, hungry for more.

He growled my name against my neck as he'd leaned over to tease where my pulse was. Whenever he played with my neck, I struggled to contain my arousal.

No matter what I did, even if I gritted my teeth, I had to moan, I had to do something because it felt so good, and I didn't want it to stop.

"Please," I said.

The two fingers that were inside me moved, slid up toward my clit, and he began to massage my nub, and I felt so close. It always embarrassed me, because Peter lasted a long time through sex. Just a few seconds of Peter's magical touch and I was ready to orgasm. It never took long for me to be ready, and sure enough, brief moments later, I screamed his name as an orgasm tore through my body.

It felt so good.

I didn't want it to stop.

Not for a second.

And he didn't let it stop.

He prolonged my orgasm, teasing my clit, but he

took his time stroking me, allowing me to get accustomed to the feel of his touch. I wanted it all. So hungry. So desperate for everything he was doing to me.

Before long, he'd sent me into a second orgasm, and the sheer force of it took me by surprise. This time, my release hadn't even finished, and I felt Peter stop, and the press of his cock as inch by inch, he began to sink inside me.

I moaned for more.

Peter put his hands on my hips, and slammed the last couple of inches inside me, making me scream in pleasure. My whole body felt on fire and not in a bad way. It was heady. I loved this part.

The hands on my hips didn't stay there. Peter sat to the hilt inside me, and he slowly ran his hands up my body, sliding beneath me, cupping my tits, and playing with them. Tweaking the nipples which sent a pulse right between my thighs, startling me.

It felt so good, and then he moved down, going back to my hips to hold onto me as he started to pull out until only the tip of his dick remained. Then, achingly slowly, he started to fill me.

His strokes began slow, and he'd been doing this for some time, allowing me to get accustomed to the feel of him inside me. It always felt too good to be true, and as he worked that impressive length, I didn't know if I would be able to stand it much longer.

Then, he picked up the pace, and the sounds of our bodies slapping together filled the air. I cried out, the pleasure taking me by surprise, and there was no pain. I knew Peter wasn't capable of causing me any pain.

There was that pesky little thought—I knew in that moment I was in love with this man. How could I not be? He'd done everything for me, and he'd be willing to leave with me as well. Coming on the road, traveling with me, it seemed so strange to think he would do that for me. That anyone would care enough about me to come with me.

And yes, I had fallen in love with Peter Shadows, and I wanted to hold onto these moments for a long time.

## Chapter Ten

*The Beast*

"You could have called me," I said, looking toward Ivan.

"And when I need you, trust me, I will call you." Ivan was sitting in the far corner of the room, sipping a glass of whiskey.

This was not the kind of place I imagined Ivan seeming so comfortable. It was a rundown farmhouse where we'd taken shelter for the past couple of weeks. I truly didn't get this man.

The boss of any Bratva did not spend time waiting for threats from a woman who was not even his kin, to help his Brigadier. All the Brigadiers, soldiers, associates, they bent over backward for the boss, for their king.

Ivan Volkov was their king, and yet, in a rundown farmhouse, after killing another two bounty hunters today, with The Butcher taking care of the cleanup, Ivan sat, drinking shitty whiskey after enjoying a boxed takeout meal. This man was full of surprises.

I was pissed off.

Ivan had approached me and The Butcher about taking over his section that had been left vacant from the betrayal of one of his Brigadiers. I knew why he'd approached us, but I didn't like the offer he'd given us. The Butcher and I didn't play well together. It didn't help that I liked to have more kills than her, and I do believe she did in fact rival me on just how bloody she could be.

"So, all the work you had ready was for The Butcher?" I asked.

Ivan chuckled. "You're feeling jealous."

I glared at him.

I was aware that when I didn't get a call to complete a job, it was simply because they needed The Butcher's finesse. I took a drink of my whiskey. Or, they simply wanted to see her curvy fucking ass doing the hard work. I had a feeling Ivan wasn't keeping The Butcher around because of her big tits and ass, though.

Ivan sighed and leaned forward. "I'll break it down for you. You attract too much attention. The Butcher doesn't attract a lot of attention. A lot of men and women will glance at her, but she is able to blend in. No one gives her a second glance."

Trust me, I do, but then I know what she is capable of.

"For this, I needed her to distract and kill. I needed someone to get close and handle those kills without drawing attention. She could do that. You're noticeable. You are a problem, which is why I only called you when the need for the duffel bag was necessary."

And I had stuck around as well, because I didn't like the possibility of The Butcher and Ivan getting close.

I couldn't read this bastard. There were a lot of rumors surrounding him. Talk about him potentially already being with someone, having been married, or some shit. The details were never very clear, and the reason I stuck close to Ivan these past few months, and was even considering his offer, was because of how little I was able to learn.

Ivan took care of himself and his Bratva. He didn't miss any corner, or leave any stone unturned. He looked at all the details. He knew the risks involved, but he kept doing it.

Like now, he wanted Peter to knock up Finn

Byrne's daughter. I didn't even see why that was important to him. I got wanting to take out Finn as he was a threat, but how would knocking up his daughter accomplish that?

There was also another little more interesting business, like how the fuck did Ivan even know about Finn Byrne's daughter?

Finn Byrne was a horrible bastard, cruel, and someone I'd considered very much evil. He kept the identity of his kids very quiet. No one could know about them. Yet, against those odds, Ivan had been able to find out exactly who Niamh was.

How the fuck did that happen? I'd even attempted to do some digging, and I couldn't find anything. Everyone had a paper trail, everyone left a tiny crumb that was just sizeable enough to follow.

Not Ivan. It was why I respected the fuck out of him. He'd been the one and only person where I had to speculate about rumors, and try to piece together the man who sat before me.

"When I need a distraction of a volcano, you'll be the first one I'll call," Ivan said.

I smiled, because in truth, I did like to make an entrance.

****

*Peter*

*A Few Weeks Later*

It was hot as fuck, and I decided to do something I had never done before. It was Sunday, which meant no diner, and no gym.

Niamh and I were in the clear, and to celebrate,

I'd packed a little picnic. There was a small fair in town, out near the school's football field.

There was a small park across from the small church and graveyard, along a small woodland. It was private, giving us some space away from the prying eyes of the locals. Although, there were several people still milling about.

Holding Niamh's hand, I knew we'd become the local couple. It seemed to have broken down quite a few barriers, which I wasn't entirely sure I was happy about, but I knew Niamh was happy, and I didn't want to spoil it.

I also had a feeling Niamh was pregnant. We hadn't stopped having sex, and I made sure each time that I came balls-deep inside her. Even stopping her from sucking my dick, so that I could complete my mission.

She wasn't starting to show, however, she'd not had a menstrual cycle in nearly two months. I'd also noticed over the past couple of days, she did start to get tired, and a couple of times this week, she had started to experience morning sickness.

Neither of us had said anything. I wasn't even sure if Niamh was aware of what was going on. I wasn't going to spoil our fun by telling her what was happening. There would be plenty of time for that, I was sure of it.

The picnic I'd arranged wasn't too big—a couple of sandwiches, some pastries. A few bits of finger foods I had organized at the local bakery. Nothing too special, but enough for both of us to enjoy. I'd also foregone the bottle of wine for a bottle of water. Niamh didn't enjoy soda a lot.

Now, perched up against a tree, Niamh between my spread legs, I wrapped my arms around her, holding her close.

"This is nice, isn't it?" she asked.

I knew what she was thinking as she'd mentioned it a few times over the past week. Our time in Pickle Quest was coming to an end. What Niamh didn't know, was during this time, I'd killed an additional two men.

Ivan and this little group of killers had also dealt with several bounty hunters. I didn't know what the fuck Finn offered them, but their dead rivals didn't seem to stop them in their tracks, which fucking sucked big time. It pissed me off. And yet, there was nothing I could do about it.

All I could do was wait and hope Niamh stayed pregnant. She wasn't ready to know she was pregnant, even though I had a feeling she did know.

"Yeah, we've been too busy for a long time. It's nice just taking our time, slowing down." I kissed the column of her neck. "Enjoying the views."

She laughed.

Most Sundays we were naked, enjoying the view of each other. It had taken some time, but eventually I'd been able to break down her walls about being naked in front of me. She was so nervous and embarrassed about her body.

I'd spent an entire Sunday making love, kissing, and fucking every inch of her body. I didn't give a fuck what other men said. Niamh was fucking beautiful, and I loved her large tits, the fullness of her thighs as they wrapped around me, how juicy her ass was. I didn't want a woman who complained about how I was hurting her and seeing as I wasn't a small man, that would undoubtedly happen. Niamh could take everything I gave her and beg for more, which was exactly how I liked it.

"There is something I wanted to talk to you about," Niamh said.

"If this is about us moving, I already figured you wanted to move. Tomorrow? End of this week?"

"You're not going to ask me why?" Niamh asked, moving so she faced me.

I reached out and cupped her cheek, stroking my thumb across the delicate skin. "Why would I ask you? You have your reasons, and I don't care, just so long as I'm with you."

I never watched romance movies. Niamh did, and I kind of picked up a few tips along the way. As long as I didn't hold back my imaginary feelings for her, and spoke softly, she fell for everything I said.

I cared about Niamh, but I didn't know what love was. I'd watched the movies with her, but again, the whole concept of love was so foreign to me. Love was a fairytale people spun to keep others in line.

"When do you want to leave?" I asked.

"Tomorrow. I have already handed in my notice. I can wait, if you need to give your notice at the gym," Niamh said.

"No, that's fine. We can both go."

I was aware Niamh had handed in her notice. I'd seen her sneak downstairs late one night, and when she had fallen asleep, I went to see what she'd been doing, and sure enough, she was being thoughtful, even in running away. I still didn't know how Finn Byrne was able to create such a daughter, but Niamh was nothing like her parents. She was kind, sweet, loving, charming, and everything I knew I should stay away from.

For whatever reason, Ivan had chosen her for me, and when the truth finally came out, Niamh was going to see that she'd been given to someone who would never be able to give her what she wanted. I didn't do love. I was not her knight in shining armor. I was a killer through and through.

She leaned up and kissed me. "I need to use the bathroom."

I held onto her hand, and she gave a little giggle as she pulled away, and I tried to hold on, but she let go.

"I'll be right back."

I watched her walk away, heading toward the small building near the church where the toilets were. Leaning against the tree, I took a deep breath, and as I did, my cell phone vibrated. I was tempted to ignore it. Whenever my cell phone went off, it usually meant bad news.

Niamh and I were having a good day.

She wasn't going to be happy for long, if tomorrow she thought we were leaving. The truth was, I intended to drug her and take her back to my sector. I was convinced I had knocked her up.

Checking the caller, I saw it was Ivan. There was that temptation to ignore it completely, but he was the boss, and I still had to answer to him.

"Hello," I said, being awfully polite.

"Where's Niamh?" Ivan asked, and he didn't sound happy.

This put me instantly on high alert as I sat up. "Why?"

"The slippery fuck made his way into town. Finn Byrne is in Pickle Quest. He intends to get Niamh."

And that was when I heard it. The scream. Niamh's scream.

I was on my feet running, and I already knew it was too late. I'd already dropped the cell phone in my hand and retrieved my gun.

One of Finn's goons was shoving Niamh into the back of a blue truck. I ran as hard and as fast as I could. Aiming my gun, I took a shot, not going for the head, but the knee of the guy waiting to climb into the truck. The truck was already starting to pull away, and the deep growl of the man I shot echoed close to me.

Anger tore through me, as I looked up and watched Niamh fighting for her freedom. She was hit hard enough that she suddenly slumped to the ground. I was not close enough, even though I kept running, but it was no use. All I'd gotten was the guy I'd hurt.

I acted, I didn't think.

Grabbing the bastard who was trying to get away, I pulled back my fist and hit him hard. I expected I was going to have to hit him again and again, but much to my surprise, he was knocked clean out with one punch.

As if by magic, there was no one around as I dragged his body to the back of my car. Slamming the trunk down, I was tempted to take one of my crowbars and start attacking the knocked-out bastard, but I knew that would not work.

I needed to think clearly right now. Killing him wouldn't get me back to Niamh.

I'd done the ultimate mistake and let my fucking guard down and now, Niamh was back in her father's clutches and I was pissed off.

I gathered up our picnic and saw that my cell phone was on the ground where I dropped it. I picked it up and expected the call to be ended, but Ivan was still on the line.

"They have her," I said.

"We'll be there in twenty minutes."

I hang up, that was more than fine, because for the next twenty minutes, I was going to be busy.

**\*\*\*\***

*Niamh*

Peter had a gun. I'd seen that with my own two eyes.

Peter had been chasing me down, and he didn't seem surprised that there had been men to take me. I should have known this was coming.

Fear traveled up my spine.

I'd already come to, inside the truck where they'd taken me. We were still driving so I didn't know for sure how long I'd been out of it. There was silence in the car. No one was talking and I was staying perfectly still on the floor, while I came to terms with the fact that Peter had a gun. Why did Peter have a gun? He'd aimed it, of that I was sure. Surer than anything, which was crazy, because that would mean he knew exactly how to shoot a gun, and how was that possible if … he was just an ordinary guy who worked at a gym? My only conclusion could be that Peter wasn't an ordinary guy.

The truck came to a stop and now I felt the panic rising My dad was not a nice guy even when everything was going his way. I'd been a runaway for awhile now, and he'd come to get me himself, which meant this was going to hurt.

My heart raced and I felt the tears coming, but tears and begging never helped me.

The back of the truck opened and I felt the other men climb out. I stayed perfectly still, trying to perfect my breathing in the hope he would ignore me.

I felt someone climb into the back of the truck and I knew without opening my eyes that it was my dad. He tutted and then pain exploded as he grabbed my hair and began to drag me out of the car. I couldn't pretend anymore as he pulled at my hair. I tried to stop him, and had no choice but to follow him out.

At least he'd grabbed my hair in one chunk, but that didn't stop it being painful. Pain filled my head from the force of his grip. I tried not to scream or whimper, but that was impossible. Even as I cleared the truck, he didn't let go.

My father didn't let go until I was on my knees, and then he used the grip he had on my hair to slap me hard, right across the face. Once one way, then going back the other way. He did that again, and my face was burning. I couldn't get away, and no one was willing to help me. They were all my father's minions. His goons.

Finally, he let me go, but this wasn't for a reprieve. No, this was for him to kick me hard. I curled up in a ball, and his foot connected with my stomach and then my chest, and I turned over for him to stomp on my back.

"Useless fucking slut," he said.

Then I heard his belt buckle.

"Please," I said.

I should have known begging for mercy or asking him to stop wouldn't do me any good.

"Please?" He burst out laughing and that was when I screamed.

The dress I wore didn't provide any kind of protection from the buckle of his belt as it hit me. I was in for the beating of my life.

All the while, I couldn't rid my mind of the memory of Peter with his gun. Who exactly was Peter Shadows?

## Chapter Eleven

*Peter*

I'd arrived at my place with time to spare. With the fair in town, no one was around, so I was able to carry the body of the still knocked-out man into the main house. Within minutes, I had my area set up, and I grabbed a glass of ice-cold water and slammed it in his face.

He came to, so I decided to crush the glass onto his face, making him scream, and I now was doubly sure he was very much awake and alert. Crouching down to be at eye level, I smiled at him.

"Hello," I said. "So, you and I, we're going to have a little chat."

"I'm not telling you fucking nothing." He spat in my face, and I wiped the spittle off, rubbing it between my fingers.

I was a patient man, well, in most situations, I was a patient man, but all of that had ran out when Niamh was taken. Now, I wasn't Peter Shadows, the personal trainer employed by the gym and Niamh's boyfriend. That cover was gone. I was Peter Orlov, and I didn't have to put the monster that I was to bed. In fact, I walked toward the kitchen counter, grabbed a knife, and then plunged it into his genital area.

"If you ever make it out of here alive, I imagine you're going to want the use of your cock, but I'm going to want it as a trophy. I hope the last time you used this thing was worth it."

I debated pulling the blade out, but instead decided to leave it right there. It looked like I had actually pinned his dick to the chair, even through his baggy pants. This is why men shouldn't wear baggy pants. The screams filled the room, but to me they were sweet sounds of Heaven.

Blood soaked my hand, and then I decided to grab a few more knives.

"You know, in my time, I've enjoyed a lot of knife work," I said.

The man was still screaming and blubbering like a baby, but I wasn't going to allow it to distract me from my work, so I kept talking.

"You know how when you grab a bucket and it has a hole in it, and water leaks out in a perfect united unit, and then you add another hole, and it's like the two holes are competing for who could empty the most water? I've always been curious about a person and when it comes to their blood." I held the small knife in my hand, the kind often used to prepare vegetables. Like a hand knife. "Do you think that is going to work on a person?" I asked, and then I stabbed him three times, going for places that wouldn't cause him a quick death, but would hurt a hell of a lot.

His screams started. "Stop, please, fucking stop!" he said.

I looked at my masterpiece and clicked my tongue. "Not quite working how I wanted it to. Maybe there's like a plug, and you have to unclog it to make it go glug-glug." I stabbed him a few more times.

I knew exactly what I was doing, and I was really enjoying myself. I liked stabbing this man. It had been too long that I'd gone without killing, and I wanted to enjoy the experience again, and again, and again. I had not been able to take out every bounty hunter, and that upset me.

At the sound of my front door opening, I didn't

even bother to turn around to know that Ivan, The Beast, and The Butcher had entered my home.

"Where is he taking her?" I asked.

The man in the chair had just pissed himself.

"I can't tell you," he said.

I reached down and grabbed the hilt of the blade that had his cock imbedded on the chair. I gave it just a little twist, reminding him of exactly what he was going to lose. This man was dead, but there was always that faint glimmer of hope that for whatever reason, they might survive and make it out alive. It was kind of charming, at least I thought so. Never saw it myself.

I waited, and then I twisted, and his screams filled the air.

"You're going to tell me where she is, or you're going to suffer."

I knew without a doubt that Finn was going to make her hurt. I also had an inkling that she was pregnant with my child. If he hurt her, beat her, there was a risk of our baby being hurt. I couldn't allow that to happen.

The clock was ticking.

"Fuck you," the man said, and then went to spit on me again.

"Allow me," The Butcher said, and I turned toward her, not wanting her to interfere.

The man looked … happy as she stepped forward, and I watched, a little baffled, as she stroked his face. She was soothing at first. "There, there, it's going to be okay."

And then, I was amazed, as she made him scream in pain, and because she had stepped in front of him, I didn't see what she had done, but as she stepped back, I saw that she'd removed one of his eyes. Holy fuck.

The Butcher didn't look at all fazed by what she

had done, as she wiped her hands on a towel. I didn't think she'd gouged it out, but had crushed it inside his eye socket.

She looked up at me.

At first, I saw what she had done as pointless, but then he started to talk.

"I don't know where he is. He planned to take his daughter to his secure location, but he isn't going to stay there long. The plan is to transfer to another car, and then he's taking her back, but I wasn't privy to any of the other details," he said. "I only know he wanted his daughter back. Please, just kill me. I ... don't let her ... fucking Butcher."

And then I glanced over to The Butcher and saw her smile. She knew that was going to happen.

Okay, now I was impressed. When it came to The Butcher and The Beast, their reputations were rumors, but now I was starting to see why. They were willing to do whatever it took to get the job done. I'd just watched her take out a guy's eye and she didn't even care. There was no love in her eyes, no feeling, and for a split-second, I wondered why. How did a woman get like that?

But then, I knew it was exactly the same for a man.

The Butcher had been raised this way. She'd been taught to be unfeeling, to do damage, to hurt, to maim, to kill, and that is why she was as scary as she was, and as deadly.

I looked toward Ivan. "Do we need him?" I asked.

"No, we don't. I already have leverage for Finn Byrne." He glanced down at his watch. "And I should be getting a call in three, two, one."

As if by magic, Ivan's cell phone began to ring.

I was angry, because he didn't reach for it.

"Answer it," I said.

"All in good time. Take care of that asshole first. I want to see how you end him," Ivan said.

I wanted to argue with him. Ivan always got what he wanted, and the longer I stood here arguing about following orders, the more Niamh was at risk of being at the mercy of her father, and that I couldn't allow. Going to the man I'd taken, I looked him in his single eye, and then reached out to him, and with all my force, I twisted, snapping his neck. There was no satisfaction with his death.

Ivan's cell phone stopped ringing and I turned toward him.

"It went to voicemail, how rude." He gave a little tut. "No one knows patience anymore, have you noticed that?"

"The world wants answers and they want them yesterday," The Beast said.

I wasn't interested in righting the world, or even talking about patience or people not having it. Niamh's life was on the line.

Ivan's cell phone rang again, and this time he waited several rings. My patience was being strained to a whole new level, and I was about ready to snap when Ivan answered the call. He'd put it on speaker.

"You have something of mine," Finn Byrne said.

"I have something of yours, but you don't tell me who you are?" There is another tut from Ivan. "I don't like playing these guessing games, because if you want to get truly technical, then I have a whole lot of everyone's things."

Running a hand down my face, I was close to losing it.

The Butcher and The Beast looked calm, also mildly entertained. I was the fucking furthest from any of it. I was ready to explode.

"You have my son, and you know exactly who this is," Finn said.

Ivan clicked his tongue. "Finn, Finn, ah, you're talking about Finn Byrne, is that correct?"

"Yes."

"Yes, I do have your son. He's in a rather uncomfortable position at the moment." Ivan let out a little chuckle.

I didn't see a third member, but The Butcher had left, only to come back seconds later with a man whose arm looked to be in the wrong position. There was also blood oozing out of his nose, and it looked like a couple of teeth were missing.

"I had a little fun," The Beast said.

"Dad," Finn the son said.

"Finn!"

"There are a lot of Finns right now, I'm getting confused," Ivan said. "Maybe it's time to cull the Finn population."

I watched as The Beast walked over to Finn the son and wrapped his fingers around his throat.

"Do you love this son?" Ivan asked. "I mean, he is your oldest son, and you do plan to … what is it, allow him to take over?"

"Let him go," Finn Byrne Sr. said.

"Let him go? Do you seriously think I am just going to hand over your son? No, I want something in return," Ivan said.

"What?"

"Quite simple really, I want Niamh. You know, brown hair, brown eyes, you're her shit father, but I kind of like her," Ivan said. "You will get your son, and I will get Niamh, and I'm not negotiating."

Ivan hung up the phone, and I was ready to

fucking scream.

"What the fuck are you doing?" I asked.

"I'm waiting to see what we're dealing with."

"My dad won't call back. He doesn't do deals with the likes of you," Finn the son said.

I was already sick of thinking about the name Finn.

I didn't know for sure how much time had passed, but then Ivan's cell phone rang.

We needed to make a deal.

I had to get to Niamh.

"We have a deal," Finn Byrne said.

**** 

*Niamh*

*Present Day*

This was a trap.

My father was not going to let any man from the Volkov Bratva get the better of him. It had been hard to hear the full conversation, as it was vague. The Volkov Bratva had my half-brother, Finn—the son and child my father did want—his eldest, who he wanted to guide and build the empire with.

I didn't know exactly where we were. I've been forced onto my knees on the cold and dirty floor. The stench was making my head spin.

I had a horrible feeling I'd lost the baby I was carrying. I hadn't taken a test, but I had done the math, and I understood basic biology. I was pregnant with Peter's baby.

We were going to have a baby, or we might have

been. I didn't think … after the beating I've just been given, I didn't know if I still carried his child. There was a lot of blood between my thighs. The bottom of my white dress was now stained with blood.

My father had stopped when he saw it, and I think he might have known what he'd done. He seemed happy about it.

Pain sliced through my whole body.

I hoped Peter had gotten away, but then the memory of him with a gun … I didn't know why that bothered me so much. Guns didn't scare me, I was used to men holding guns. I'd been around them all my life. I even knew how to fire a gun myself. One of my father's men had shown me. I think he took pity on me and the fact my own father didn't love me enough to care what happened to me. Either way, guns didn't matter to me.

Peter and a gun, did matter. It meant something, but I didn't know what.

Until I watched as Peter walked into the room with another man, who for some vague reason I recognized. Then, there was my brother, who looked like our father. He considered it a curse to look exactly like Finn Byrne, but he loved being the oldest son.

I looked at Peter, and I knew he must be part of the Volkov Bratva. That was the name that kept going on repeat. I wanted to ask him what this was all about.

He didn't have a gun in his hands, but gone were the gym sweats and jeans I'd become accustomed to. Before me stood a man of business. A man I knew to avoid. The ink on his arms and chest all made perfect sense to me now.

I'd been lied to.

\*\*\*\*

*Peter*

Niamh was on her knees, on the dirty floor, and I didn't need to be a doctor to know she'd lost the baby. The blood on her thighs and coating the edge of the dress was a clear sign of that.

The bruises on her face and body already showed what she'd been through. Parts of the dress was torn, which could only come from a belt buckle, and one glance at Finn Byrne's buckle, even in the low light, I saw the staining from it. He'd whipped her with the belt. He'd beaten her. The urge to grab my gun and end that son of a bitch increased.

"Hello, Finn. I don't think we've been properly introduced. I'm Ivan Volkov—"

"Let go of my son."

Ivan stopped and he sighed. "You know if there's one thing I cannot stand, it's rudeness, and you're being so very rude." He gave another tut.

Niamh cried out as her father's grip on her hair tightened. "I want my son, or she is going to have her head blown wide open."

Ivan clapped his hands. "I do love it when the theatrics are thrown about, but I wouldn't do that if I were you."

Now, this is what I loved about Ivan Volkov. Nothing ever went down without him being one hundred percent aware of the danger, and he always made sure he had a Plan B, Plan C, and Plan fucking D.

Red lights played across Finn Byrne's chest, as well as the other men who were in the room.

Ivan tilted his head to the side. "Red looks good on you."

"What is the meaning of this?" Finn asked.

"Oh, it's quite simple really. Do you think I

didn't for a second figure this was going to be a trap?" Ivan laughed. "You chose the location, but you see, I've been keeping busy with all those bounty hunters you had finding your daughter. I searched the location, already figured out when you had started to get the clear understanding of where your daughter was, and I've had this warehouse prepared for weeks. One click of my fingers, and you all go down."

I didn't have to move. So, Ivan had been busy while I'd been doing what I needed to do, but that seemed useless now.

"I've had eyes on you for a long time. It was why young Finn boy here was so easy to find and take. You might want to consider a little more training in that regard."

"What do you want?" Finn Byrne asked.

"Well, for a start, I want your daughter, and I think for a time, I'm going to take your son as leverage, and then we might start our negotiations."

"Do you seriously think I'm going to negotiate with you?" Finn asked.

"Not right now, but in time, I have a feeling you'll come to your senses."

"No," I said, speaking up. "He dies tonight."

Finn turned his gaze toward me and then, even with all the evidence of the guns pointed at him, he smiled. "I take it, that was your baby inside her?"

I reached for my gun and was already taking aim at the smug little fuck. Tensions rose and I felt more guns had been drawn.

I stared down the barrel of my gun, and I looked directly at Finn Byrne. He'd fucked everything up, and I had a feeling he knew it, and didn't give a shit about who he had hurt in the process. I've met men like him. Just staring at his face reminds me of my father, of the men

I'd killed to free myself.

I couldn't let this bastard live. I didn't want to walk out of here knowing he was alive. I get Ivan had his reasons, but I didn't like it.

Finn Byrne must die.

He was taunting me.

I hated him.

"Not today," Ivan said.

I didn't want to listen to him. Killing Finn now would save us a lot of trouble and that was exactly what I wanted to do.

"Let her go," Ivan said.

"Tell him to lower his gun," Finn said.

"Lower your gun."

I looked at Finn, and the temptation to say no was so strong, but Ivan Volkov was the boss. He was in charge. That's what made him king and why the Bratva was strong and constantly expanding.

Lowering the gun took a lot of strength. But I knew, one day soon I was going to use it, and when I did, I was going to look into Finn Byrne's eyes and end his life. Then I'd be the one laughing.

## Chapter Twelve

*Niamh*

Laying in a hospital bed, I stared up at the ceiling, and it was kind of surreal thinking about what happened just a few hours ago.

I hated referring to that man as my father. He was no father to me. He was a monster and I hated him more than anything else in the world.

The man, Ivan Volkov, left without giving up my brother, and took me out of that hellhole. I'd been about to die. I knew my father would have gladly sent a bullet into my skull without a thought. I wasn't dead, and I was no longer pregnant either. The doctor had already come and told me that news.

I was alone. Again.

Peter hadn't stopped by. Neither had my brother, or anyone.

I should be used to this now but the biggest problem was there were so many unanswered questions. Who was Peter Shadows? Who was Ivan Volkov and why did I recognize him?

I couldn't focus as the pain in my body hadn't been quite numbed by the medication. I didn't like to take painkillers. I'd seen too many people become addicted to them, and, well, I was in pain and could easily get addicted to them.

I had no idea who was paying for all of this. I didn't have any health care insurance, and I certainly didn't earn enough to pay for this kind of treatment.

Tears filled my eyes, but I quickly blinked them away as the door to my hospital room opened. I opened my eyes, and sure enough, there was Peter Shadows. He closed the door.

Only, this wasn't the Peter Shadows I knew. This was someone different. He pulled up a chair, turned it, and straddled it.

Neither of us spoke for several minutes. I glanced at him, and then looked around the room, trying to figure out what I was supposed to say to him. I didn't know what to say, or what to do. Everything was a mess right now. We were going to have a baby and I had thought myself in love with him, but that had been a lie. I was in love with a man that didn't exist.

"I spoke to the doctor," Peter said.

This drew my attention to him.

"He said you are going to be fine. One day, you'll be able to have more child—"

"Who are you?" I asked. I already knew what the doctor had said. My pregnancy had been short and I had lost it due to the beating I took. There was nothing to suggest I couldn't have more children, or even a healthy pregnancy. All the right words were being spoken, but I didn't care.

"I know you're not Peter Shadows."

"Just like you're not Niamh Long," he said.

I smiled. "So is that it? I was trying to get away from my father. What is your excuse?"

"I was doing as I was told."

I didn't know if that was worse. I wanted to cry and I gritted my teeth. I had to keep those tears locked up inside. I wasn't going to cry in front of him.

"It was all a lie, wasn't it?" He didn't say anything, but I knew it was. "You were doing as you were told, which means your boss, I'm guessing Ivan Volkov, told you what to do."

"I was following orders, and it was simple. Get

Niamh Byrne to fall in love with me, and get her pregnant."

Pain sliced through my body, but it wasn't a physical pain. No, this was … emotional. I should have known these past few months had been a lie. A big fat, stinking lie.

"Well, I guess it's a job well done, and then my dad messed it up." I wanted to put my hand on my stomach, but I stopped myself.

I didn't think I would ever forget that moment I'd lost the baby. The pain had been … there were just no words.

They'd taken the dress from me. It was placed in a clear plastic bag, and it was in the corner on a small chair, with a few other things. Now, I was in a hospital gown, trying to preserve my dignity, although I didn't feel like I had any left. I felt so lost, so alone.

"I'm Peter Orlov," he said.

My attention went back to him.

"I work for Ivan Volkov, I'm one of his Brigadiers, and my loyalty is to him and him alone."

I should have known that anyone who had any interest in me was only doing it because they'd been ordered to. Thinking back to that moment when he walked into the diner, I couldn't help but snort. My initial instincts had been accurate. Peter had been a threat to me, but for all the wrong reasons.

"I get it," I said. "You don't have to keep reminding me. You will do whatever your boss says, and if that means sleep with me, get me pregnant, then you'll do it. To hell with the consequences, right?"

He didn't argue with me.

I meant nothing to him.

I was nothing.

Clenching my hands into fists, I sunk my nails

into the flesh of my palm, doing anything to keep a lid on this pain. Did he not see what he was saying to me? I wasn't worth caring for. He was following orders. He didn't want me, not really. I was just a job.

The door to my hospital room opened, and this time I saw Ivan Volkov as he stepped inside. He spoke to Peter, and a second later he turned and walked out of the room, leaving me with Ivan. A stranger, and yet not.

"How are you feeling?" Ivan asked.

"Why do I feel like I know you?" I asked. At first, I wanted to tell him to go fuck himself, but that wasn't polite. No matter who raised me, I wasn't going to be rude to anyone.

"We'll get to that soon," Ivan said, moving toward the side of my bed to take a seat. "Tell me, how are you feeling?"

I didn't see the point in lying, nor did I see the point in ignoring him. I'm not rude, and besides, in a strange way, this man saved my life. I wasn't stupid, I was aware my father intended to kill me, and it was Ivan Volkov who saved me, bargained for me.

"How's my brother?" I asked.

"Don't worry about him."

It was the first time I had seen anyone get away from my father without having to give something up. Ivan had been in control, not my father, and that was kind of fun.

"Please, Niamh, tell me how you're feeling?"

He seemed to genuinely want to know, and staring at him, I didn't want to argue. It had been a long day and night. The pain hadn't been fun.

"Not so good and I don't want the meds increased. I don't know if it would be right to say I've had worse, or if that would be a lie as well." I glanced down at my hospital-gowned body. Half of me was covered by the bedsheet as well. I didn't imagine I looked that great. With my dad pulling my hair, I was pretty sure a couple of pieces had been torn out. Then of course, I didn't imagine my face was bruise-free. When he pulled me out of the truck and slapped me around, he didn't stop there. Whenever he got angry, he'd come back and hurt me.

I was always an easy target for my father's wrath, and that hadn't changed once in the last few years, not even with me running away. If anything, it had made him angrier. I had truly believed that today I was going to die.

He'd been so angry, and there had been no stopping him. Not that any of his soldiers or men had attempted to do so.

I was trying not to think about the baby. I'd not even known for sure I was pregnant and now I had lost it, and that saddened me. I didn't want to lose my baby, any baby. The temptation to put my hand on my stomach was strong, but I held back. Ivan was a stranger. He didn't need to see my weakness.

"You will be able to have more children," Ivan said. "I didn't mean for this to happen. I got the information on your father's location too late. You were never meant to be harmed."

"So, you and Peter knew exactly who I was?" I asked.

"Yes."

"And you planned this?"

"Yes."

There was no sadness or regret. He just looked at me like it made him feel nothing. Tears filled my eyes as I let the experience wash over me, because the truth was, it had sucked, big time.

There wasn't a single moment through any of this where it had felt good. All those times I thought Peter was a good man—a gentleman, charming—it had all been a lie.

"Why?" I asked. "Why go to those extremes? Why lie to me? What did I ever do to you?"

Ivan sat there in a chair and stared at me for what felt like the longest time. I didn't even know if he heard me, but then, in slow movements, he reached into his jacket pocket and pulled out something I hadn't seen in a long time.

On a cheap piece of rope, dangling in the center, was a cross. I had won it at a fair that had come to town when I was a child. The woman behind the counter hadn't liked my mom, who'd been irritated that I had won anything. When I won that cross, it had a metal chain, but halfway around the fair, it snapped. My mother didn't care and she was only interested in getting another drink. While she'd been distracted at the bar, I ran back to the woman and asked what I could do to fix it.

She took a piece of black rope, tiny, the kind used for crafting, slid the cross onto the rope, tied it up, and slid it right over my neck. She told me if I was ever feeling scared or alone, or worried, then I was to hold onto the cross and know I was being taken care of. That someone out there did love me.

I kept that chain until five years ago, when I was at a hospital. My mother had been drinking again, but it had gotten bad, and resulted in me having no choice but to take her to the hospital to get her stomach pumped. I'd been in the waiting room, and that was when I remembered the man before me. He looked colder now, scarier.

In the waiting room, Ivan Volkov had looked like a man ready to give up, ready for anyone to kill him.

"In my moment of darkness, of weakness, you

came and sat with me," Ivan said. "I know you remember it now. You could have left me alone. You could have ignored me the way everyone else intended to. You didn't. You, Niamh, a young and slightly terrified woman, came to sit next to me. You offered me comfort when I needed it most."

**** 

*Ivan*

*Five Years Ago*

She was gone.

I felt like I couldn't breathe.

The pain was unlike anything I had ever imagined.

After everything I had done, this was the worst feeling in the world. This was helplessness. This was pain and torture mingled into one, because I couldn't save her from this. I couldn't protect her. I couldn't even stop it. There was nothing I could do.

I had a gun. A knife. There were drugs I could get.

It would be so easy to end it all and join her.

The world didn't need another fucked-up monster. All I wanted to do was hurt people. To hurt anyone that had lived, while she had died.

Lost in my own world of pain and torture, I didn't realize I had been seen until someone sat down beside me. I was about to lose my shit and scream at whoever had thought they could approach. Could I not have a moment's peace to mourn? To kill myself? To plot the way I was going to die?

"Are you okay?" a feminine voice asked.

I was ready to growl at that voice, and I was just about to do that, when I turned and saw a sad smile looking back at me. She was young, late teens, possibly early twenties. I wasn't sure. I'd never seen her before.

"I'm fine," I said.

"Yeah, me too. My mother is in the hospital getting her stomach pumped for the hundredth time. She's never happy when they do that. She always said alcohol is used to get drunk, not tossed down some drain or put in a medical bag."

The woman beside me gave a sad smile.

"Why are you here?" she asked.

I wanted to ignore her. I intended to ignore her, but something just … it … I had to tell her what was going on. I didn't understand it. None of this made any sense to me, and so I did.

"The love of my life has just died."

"I'm so sorry." She reached out and put a hand on my arm. "That is so awful."

I nodded.

We both sat in silence.

"She was my wife," I said. No one knew we had gotten married in secret. She had known who I was, what I was capable of, and yet she had still loved me. From the moment she had met me, she'd blown my world completely apart. And now she was gone, as if she never existed. The world was never going to know her, or know us.

Everything I had built and the man I'd become was because of her.

When the woman began moving, I turned toward her and watched as she removed a necklace from around her neck. It was an ugly looking thing. A faded rope, with a cross dangling from it. "I'm not the religious type," I said, when she held it out.

"I'm not much of a religious type either. Never even been inside a church." She licked her lips. "I won this at a fair when I was about eight years old, I think. I've had to change the rope once as it snapped. My dad, he'd been … well, it doesn't matter. What matters is the woman that gifted this to me when I won it, told me if I ever felt alone or scared, then I should hold onto it, and know that I was never alone."

It was a silly tale.

"Maybe your wife is wherever she is, and you can hold this because we share this moment together, and whenever you feel alone or sad, or in need of feeling close to her, this could help."

I wasn't a child. I didn't need little trinkets.

"For fuck's sake, Niamh, get your useless fat ass out of that fucking chair, and get over here."

That voice angered me.

Niamh got scared, and slid that cross into my hands. In that moment, I knew a perfect stranger had gifted me with something precious of hers, in my moment of need. And in that moment, I knew I had to do something to protect her.

\*\*\*\*

*Niamh*

*Present Day*

"You didn't need to do anything. I didn't give you that necklace in the hope of getting anything in return. I gave you that necklace so it would bring you peace."

I'd never told a soul about the strange man who looked ready to kill himself. Over the years, I wondered what happened to him and whether my necklace had helped. It was easy to remember him when I had reached for my necklace, only to find my chest empty.

Ivan got to his feet and stepped closer.

Having the memory of who he was, I no longer felt afraid of him. "Does Peter know how we know each other?" I asked.

"No," Ivan said. "No one knows anything about how you and I know each other. No one knows that I was … married. No one knows I was in love."

This made me sad and in that moment I felt pity for this man, which was completely insane because he'd sent a man to manipulate me. I didn't want to reason with him, or attempt to even understand him.

"What is going to happen to me?" I asked. I had to stay on track. It was going to be the only way I would survive.

Ivan took hold of my wrist and put the necklace back into my hand. "You need this more than I do," he said.

I held the necklace within my grasp. At first, I didn't look at it, but then, I couldn't help but chance a glance at it. I hadn't seen this necklace in five years. I'd given it to this strange, lonely, and heartbroken man, without even realizing I needed it. I hadn't thought about myself. All I wanted to do was make it better for him. He'd been so lost and alone.

All that time, I'd been helping Ivan Volkov. That was insane.

"You've not changed anything," I said.

"No, I never needed to." He stepped back and took a seat. "I'm sorry about you losing the baby, but I am not sorry for sending my man to you."

I wanted to scoff, to do or say something, but I just shook my head. "You sent me a lie. Do you have any idea what that is like? Peter … everything about him is a lie."

"You're going to marry him," Ivan said.

I shook my head. "No, I'm not. I'm not going to marry a man who has lied to me. Who has completely betrayed my trust. I cannot do that."

"You're going to, because he is going to be able to protect you. I'm aware of your father and what he is capable of. I know he's got some favors to call in, and he will not have a problem hurting you. Not that he knows how important you are to me."

This felt so surreal.

"I'm not important."

"But you are, Niamh Byrne."

## Chapter Thirteen

*Peter*

I waited outside Niamh's hospital room and I heard her and Ivan talking, but their voices were muffled. I didn't know for sure what was going on. She lost the baby. Normally, I didn't care. There was no reason for me to care, or even to concern myself like this.

There had been a baby and now there wasn't.

She wasn't even pregnant long enough for us to know what the sex of the baby was, or if she was even pregnant. The doctors had confirmed it, along with her miscarriage. I kept seeing Finn Byrne's face. It played over and over in my mind, and I didn't know what kind of game Ivan was playing, all I knew for sure was that it pissed me off.

I needed to kill that useless, pathetic son of a bitch. I wanted to hurt Finn, run my blade into the delicate parts of his body.

"Here."

I looked up to see The Butcher once again blending in and holding out a coffee for me to take. I was tempted to ignore it, but instead I reached out and grabbed it.

"It's shit. Hospital coffee and food is the worst, and it doesn't matter if you go private or public." She took a seat beside me, and was already drinking her coffee.

I took a sip and that shit was nasty.

"But it does the job in keeping you wide awake."

"Why the fuck are you even here?" I asked, taking another sip of the nasty coffee.

"Keeping Niamh safe. Finn Byrne is a sneaky little bastard."

"Do you think he plans to come and kill his daughter?" If he came to this hospital and tried, there was no way I was going to allow Ivan to hold me back. I would kill that son of a bitch, and I would take my own sweet time about it as well.

"Yeah, it's Finn Byrne. In case you didn't know, the man has a reputation for being unreasonable and seeing as he was quite happy to beat the living shit out of his daughter, I'd say he's capable of anything."

This made me angry. Niamh had endured enough. I glanced down the corridor and kind of willed the bastard to show up, just so I could finally have the pleasure of ending him, and that would be a lot of fun. It was what I wanted to do, so damn much.

"You know, don't you find it odd?" The Butcher asked.

To me, it was strange to be sitting side by side with The Butcher, let alone having a normal conversation with her. This woman was known for being surrounded in mystery. All the information about her was based on rumor or gossip. She was a freaking ghost, and I was starting to understand why.

"Find what odd?"

"Niamh ran away from her father. He clearly saw who you were, and I'm guessing he knew what was going on, and yet he didn't kill his daughter."

This made me stop and I turned to glance over at The Butcher.

She held her hands up as if in surrender. "Don't look at me all judgey. I'm just saying, a guy who has no qualms in beating and whipping his daughter, why didn't he kill her? He clearly doesn't love her, because if he did, Niamh wouldn't have run away."

"Maybe he does love her, and she ran away because she couldn't stand the beatings."

"True, but even the bounty hunters were ordered to keep her alive. In my experience, that is odd. There is always a bounty dead or alive, or even located. Finn Byrne was explicit in his instructions. He wanted his daughter back or located, and he wanted her in one piece. She had to be breathing."

Now that she talked about it in that way, I did find it odd. Especially considering he'd held a gun to her head.

"You don't think he was going to kill her?"

"A man like Finn Byrne doesn't negotiate. Even if you do have his son. I've met a lot of Finn Byrnes in my time and as far as they're concerned, they can have more children. We know he's got a lot of kids, and it wouldn't be hard for him to father another one, or two. At the same time in doing my research, Finn doesn't like his daughters. None of his daughters or their mothers are seen by him, yet, Niamh is different, why?"

I had no idea. I didn't get a chance to ask any more questions as Ivan stepped out.

"We need to talk," Ivan said. "Keep an eye."

The Butcher put two fingers against her temple and saluted Ivan, who didn't even bat an eyelid at the action. I expected Ivan to take us back into Niamh's room, but we walked further down the corridor, going to a quiet room. I'm not sure how Ivan knew it was vacant, but we stepped inside, and he closed the door behind us.

I stood there, looked at him, waited, and he ran fingers through his hair as he glanced around the room. My patience was fading, and I want him to tell me what the fuck was going on, but as always, he was silent. I didn't know what to say.

"You and Niamh are going to get married," Ivan

said. "I'm going to make all the arrangements and within the next month, you'll be married. You don't need to go back to Pickle Quest. You can return to your section and continue as normal."

"Is that it?" I asked. "You expect me and Niamh to work this shit out? I lied to her."

"And I've already started to mend the pain, but there is only so much I can do. It is now up to you."

"For fuck's sake, Ivan, what is going on? Tell me what you know about her. Tell me why this is important to you!"

I didn't like feeling out of the loop and all I got for my rant was Ivan smiling. "I guess The Butcher has been whispering in your ear."

"She has a point," I said, gritting my teeth. I didn't like it being insinuated that I was being manipulated. Anything else, I wouldn't even question, but there was no getting away from the truth. "Why didn't Finn kill Niamh?"

I didn't even want to think about anything bad happening to Niamh. She didn't deserve to die. She was a kind woman, caring, considerate, sweet, and I didn't want to think of her as dying or dead.

"She's his daughter?" Ivan asked.

"You and I both know a man that treats his daughter like that is no man at all. Damn it, Ivan, tell me, or is this going to hurt her? The truth is, you're giving me a wife, and you're going to let her die on me."

Ivan stared at me, and slowly I saw the monster appear before my eyes. It was strange, because there were no changes. It wasn't like he suddenly became a big scary monster. It was in the eyes.

"Niamh was never supposed to lose her child. I'm a lot of things, but I will not allow children to be used as pawns. I didn't think Finn Byrne would come for his daughter."

"Then tell me why he did," I said.

None of this was making any sense.

Ivan glanced around the room. "The Byrne name has a long line of strong men and strong women. Finn, himself, and Niamh's grandmother were direct descendants of the Byrne name."

I hadn't followed the name or family tradition. As far as I knew, Finn was the only living descendant of the family line. It was why they were so hell-bent on having a son, which was why we had his son.

"It would seem Finn's mother was called Niamh Byrne, and she didn't like the bastard her son had become. As it happens, before she died, she decided to go and see all of Finn's children, boys and girls. She happened to stumble onto a young girl, little Niamh, who was probably about five at this point. From what my sources tell me, Niamh's grandmother didn't even approach as such. She approached as an older lady, intent on seeing the truth of her grandchildren."

I didn't know why Ivan was telling me this as if it was some kind of bedtime story.

"As you can imagine, kids can be kids, and that means they can be cruel. Niamh Sr., was seeing that this evilness within her family line was in her son, as it was in his sons and daughters, and then one day, she happened by a small apartment complex, where little Niamh Byrne was outside, playing with her dolls. Or what she could call dolls, whatever the fuck Niamh was playing with. Probably daisies in the grass. I don't know. Either way, on that day, Grandmother saw something in Granddaughter that made her change her will."

This made me pause. Finn Byrne had been a hard man to ride out of the city, but his strength and power had weakened in what seemed like overnight.

I frowned, and looked toward Ivan, who nodded.

"Everything that is in the Byrne name belongs to Niamh," Ivan said. "All the money and wealth didn't disappear overnight. On his mother's deathbed, when he was gleeful, she had the last laugh, because not only did she transfer all ownership to little Niamh Byrne, but she also locked it up solid and tight so that Finn couldn't take it. If the funds started to leave the account in too big of a sum, someone was alerted and would stop transactions. That's the first thing Finn tried to do. If Niamh signed over anything to anyone, that was another alert. Everything Finn tried to do would result in him getting less and less, which is why I was able to take his turf and push him back."

"Niamh doesn't have a clue," I said.

"She does now," Ivan said.

"Why didn't he kill her?" I asked. "Wouldn't it have transferred to him?"

"No. It would seem Niamh Sr. was not to be trifled with. The inheritance of the Byrne name comes with a lot of responsibility. Something Finn didn't take seriously. He thought the wealth, the power, all of it was coming to him, and it was, until the day he slapped his mother around and opened her eyes to the man he had become."

I did not know how Ivan knew this.

"You see, Peter, leaders need to be monsters, but they also need to know when to keep that monster locked up tight, and then there are other times when that monster is coming, no matter what."

"Niamh's a powerful woman."

"I met Niamh's grandmother," Ivan said. "I met her a few times. She was a lovely woman. She told me I would make a fine leader. She also wished I was her son, but she had to stick to tradition. The only way to do that was to keep the power in the Byrne name, but in marriage, that power can be utilized. Finn couldn't kill his daughter, but he was trying to find a way of gaining that power."

"Are you telling me he planned to marry her off?" I asked.

"Yes, and then Niamh decided to take off. He had everything in place, and then she did what she did, and the guy in question—the weak sap who was going to be told what to do—met an untimely end." Ivan clicked his tongue. "You're going to marry Niamh. You're going to protect her, and in time, you're going to give her a child, many children. You will give her exactly what she wants, because in return she is going to provide us with the power of the Byrne name."

Ivan moved past me, going toward the door.

I realized in that moment how important it was to keep Niamh safe. Her father was never going to kill her. He couldn't do it, not if he wanted to forego everything that was Byrne.

"There's going to be a target on her head."

"Oh, trust me, there already is, which is why we need to have you married as soon as possible. Now, I suggest you go and check on your future bride."

Ivan opened the door and I stepped through. I didn't linger to try and get more information out of Ivan. There was no point. He'd already given me a lot of details. I was still curious as to how he and Niamh knew each other, but there would come a time for that. For now, I had to see Niamh.

I passed The Butcher, who was sipping on that nasty coffee, and I stepped into her room and closed the door behind me.

Niamh turned her head to look at me. "Has Ivan

given you the news?"

"Yes."

She laughed and shook her head. "You'd think if I had that much power, I might have been able to stop this. To stop all of this."

"Your dad kept you out of the loop on purpose. He couldn't allow you to know the kind of power you wielded."

"And now Ivan Volkov wants it."

"No, I don't think he wants it for himself," I said.

I stayed by the door, not wanting to get any closer.

"You lied," she said.

"So did you."

"True. Yeah, so true. I was Niamh Long and you were Peter Shadows." She started laughing. "I should have known it was all a trick."

I didn't say anything.

"We're going to be married," I said.

"I know." She pressed her lips together. "I don't want to be married to you. I don't want to have anything to do with you, but I also know I don't have a choice."

"This is for your safety," I said.

"You know, I was falling in love with you," she said. "I thought you and I could have a future but that's all a lie. There is no way you and I could have any future now."

This time, I moved and took a seat beside the bed. "Why?" I asked.

"Because it was all a lie."

"The names were a lie, the gym, I'm not a personal trainer. Everything else I told you *wasn't* a lie. I did own that house. It is mine," I said.

"What about running away with me, traveling?"

"That wasn't a lie."

"Did you have feelings for me?" Niamh asked.

"I don't do feelings," I said.

This made her laugh.

"I don't know what love is." I wouldn't go into details as to the type of man I'd become. There was no point in that. Staring at Niamh, I knew I'd caused her a lot of pain.

"You know, I had always wished for a man to love me for me. Who wanted no one else but me. Who wanted to grow old with me."

"I will be that man," I said. "I just don't do love."

Tears fell down Niamh's cheeks. I was breaking her heart and there was nothing I could do about it.

"We don't have a choice, do we?" she asked.

"No"

She nodded. "Then I guess you and I are getting married."

## Chapter Fourteen

*Niamh*

*One Month Later*

I'm no longer Niamh Byrne.

Nope.

Staring down at my wedding band as I sat on the toilet, trying to avoid the wedding reception, I'm Niamh Byrne-Orlov. At Ivan's insistence, I was to keep my last name and just add that touch of Peter. Peter didn't argue. Neither did I. There was no point.

I was at a wedding where I didn't know a single wedding guest. I'd not invited any of my family because in the past month, my mom had phoned five times, attempting to lure me away from Peter's home.

My father wanted me back in his care, but he had no intention of caring for me. I saw that now. The only reason Finn had ever come around was because of the inheritance, which I'd not been aware of. I couldn't help but wonder if my mom knew the truth. I doubted it, because she would have found some way to use me to get money for herself.

That was all it was about with my family—money and power.

The sound of feminine giggles filled the bathroom, but I didn't go out to join them. Ivan had helped me choose my bridesmaids. They had been the wives of the other Brigadiers. I had only met them a couple of times. All three of them seemed nice, so too did a woman who asked me to call her Butcher.

Again, I was not going to question it.

At the moment, I preferred to be on autopilot. It made life a lot safer for me, and I didn't have to think.

I put my hand on my stomach. I tried not to have moments like these where I started to think about what I had lost. A baby. My baby. Someone I could love and who might, if I was a good mom, love me back. I didn't want to force anyone to love me, but just for once, it

would be nice to meet someone who could potentially love me for me. No one else ever had. Not even Peter.

Tears filled my eyes, and with the makeup I wore, I didn't want anyone asking questions. Someone walked into the bathroom and in a calm, collected voice, ordered everyone out. This made me frown.

"You can come out, Niamh."

I wanted to stay inside the bathroom and not come out, but at that instruction, I was a little pissed, so I unlocked the door of the cubicle and opened it to find The Butcher standing with her arms folded.

"Why are you hidden away in here?" she asked.

"I'm not hiding. I had to use the bathroom."

"You've been locked away for half an hour. Did you have to do a number two?"

This made me frown. "What? Why are you asking me that?"

"If you're struggling to go, then I recommend some water or fiber."

I put my hand over my ears and frowned. "No, please stop."

She shrugged. "I'm only trying to help. So, if you're not taking the world's largest dump, why are you keeping yourself in the bathroom?"

I had never met a woman like her. She wouldn't tell me her real name, and in the last month, I had seen a lot of The Butcher. Peter told me to be careful around her. I didn't know why. She'd only ever been kind to me.

"I'm not locking myself away."

She raised both her eyebrows and didn't say a word. She looked so beautiful. The lilac bridesmaid dresses Ivan had picked out made all the women at my wedding look stunning.

The Butcher had her hair pinned back at the nape of her neck, with ringlets cascading down her face. She looked stunning.

The dress molded to her curves, and she had a figure I wished I had. She had full breasts and hips, and to me, she had the body of a curvy model. Peter told me not to be easily fooled. The Butcher was a cold-blooded killer. She had more kills than anyone else he knew, apart from perhaps The Beast, but apparently there was a great deal of debate in how many kills either of them had.

Again, this was not a topic of conversation I was ever going to have. Ivan had already made me aware that The Butcher was sticking close because of Finn. The Volkov Bratva had promised to take care of me, and I was never going to be hurt like I was last time. Again, I wanted to touch my stomach, but I stopped myself from doing that, and instead glanced over at the woman who was in the bathroom with me.

"You do know I can tell you're lying," she said.

"I'm fine, I wanted to be alone. Is that a crime?"

"I don't think it's a crime, but why do you want to be alone? It's your wedding day."

This made me laugh. "You do realize that Peter and I didn't have a choice."

The Butcher frowned. "Why not? You had a choice back in that weird town and you chose each other."

I took a deep breath. I didn't want to be reminded

of that. "Look, that was different. I didn't realize who Peter was, and that it was all a lie."

"But you're still the same people," The Butcher said.

"We're not, okay? The Peter I knew was a kind man, gentle, and sweet. He worked at a gym, and he liked helping people. The Peter out there is…"

"He's no different. Okay, maybe he is different because he's not a kind, gentle, or sweet guy," The Butcher said. "But, you're not some random girl who works at a diner either."

"I know, but I didn't seek him out. I was just trying to survive."

"And now you both have to learn to survive this. I don't know a lot about marriage, but I do know it's fucking hard work."

"And it's supposed to be with people who love each other," I countered.

The Butcher burst out laughing. This didn't make me feel any better.

She put a hand to her stomach and she waved the other one across my face, as if it was the funniest thing she had ever heard. "Seriously, do you even know history and understand what marriage is? It's a contract. A biding contract that brings families together, but it also produces wealth and all that shit. It is rare, so very rare for love to even enter the equation. Even if it does enter the equation, it is rare for marriage to last. In this day and age, there is always divorce and it is so easy to get one."

I looked toward this woman and sighed. "You're not good at giving pep talks, are you?"

"No one needs a pep talk, Niamh. It's a cold sense of reality right now. Peter is your only chance of having any semblance of happiness. Is it ideal? Probably not. Think of the alternative—your father decides and then your life would be miserable. You'd be with a man who is at the mercy of your father. Spitting kids out, wishing for death, and not being allowed it. Men like your father make you pay. They make you crave death, and they don't allow it. Even though you didn't do anything wrong, he will make you suffer."

"You're saying it's going to be different with Peter? Part of the Volkov Bratva?" I asked.

"Yeah, I am." The Butcher stared at me for several minutes and I had no idea what she was thinking. "Look, I don't do the whole friend thing, or the talking thing, or any of that shit. Life sent me down a path I wouldn't wish on anyone. I know of the evil shits of this world, and your father is not even the worst kind. There are men far worse, and women. Ivan Volkov is a mystery, there's no doubt about it. He is scary as fuck and what makes him even more so, is no one is ever prepared for what that man is willing to do."

This was not making me feel any better. If anything, this was terrifying me even more, but I didn't interrupt as she seemed to be on some kind of roll.

"What I have learned about Ivan Volkov, is no one can mess with those he cares about. They make an enemy of him, and he is loyal. He is not just chasing power or wealth. He is building a family. That is something no one has ever tried before. What I also see is Ivan builds from the broken, the damaged, the unwanted. It's what everyone seems to have in common."

I couldn't help but think about Peter. "Everyone?" I asked.

"Ivan Volkov himself was thrown out like garbage. There are rumors as to why, that he was damaged or defective. His dad didn't like that he wasn't perfect. Ivan wasn't killed, but he rose up the ranks, took the Bratva, and made it what it is now, and you're married into it. You're a Volkov now, but you do need to earn your place. When you are a true Volkov, you'll know it."

I looked at The Butcher. "Are you a Volkov?"

"Nope, not yet, I'm still only a candidate for an area." She clapped her hands together. "Don't worry, I have no doubts I am going to win it." She winked at me, and then moved toward the door. "So, are you going to come out and enjoy your wedding, or are you going to stay locked up in this bathroom with no way out?"

****

*Peter*

"Shut the fuck up, it won't be long before it's your wedding we're attending, and then I will be the one gloating," I said, as Victor continued to laugh.

"I don't think so. In case you didn't notice, Ivan went in order, and he's skipped me, which means I don't have to worry my little head about getting a wife."

I sipped my glass of whiskey and glanced over at Victor. I expected him to be the next one to be married off, but no, Ivan had other plans.

"Unless he plans to give you to The Butcher to play with, and gives your domain to her." I winked at him, and that soon wiped the smile off Victor's face.

It wasn't lost on me that The Butcher was spending a lot of time around my home, near Niamh, which could only mean one thing. Ivan had put The Butcher in charge of protection detail for Niamh. I had my men guarding her, as well as three men less then five feet away from her at all times. This had caused Niamh to complain, especially when she wanted to go out into the garden, or even use the bathroom, or take a shower.

The men were on a rotation between the day shift and the night shift. Six of my finest men. Nothing was going to happen to Niamh.

I also protected her. Like now, I knew Niamh had been in the bathroom for quite some time. So much that The Butcher had gone inside, and neither of them had come out.

Ivan had set our wedding day up, and of course it was extravagant, and I didn't expect anything less from him.

I finished my glass of whiskey and placed it on the tray of a passing waiter. Ivan was doing the rounds, and I saw the respect he got from everyone.

The only person here from Niamh's family was her brother, and he was under guard also. Ivan had taken over the negotiations with Finn Sr., and he'd kept Finn Jr. as well.

I moved toward Finn, with no other intention than to distract myself from worrying about Niamh. I wanted to go into the bathroom and find out what she was doing, but at the same time, I wanted to give her privacy.

"Enjoying the wedding?" I asked.

"It's a beautiful … day," he said. "It would greatly piss off my father to see it like this."

This made me happy.

"He never liked Niamh," Finn Jr. said. "It always pissed him off that he had to be nice to her. It's why he would hurt her, as that gave him pleasure. He will enjoy taking whatever happiness she has, and trust me, my father has a way of getting what he wants."

I turned to look at him, staring him in the eye. There is this smug look on Finn Jr.'s face that fades when he realized I am taller than him, bigger, and no one can protect him.

For several seconds I didn't make a sound. I just stared at him, and let his imagination run wild.

Ivan would stop me, unless it was a power trip for Ivan to have Junior here.

"I find it fascinating that you have so much respect for a man who cannot save you," I said. "He has made no effort to come and get you. Hasn't even asked for proof that you're alive. Your father never told you that the one person with all the power here is your sister. Did you know that? Niamh has the power to kill all of you, to take everything. She owns it all, which is why she was never gotten rid of. You've got sisters and brothers all over. Your father has never been known for his faithfulness. You're at her mercy, and if she so decides, your life is over. I will kill your father for what he did to Niamh, not just for the beating he gave her a month ago, or my baby that he took. No, I'm going to make sure that every time he hurt Niamh in the past, he suffers, and it will be long and slow. I like that. Everyone says revenge is a dish best served cold. For me, revenge is something you take a long time administering. I know how to make him stay alive, while piece by piece I break him. You should also know, Finn, that anyone who ever hurt her is now my target. Her slut of a mother is going to die, and if she so much as says you looked at her wrong, said a bad word, or hurt her, then I will take great pleasure in remembering this moment, because I don't give a fuck who you are. I will kill you, but I will do it slowly, and nothing, and no one will save you."

I pulled away from him as Niamh stepped out of the bathroom. Threatening Finn with the reality of what his future was to become, I made my way over to Niamh.

I didn't like that she'd lost a lot of weight in the past month since she'd gotten out of the hospital. According to my staff, she barely ate anything. She often skipped breakfast, and rarely touched her dinner.

In the past month I had come to realize that Niamh didn't like to make any kind of scene in public. Even though she was upset with me, because we had an audience, she didn't fight me.

"Are you all right?" I asked.

Niamh looked at me and then past my shoulder. I'd not seen her smile in so long, nor did she look relaxed in my company.

"Yes."

"Dance with me," I said. I held my hand out for her to take and I know she debated ignoring it, but again, we were in public. Ivan was there, friends and family. A lot of people she didn't know, and Niamh didn't like to embarrass anyone.

She slid her hand into mine, and I held onto hers tightly, not wanting to let her go. Leading the way onto the dance floor, no one stopped us as I pulled her in close. Niamh tensed as I placed my hand on the base of her back.

"What was The Butcher doing in the bathroom?" I asked.

The music had started up and I had to figure out something to say to start the conversation.

"Doing her impression of really bad pep talks," she said. "I don't think she has had many friends, and considering I don't have a lot of friends, that is saying something."

This made me smile.

"Why do you want to know?"

"I don't trust her," I said.

"She's working for Ivan."

"Yeah, but I don't trust anyone and it has not steered me wrong." I had no doubt in Ivan's choosing, but it didn't change my feelings. I wasn't going to trust

The Butcher until she and The Beast had proven themselves completely.

I knew they'd been there for Ivan when he needed them, but that didn't matter to me. Time and loyalty, when put to the test, was what I cared about.

Loyalty could be bought, and with both of them always taking a paycheck for their next kill, I wasn't going to trust them. They were no different than any assassin or bounty hunter. They were not Brigadiers.

"You don't trust me?" Niamh asked.

I looked into her eyes. "I do trust you."

She snorted. "I highly doubt that."

"You can doubt all you want. I still trust you."

"How can you trust me when I lied to you from the start?" Niamh asked.

"Simple. You lied to protect yourself and others. You knew what your father was capable of. If you were given the choice, would you have still lied?"

"What?" Niamh asked.

"If you had the choice to tell me the truth without any consequences for my safety, would you have told me the lie or the truth?"

She pressed her lips together.

"Exactly. You don't need to answer, I know the truth."

"Would you have still lied to me?" she asked.

*Shit!*

"I would have done whatever Ivan told me to," I said.

"So, that's a yes. That means I cannot trust you."

We had stopped dancing as we talked, and I quickly changed that, drawing Niamh into me.

"You can trust me."

Niamh suddenly stopped and I looked at her.

"No, because you will do whatever Ivan Volkov

tells you to do, and if one day he tells you I'm not needed and you have to kill me, you will."

She pulled away from me, ending our dance.

## Chapter Fifteen

*Niamh*

My wedding night.

Growing up, I had moments when I would think about my wedding and the man I was going to marry. It was strange, as I could barely picture him. I'd always been able to picture the future. I could imagine a couple of kids. I didn't care what sex they were, as long as they were healthy. I'd think about special events like Halloween, Thanksgiving, Christmas, Easter, even New Years, and then of course there were special birthdays. I wanted to be the kind of mom my kids could come to for anything. Needed brownies for a bake sale, I was your gal. A costume for a Halloween party, I totally could whip one up. Gifts at Christmas, I was the queen of the shopping mall. I'd have a man who loved me for me. The perfect family. In my head, that was.

Instead, I was sitting on the edge of a bed in a very expensive hotel, with complete strangers around me. Well, not in the hotel room, but all the guests were complete strangers. Even my half-brother was a stranger. I also knew he didn't like me. He certainly didn't like that I was now married into the Volkov Bratva.

It was hard for me to wrap my head around, because I'd never even heard of the Volkov Bratva, but then I'd been kept out of the loop about everything. I wasn't allowed to know anything or anyone. My place was just to serve, and that was exactly what I did—served.

I didn't have a clue what my place was here. What did they expect of me?

The door to the bedroom closed and I glanced over to see Peter flicking the lock into place.

"Do we have to worry about them … breaking in?"

"No, but I figured you'd be happier with a lock on the door."

I didn't know if he was right or not.

Rubbing my head, I tried to stifle a yawn. I was exhausted. I hadn't been sleeping well, and I knew I'd lost a little bit of weight as my clothes were hanging off me. Eating didn't appeal to me, not in the slightest.

"Are you okay?" Peter asked.

I took a deep breath and shrugged. "I don't know. I'm just trying to figure everything out, you know." I rubbed at my temple. I didn't know if I was ready to do this. I'd done everything in my power to avoid this man for the past month.

So much had happened in such little time, and I didn't know what to do or think. I'd not had time to comprehend either option.

I tensed up as Peter came to sit on the edge of the bed, right next to me. I wrapped my arms around myself, I didn't know what or who I was protecting myself from.

"Do you want to talk about it?" he asked.

"You don't have to do that."

"What?"

"Pretend to be him?"

"Who?"

"Peter Shadows," I said. The truth was, I missed him so much. My father had truly come into our lives and made a total mess of everything. I felt tears fill my eyes and I quickly glanced down. I was not going to cry.

"I'm still here."

"No, you're not. He was a lie. You said so yourself. You were just acting the part. He doesn't exist.

Peter Shadows had never killed anyone. Peter was a nice guy." I still couldn't bring myself to look at him as I was attempting to control the tears that filled my eyes. They were being stubborn.

"Peter Shadows didn't exist, Niamh. You can pretend all you want, but I was that man, and I am still that man."

At first, I didn't know how to respond, so a few seconds passed as I tried to get my bearings.

"You're right, and that man was ordered to have sex with me. Just like now. You're not here of your own free will. You are being forced to be with me, and do you know what that feels like?" I asked, but I didn't give him time to answer. "It sucks, in a real big way. It sucks more than you could imagine."

I hated to admit it, but it did. Knowing he'd been forced to be with me. I was nothing more than a job to him, and it hurt. Staring down at the floor, I willed myself not to let the tears fall, but it would seem my tears had other ideas, and that pissed me off. I didn't want to cry. I didn't want to feel this way.

"Niamh, I may have gone to Pickle Quest to find you, to protect you, and to put a baby inside you. It was an order, but I didn't do it out of force."

I shook my head. "Stop."

"I did it because I wanted to."

"I said stop!" I got up from the bed, and then pressed my hands to my ears. "I get it, okay? I know I'm not beautiful. I know I'm not pretty, and I know you were only there because your boss ordered you to be. It's the only reason you're married to me."

I didn't know why I was freaking out. In that moment, I felt so tired. So ... lost.

All my life, I'd grown accustomed to feeling unwanted. My mother had told me regularly that she had thought about aborting me. She'd even considered killing me as a baby, but my father had always shown up at the right moment, which convinced her to keep me alive.

It was strange, because I only had a vague memory of the older lady coming to see me. A woman who said she was my grandmother, and from the moment she said those words, I'd loved her. I ran into her arms and instantly told her I loved her. She stayed with me for a couple of days—sporadic visits that I always looked forward to—until she eventually stopped coming.

My father told me cruelly that she was now dead and wasn't coming back. He'd told me she'd been getting senile and she didn't love me at all. She didn't even remember who I was.

I'd gotten used to experiencing a lot of hate. Knowing no one was capable of loving me.

Then Peter Shadows came along.

I tried to keep him at arm's length. To not have anything to do with him. It was odd, because I wasn't angry at him for following orders. I wasn't angry at Peter for anything. I was angry at myself for believing it.

Only one person in my life showed me love. Then out of nowhere an amazing guy suddenly showed an interest in me, and I lapped it up like a puppy dog after a bone. I was pathetic.

Peter had given me a taste of something I'd been trying to bury deep. He'd given me a taste of love. He'd made me feel wanted, cared for, needed, and that hurt more than rejection, especially now. Because it had all been a lie.

I felt like I was losing my mind. I certainly was losing my senses, but then, all too soon, Peter's there, and he slid his hands beneath mine and cupped my face.

"No," he said. "I'm not going to stop."

He slammed us both against the wall and tilted my head back. I didn't get time to ask him what he was doing before his lips were on mine. He kissed me hard.

He'd not kissed me since that day at the picnic. *The picnic*—it already felt like a lifetime ago.

All sense of reasoning left my mind as he kissed me. I knew I should fight him, tell him to let me go, tell him to fuck off. But in the craziness of our world right now, this felt like the only thing that was right.

I could make sense of this.

I knew what he wanted.

I knew who I was.

I belonged to Peter.

The only problem was, this wasn't the Peter I wanted.

\*\*\*\*

*Peter*

Ivan had told me it was now my time to take care of her. I had no problem doing that, because in the last month I had gotten a clear picture of who Niamh Byrne was.

She was scared. Lost. Alone. And I knew for a fact she was unwanted. At least, that was what she thought.

Ivan had sent me to collect her, to knock her up. She'd been a job, but when it came down to the final act, I'd never wanted to do anything more than I did with her. I wasn't acting with Niamh. I wasn't faking it. The moment I touched her, I wanted her.

Even now as I tried to handle her emotions, I took possession of her lips, kissed her, and had no intention of doing anything more tonight, even though I wanted to. I wanted to break this fucking void between us, which I knew would happen the moment she found out the truth.

Ivan was just too fucking stubborn to accept that this kind of shit was going to happen regardless of what he did.

It was a fucked-up mess with Niamh and me. That I could accept, but I refused to give up on her.

Breaking the kiss, I stared down into her tear-stained face. Some of her makeup had started to smudge. The last thing I ever wanted to do was to hurt her. Stroking her cheek, I couldn't look away. I needed to take care of her.

As I reached for her hand, Niamh didn't fight me, which I was thankful for. I'd still fight her if I had to.

I walked with her through to our en-suite bathroom, and I didn't say a word. Ivan loved his creature comforts, so the weddings were always luxurious. I didn't know if this was his way of trying to win women over, or just because he liked to show off his power and influence.

There were many rumors, some true. I was aware that Ivan had spent a lot of time on the streets after being rejected by his father. He had to learn to survive. I believe he lived with Slavik, as well as a woman. I feel her name was Cara, who would later betray him.

I also believed this was Ivan's way of giving the women he was taking under his wing, the perfect day. The perfect wedding. I didn't know why it mattered to him. I couldn't wait to see the look on Victor's face when it came time to his wedding.

Letting go of Niamh, I stepped toward the shower and switched it on. I tested the water to make sure it was at the right temperature, and then I turned toward Niamh. Tears fell down her face, and she wasn't making a sound. I saw her heartache. There was no room for words.

I walked behind her and reached for the zipper of her dress. The seamstress had complained about this dress. When Niamh first tried it on, it had fit like a dream. Niamh had lost too much weight in the past months, and they had to quickly pin and tuck it all in to fit.

With the zipper released, the dress fell to Niamh's hips. I stepped close, and with her unable to see me, I couldn't resist leaning in and sniffing her hair. She smelled so good. Like vanilla and honey. I'd missed being this close to her.

Pushing the dress past her hips, she wore a white padded bra and a thong that was not helping the state of my dick.

She wasn't ready for us, for a true wedding night. I'd already taken her virginity, I didn't need to fuck her again until we were both damn good and ready. Although I wanted to. Tonight was certainly not the night.

I took care of her bra, flicking open the clasp, and then helping it find its way onto the floor. Her thong was easy. The flimsy fabric gave way, and I tossed it to the floor.

I stayed behind her, staring at her naked back, not liking the weight she had lost, but also knowing there was nothing I could do about it. I stripped out of my clothes, and then put my hands on her hips and guided her into the shower. She didn't fight me.

When I touched her, I felt her tense. I moved her into the shower, and the water had now gotten nice and warm. We stepped beneath the water and I closed the door.

Niamh tilted her head back, eyes closed, and allowed the water to wash over her. I was able to just watch her. I didn't need to talk or to ruin the moment. Neither of us did.

With her distracted, I reached for the soap and a sponge, lathering it up. I pulled Niamh into my arms, and the moment I touched her, she flinched, which I wasn't happy about, but there was nothing I could do.

Keeping one hand on her at all times, I began to soap her body.

"Do you ever wonder what our kid would be like?" I asked.

"Don't," she said.

"Just the other day, I was in my office at the penthouse. I've not taken you to my other home yet, but I've got a yard. Even a basketball court and a tennis court. I couldn't help but imagine our son shooting hoops on that court. Our daughter dribbling the ball down the court."

"Please," she said.

I never planned to tell her about my past, about who I was. My past was exactly that, in the past. "I don't know how to be a father. I'm not going to compare or compete with your father. Your father is an asshole. My father is dead and I killed him. Don't feel any kind of sadness or pity. My dad was evil to the core." She didn't make a sound. I'd always tried to avoid talking about my personal life back in Pickle Quest. "My dad was a different kind of father. To him, he didn't want anyone weak or feeble. To him, there was nothing worse than having a weak kid, because they were going to grow into a weak adult. He couldn't stand that. So, he came up with this marvelous idea where he would test his children's strength. I was put through a lot of tests by my father."

I massaged the sponge into her flesh, and waited for my words to sink in.

"I know what you're thinking. Math tests? Spelling? Arithmetic? My dad didn't give a fuck about how educated we were. I'll tell you about one of the tests. None of us could learn to swim, and he always felt that the best way to learn was by throwing you into the deep end. That is how I learned to swim."

Niamh gasped and she tried to turn, but I didn't want to look at her while I talked about a time I promised myself I would never speak of again. This was all in the past. I was more than happy to let it go. The people were all dead.

"He grabbed me, threw me in the deep end of the pool, and told me I'd win by learning to swim and not drown. I was so tired by the end of that day. My arms ached like I'd been fighting a superhero or something. And to make sure I knew how to swim, he did it again, immediately after. So even tired, I had no choice but to fight for my life."

"That is awful."

"My sister and brother were not so lucky."

This made Niamh gasp. "They died."

"Yes."

"Another test—he dumped me and other kids out into the woods to survive. It was freezing cold, so not only was I fighting the elements to survive, he'd also sent men in there to hunt us down."

"You've got to be kidding. There is no way that could happen."

"I got out. I killed the hunter, and I knew there were others that didn't survive. He attempted to brand me." This time, I did spin her around, taking hold of her fingers, and placing it at a patch of my thigh I had covered with ink. "Some of us died of sepsis. He refused to treat us, and he even left us outside. I was able to take care of myself. Others were not so lucky." I hadn't thought of the other boys and girls, who had struggled against the fever.

Some had gotten the wounds infected and it had

spread through their bodies, until eventually they couldn't fight any longer.

They had gone.

"You speak as if you had … so many brothers and sisters."

"I did, or at least that is what I was told. I would later find that my father was paying an orphanage to send their unwanted children to him. He'd turned his tests into a game, and he was recording it. There were others, wealthy men and women, who were paying to watch. Seeing who would be able to survive. We were like a bunch of dogs in a cage, and they were priming us ready to fight. The only thing I know for sure is I am an Orlov."

Niamh had tears in her eyes and she reached up and touched my cheek. "I'm so sorry."

"You do not have to cry. I dealt with it. That man is no longer alive and he's never going to hurt another child again."

"But, don't you get it? Your father. My father. I don't imagine it stops there, does it?"

"The world is full of men that do evil things. We're not going to be able to change that," I said.

"Why did you tell me this?" she asked.

"I wanted you to know who I am, so you could understand."

## Chapter Sixteen

*The Butcher*

"Are you going to tell me why we're not just killing this sick little shit?" I asked, turning to look at Ivan.

I pointed at the television screen that showed Finn Jr., locked up in his cage once again. He'd been allowed to attend his sister's wedding and between myself and The Beast, I'd been able to keep an eye on him. The only time I didn't was when I went to see what was taking Niamh so long in the bathroom.

"All in good time."

"Have you noticed that is what you say a lot?" I asked.

"I also noticed that when you get familiar with a person, you talk a lot."

I rolled my eyes at him, because I didn't care what he said. I was not known for talking, apart from those that knew me well. There were few people that did.

Shrugging my shoulders, I shoved my hand into a family-sized bag of cheesy potato chips, which were my favorite snack for watching an asshole on screen. I didn't even know where he had sent The Beast off to, and I didn't care to know.

I stared at the screen and thought of ways I could end this bully. Finn Jr. was a piece of shit. I didn't realize how bad he was when I took him. Ivan's orders had been to take him alive, but I'd be quite happy to see this little shit dead.

With his father's reputation, this sick little shit had used it to his advantage over time. He was only a year older than Niamh, and yet the two couldn't be more chalk and cheese.

Niamh was a nice person. I sensed that.

I had a way of knowing good people from bad, and Niamh was nice. Her half-brother on the other hand, needed to be killed. There was no nice way to put it.

Finn Jr. liked power, and he was evil with it. I had uncovered several girls who worked for his father, as well as at the high school where he went growing up. Whenever Finn liked a girl, they didn't get a choice. That was taken from them. If they wanted him or not, he was going to have them, and he wasn't above using force.

To put it bluntly, he'd raped a lot of women and had been doing so since he was eighteen. I think I might have found his first victim. It had been the school nice girl. She'd been sweet and kind, a tutor, helping all of those in need. She caught the eye of Finn, even though she wasn't interested in boyfriends, and she rejected him. That had been her biggest mistake.

She'd been working late at the library, and on her way to her car, he grabbed her. All night long, Finn Jr. raped her, humiliated her, and slowly broke her. He returned her home, as if it was just a date. His father was at her parents' house, and told her if she went to the cops, her parents would be dead. He'd hunt them down. She didn't go to the cops, and instead the family lived in fear.

I got this information from the woman's sister. Finn didn't just have his fun once. Now that the family was afraid of him, he used her multiple times until she finally couldn't take it and killed herself. This smug little shit believed his father was going to get him out of this mess.

He didn't realize that he was now on *my* radar, and he wasn't going to be free very long. I was going to be the one to end him.

# A MONSTER IS COMING

****

*Niamh*

*Two Weeks Later*

I was bored.

Peter was out doing whatever kind of job he had to do, and I was stuck in here, in his penthouse apartment suite, and yes, it was nice. I'd been stuck here since before the wedding, and now I was stuck here again.

I was sitting on the pristine white sofa, aware that less than five feet away were three guys. I had tried to get to know the men who were on my guard duty, but none of them were willing to talk.

Did they even realize how scary it was to have three men staring at me? This was why I was on the sofa, staring at the blank TV screen. I could see them all, perfectly poised, ready to strike if someone even knocked at the door.

With my hands on my thighs, I took a deep breath and allowed the flow of boredom to wash over me once again. According to Peter, my life was at risk because my father was still alive. I didn't know why Ivan was keeping him alive, or what reason he had to see me married.

I hated this confusion.

I hated this kind of boredom.

I'd attempted to talk to Peter about the men, but he wouldn't hear of it. The men were here to stay. It didn't exactly fill me with confidence that it took three men to watch me.

When the main door opened and all three men aimed their gun at the door, stepping closer to me, I was a little startled. I didn't need to be, as seconds later, Ivan Volkov appeared.

"Are you going to shoot me?" he asked.

I'd moved onto my knees and I now looked toward the scene unfolding. The men put away their guns.

"I'm here now, I can take care of Niamh. You can all wait outside," Ivan said.

I expected them to argue. There were multiple times I'd tried to order them to leave, and none of them would listen to me. Don't get me wrong, I knew they couldn't listen to me, and that sucked.

They were following orders. Peter's orders.

Now they were following Ivan's orders.

One by one, they left the apartment, and I turned my head back toward Ivan's. "Is there any way you can teach me that?" I asked.

"I can teach you, but it is never going to work."

"Try me."

"First, you have to become me, and then everyone has to bow down to you," he said.

I wrinkled my nose. "I think I'll pass."

"You don't think you could be me for a day?" he asked.

I remembered him in the hospital. It was a vague memory but one I still had. He'd been so broken. Even though the man who stood before me now was a strong, self-assured, confident specimen, he hadn't always been.

"Why doesn't anyone know you've been married?" I asked.

Ivan looked at me. "Have you told Peter?"

"No. It's not my news to tell and if you wanted them to know, you would have been the one to tell them." I glanced down at the brown paper bags in Ivan's hands and my curiosity got the better of me. "What do you have?"

"Lunch."

He moved toward the dining room.

I was tempted to ignore him and just stay kneeling on the sofa. Ivan was too much of a temptation.

My guards didn't talk to me. I didn't have a lot of conversation and I was still pissed at Peter.

Climbing off the sofa, the temptation to run to the dining room just so I could keep talking to him, was strong. What kind of loser did this make me?

I arrived at the dining table, and Ivan was setting it for not just two people, but three.

"Who else is joining us for lunch?" I asked.

"Peter will be along shortly."

"How do you know?"

"I have my ways of knowing what irritates husbands. I seem to have that effect on people when they want to keep their wives close." Ivan did that wink thing again.

I rounded the table so I was on the opposite side, and lowered down into my chair. I didn't know if I could trust Ivan.

"You enjoy irritating other men?"

"I do," Ivan said.

Truthfully, I was surprised.

"You're not going to answer my previous question."

"No."

"Do you always get what you want?" I asked.

"No."

He finished unpacking the lunch, and then sat down in the seat opposite me. Neither of us broke eye contact. "With how the two of us met, you know I don't get everything I want."

I pressed my lips together because he was right.

He'd lost someone he loved.

"I'm so sorry," I said.

"Don't be. There is nothing I can do to change it. All I can do now is look forward to the future. So, you and Peter, when are you trying again?"

He nudged several wrapped packages toward me.

"Are you kidding me?" I asked.

"Not at all. That food is for you, and seeing as you're not eating, I'm going to make sure you start doing so."

I rolled my eyes. "You're not my dad."

"I know. But that doesn't mean I can't act like it now. You clearly need someone to take care of you."

I laughed. "Please, I've been taking care of myself my whole life. I don't need anyone to start now." I hated how hard I sounded. I reached for the drink and wrapped my fingers around it, feeling the warmth. I took a sniff, and the aroma of coffee was so heavenly. My mouth watered for a taste, and I took a quick drink of the liquid, and it tasted so good.

"It's good coffee."

"The bakery is the best in Peter's territory."

"Do you have different bakeries you love?" I asked.

"Yes, in each territory, I have found several that I like, and yes, I take each wife to all of them."

"You're close with each of your men's wives?"

Ivan nodded. "Yes, I am well liked. It's a gift." He laughed. "It helps to remind them all of what they've got. They never take their women for granted."

I stared at him and knew he did it for a reason. I didn't for a second believe Ivan took his wife for granted. I had a feeling when it came to Ivan, he had loved his wife with all his heart. I didn't know who she was, but anyone who enjoyed that kind of devotion would be a lucky woman.

"What about the men who are forced to marry? Do they feel the same way?" I asked.

Ivan smiled. "You think Peter's been forced into this relationship?"

"You cannot try to pretend he hasn't been."

"Do you think I'm so careless when it comes to a man and woman that I don't know what's best for them?"

I smiled. "So, now you're an expert on what is good and bad for people?"

"Yes."

It felt so good to talk to someone. Even though I was pretty sure Ivan was a terrifying person. Men were afraid of him. I knew Peter respected him.

"You have no doubts, do you?" I asked.

"Eat your sandwich."

I shook my head and unwrapped the paper bag it had come in. The scents of tomato, garlic, beef, and provolone assailed my senses. "A meatball sub?" I asked.

"Yes, only the best for you."

I was growing partial to that little wink he gave. Ignoring that spark of happiness building in my chest, I lifted the sub and took a large bite. The flavors ignited on my tongue.

"I am going to kill your father."

With a mouthful of food, it wasn't exactly the greatest conversation starter. I coughed a little and then quickly chewed my food and looked toward Ivan. He took a bite out of his own sandwich. I wasn't sure what he had gotten for himself.

"What?"

"Your father and indeed your mother, both are going to die. I predict Peter is going to be the one to kill your father."

I had no idea what to say to that. Did I just keep eating and hope he didn't ask any questions?

"Once your family is taken care of, you should be able to make your choice," Ivan said.

"My choice?"

"Yes. You're not aware of it now, but you are a very wealthy woman. You've inherited the Byrne fortune. It doesn't make you the richest woman in the world, but it will give you a good life."

This made me frown. "What about my marriage?" I held up my wedding ring finger.

"That is your choice. There is going to come a time when the threat to your life is no longer there. I'll have dealt with the Byrnes, after I get what I want from them. That is the only reason they are still alive."

"Can't you take what you want?"

"I like to play the long game. I go for what I want, people end up killed." Ivan took a bite of his sandwich. "When the time comes, you're going to have to make a choice. You can either stay married to Peter, or you can leave. I, nor Peter, will stop you."

"That's just what every woman wants to hear," I said.

"I took the choice out of your hands once. I will not do it again."

"Why do it to me in the first place?" I asked.

"I owed you one."

"What? How is sending a man to lie and manipulate me, owing me one? I didn't do anything wrong to you. I don't even know you. I thought I was helping you."

"And you did. More than you know, you have helped me, time and time again. It's why I know Peter is a good match for you. I know he likes to believe he doesn't know what love is, but we both know that's bullshit."

"Really? Because he told me some of what he has been through. I don't expect any man to be able to love that easily. When he should have been loved as a boy, he was tested." And here I was defending him. What the fuck was my problem?

"The same could be said for you," Ivan said.

"I … it doesn't matter."

"You didn't feel love. You've never known the loving embrace of anyone other than an old lady a few times in your life. Yet, you have a lot of love to give."

"Please stop," I said.

He talked about being able to give a lot of love, and I couldn't stop thinking about the baby I had lost. It still hurt. The wound cut too deep.

"And that is another reason why your father is going to die."

"Do you plan to wipe out the Byrne line?" I asked.

"No, because I have no intention of killing you."

This conversation right now was blowing my mind. I didn't know how any of the other wives had been able to handle Ivan. I didn't know whether to laugh at him, or just weep.

"Did you give the other men's wives this choice?"

"No, they were not in a position like you."

"It all comes down to money?"

"No, it all comes down to what you desire, Niamh. If you want to be free of this world, I will help you find that way. If you want to stay married to Peter and join the Volkov, then that is open to you as well."

"Peter doesn't love me."

"Yes, he does. He just doesn't realize it yet."

And then, the main door opened and closed. It

didn't sound too gentle either as seconds later, Peter entered his penthouse apartment. He didn't look happy.

"About time you joined us. I got you lunch," Ivan said.

**\*\*\*\***

*Peter*

I'd heard the whispers of Ivan arriving at fellow Brigadiers' homes without an invite. Enjoying their wives, not in a sexual way, but in a fun and friendly way.

I couldn't quite read the atmosphere based on Niamh's facial expression, even though I wanted to know what the fuck was going on. For several seconds, my wife looked at me, and then she went back to eating her sandwich. I'd been made aware of Ivan arriving at my home, by the alarm I had on my door.

Before I'd even married Niamh, I had security placed throughout my penthouse suite. When you had enemies far and wide that wanted you dead every other week, you learned to protect yourself. Even when I wasn't home, I activated the security and I was able to keep an eye at every single residence I owned. I'd known Ivan hadn't left my territory. He'd also not come and seen me either.

Several of his spies were always around. I knew he trusted me, and sometimes he played the Bratva game just for his own personal entertainment, but I was not amused. I didn't know what Ivan had to say to Niamh.

In the past two weeks, we were … existing together. This situation wasn't ideal. I knew Niamh was hurt by my lies. At the same time, I knew she couldn't quite be so angry. She knew she had lied just as bad to me. Although, I had known who she was. Our situation was a little fucked up, but it was workable.

I'd decided to give her space, and she'd been sleeping in the spare bedroom. Only, Ivan had made the decision that not only was he going to pay us a visit, he was going to stay the night as he didn't feel like going to one of those boring hotels.

After lunch, Ivan stayed and watched a movie with Niamh. He told me I could get back to work, but I didn't want to leave Ivan alone with my wife.

After the first movie finished, and I watched as Ivan made himself comfortable, which pissed me off. I made my escape and went to the bedroom. Pulling up Slavik's number, I called him. At first, he didn't answer. It took several rings before he finally picked up.

"What's up?" Slavik asked.

"How the fuck do you get Ivan out of your home and away from your wife?" I asked.

There was silence on the line and that didn't exactly bode well for me. I didn't want silence. I wanted answers.

"Wait it out. Spend time with your wife. Go on dates with her. Show her attention," Slavik said.

"What?"

"I'm telling you what to do. You don't like the answer, then enjoy Ivan being a best friend to your wife."

He hung up and I called Andrei, who also said the same. Next I called Ive, and he pretty much said the same. I'd already been gone too long, and I made my way out of the room to find another movie put on "pause," and there was laughter coming from the kitchen.

Gritting my teeth, I walked into the kitchen, and there at the stove stood my wife and Ivan, and it was like they were two best friends as they attempted to make popcorn. The kernels were popping and Ivan chose that moment to open the lid for a couple to pop right on out.

Niamh let out a scream, and quickly put her hand on top of his. "Don't."

"Having fun?" I asked.

They both turned to look at me.

"Yeah, Dad, we're having fun making popcorn to watch a movie full of blood and guts. You want to join?" Ivan asked.

"Can you and I have a word?" I asked, not entertained at all.

The smile on Niamh's face dropped. "Here, I can take this."

Ivan sighed. "It looks like I've got to go and get my ass kicked."

Niamh chuckled and I walked with Ivan away from the kitchen, going into the dining room. "What the fuck are you doing?"

"I was making popcorn. What was hard to see about that?" Ivan asked.

"No, what are you doing with my wife?"

Ivan stared at me for several seconds. "In case you didn't know, I was making friends with your wife. I'm helping you out, seeing as I might have also caused you a little trouble?"

"What?"

He rubbed at his temple and came toward me. "Who sent you to Pickle Quest?"

"You know the answer to that."

"Exactly. Who told you what to do?"

"Damn it, Ivan, what is your point?"

"My point is this. I told you what to do because you may not see it now, but you and Niamh could be good together. That is up to you to do with as you will, but let me warn you of this." Ivan stopped and I hated fucking waiting. There was no rush with Ivan. "When all of this is over, I've told her she has a choice. She can either stay married to you, join the Volkov, or she can leave. Be free of you, and live her life without any consequences."

"What the ever-loving fuck?" I asked.

"I don't need the Byrne riches, Peter, or the wealth. I don't fucking want it. This was never about getting property or money. I've got all I need, I'm not fucking greedy. That is what removes people from power. I'm not a fucking idiot and none of this shit has gone to my head."

"Then if that is not what you want, why go for Niamh? Why go for Byrne?"

"Because I don't like him. I don't like what he represents, and I owed Niamh a debt. Making sure she can live her life, free, and away from all this shit is the least I can do."

And with that, Ivan turned on his heel and left.

He'd given my wife an out. I didn't know what the fuck I was supposed to do with that.

I heard Niamh's giggles from the kitchen, but I wasn't in the mood to keep hearing them.

## Chapter Seventeen

*Niamh*

When Ivan arrived at lunchtime, I never for a second thought I was going to have the best day of my life. Yet, hanging out with Ivan, making popcorn with him, watching a couple of movies, ordering pizza, had been so much fun.

Peter had stuck around until the popcorn, and then he'd left. It was nearly nine at night and he still hadn't returned. I was getting tired, and I'd already moved some of my stuff into Peter's room so Ivan could take the spare bedroom.

I said good night to Ivan and made my way into Peter's room. The moment I stepped inside, I could smell him. Even though the room didn't have any personal touches, I knew Peter's smell. It had become a comfort to me in Pickle Quest.

I was afraid to touch anything, so I grabbed my pajamas and made my way into the bathroom. I was tired, but I needed to take a shower.

I removed the clip from my hair, and brushed my teeth before stripping out of my clothes and stepping beneath the hot spray of water. I couldn't help but wonder what it would be like to live my own life, free of worry. Free of the fear of my father. Even as I got older, I never lost that fear of him arriving unannounced. Even now, I couldn't help but feel that small smidge of fear that threatened to curl up inside me and spill right back out. What if my father beats Ivan?

I knew how cunning and manipulative my father was. Did Ivan know what he was doing? I had no doubt he did, but I was so used to my father being at the top of the food chain, it was hard to imagine anyone else.

After the shower, I stepped out, wrapped myself in a towel, and quickly dried off. The bruises had started to fade from the beating my father had given me. Ivan had wanted them to be gone from my face for the wedding, which they had been.

Once my body was dry, I changed, ran a brush through my hair, and then grabbed the towel to dry it again so it wouldn't dampen my pillow.

Even though Peter wasn't home, I was nervous about going into that bedroom. This was Peter's bed. I'd shared his bed with him plenty of times. More than a few. I'd pretty much lived with him in Pickle Quest, and now I didn't know what to do. I had an out. When all of this was over, I could leave for good.

I clenched my hands into fists because I knew I should be excited about the prospect of being free, of not having to worry about someone hurting me. I didn't have to worry if Peter was only faking it because his boss had ordered him to. I'd be free to make my own choices, to do what I wanted to do.

But, I didn't feel happy.

I was a little scared and afraid.

I wanted to hate Peter. He had lied, but then so had I. We'd both lied for different reasons. I'd not gone out of my way to fall in love with Peter, or to make him fall in love with me. I'd not been ordered to get him pregnant.

Why did this have to be so hard?

It would be easier to hate Peter, but the sad truth was, I still loved him. That love hadn't died when the truth had come out. I couldn't just stop loving him.

I didn't want Peter to be forced to be with me. He didn't do love, and I accepted that. But at least he could like the person he was married to, or perhaps even grow to care for them.

I put the used towel in the laundry basket and stepped into the bedroom, only to come to a stop as Peter was standing at the foot of the bed. There were bloodstains on his shirt, and for a second, I didn't know what to do.

"Did you kill Ivan?" I asked.

"No. He's enjoying my whiskey in the spare bedroom," Peter said.

"Ugh, are you okay?" I didn't know what to do. My father had visited my mother a few times with blood spatter. He didn't seem to care that he'd killed someone prior to coming to see us. My mother didn't care either. I did. The blood had scared me.

"Yeah, I'm fine." He glanced down at his shirt. "Your father had sent one of his men to try and take you."

"What?" I asked.

This surprised me.

"You're a powerful woman, and he is going to try and get you, but he's not going to succeed."

Peter held his hand up as if he was going to touch me, but then he stopped, clenched his hand into a fist. "I'm going to take a shower."

I didn't stop him as he brushed past me.

"Thank you," I said quickly. I felt him stop and I turned toward him. "For not letting him hurt me anymore."

"I bet he is regretting everything he has done to you."

"No, I doubt it. I bet he wishes he kept me locked up so he could use me as a punching bag."

"It's not going to happen," Peter said.

"Thank you." I didn't know what else to say.

He nodded his head, and then turned on his heel and stepped into the bathroom.

For several seconds, I just stood in the center of the bedroom, not sure what to do. I felt at a loss for words. I wasn't used to this feeling. Not that I ever had a lot to say before.

Stepping toward the bed, I then stopped again. Which side of the bed did Peter prefer? I was truly not sure, so I climbed into the right side, when I looked at it directly. Sliding beneath the sheets, I turned and faced the door. If I turned the other way, I'd be facing Peter when he climbed into bed.

We'd not shared a bed since the day of the picnic. That day, I'd woken up with his arms wrapped around me, his face against my neck, kissing me. I'd started to experience the morning sickness off and on at that point. That day, there had been no sickness.

Peter had kissed my neck, and one of his hands had worked up to cup my breast, and the other had moved down to cup my pussy. His hands on my body felt so good. I'd not wanted him to stop, and he hadn't either.

I pulled out of the memory, because I didn't want to think about sex. Peter didn't take too long in the shower. Within what felt like minutes, he was done, and stepping into the bathroom with only a towel wrapped around his waist. It was then I remembered that Peter slept in the nude. He refused to wear anything for bed.

We were married. I was in his bed once again. The bed dipped as he climbed beneath the covers. I stayed perfectly still.

Silence fell in the darkened room. I heard his breathing. At one point, I was pretty sure I had stopped breathing.

"I've done a lot of bad things in my time, Niamh. I've never raped a woman, and I'm not going to start now. You don't have to be afraid of me."

Okay, I didn't know why, but for some reason that pissed me off more than I expected.

"What?" I asked, but I certainly wasn't calm, nor was I quiet when I suddenly yelled at him.

"You're acting like you're afraid of me. I have never attacked you, never hurt you."

"Shut up," I said. In the back of my mind, I was pretty sure my own brain was asking me what the hell I was doing. I wasn't talking to no one here. I was talking to a Brigadier. One of the scariest men alive. Even though Ivan Volkov had shown me his softer side, I didn't for a second believe it.

Ivan was deadly, and so were the men that worked for him, and that was how he wanted it.

"I'm not accusing you of attempting to attack me. I'm not … ugh, you're so frustrating." I couldn't just lie there or even sit there in the bed next to him while he appeared to be so calm. I wasn't even trying to treat him like some monster. Throwing the blankets off my legs, I climbed out of bed and then started to pace near my side of the bed. All the while, I was aware of our guest in the bedroom where I should be right now, only I couldn't be. Had Ivan done this on purpose? Was he trying to force me and Peter together? "I know you're not going to attack me, Peter. I know you're only doing what is best for the damn Bratva." As I started to pace and talk, I didn't even realize what I was saying. It was like a load of mixed words came together and made no real sense.

The truth was, I was so confused.

"Do you know what sucks?" I didn't even give him time to answer. "That I can't even be mad at you. It's not like you and I met and I told you the truth about who I was, did I? No, I lied just as much as you. I can try and dress it up inside my head, but we're both at fault, and yes, I'm angry. You didn't tell me the truth, and that even irritates me, because I can't be angry at you, as neither of us told each other the truth."

"What's your point?" Peter asked.

And then I stopped and felt the tears sting my eyes. "That … I fell in love with you and I know you didn't feel the same about me. It's fine. It doesn't matter. I don't want you to lie to me anymore, and no matter how much I try to fight it, I can't … I lost our baby."

I'd not really given myself a chance to cry. I hadn't thought about it. Even when I was alone and bored, I would think of anything and everything that had nothing to do with the baby I lost. The doctors had said it was an early pregnancy, and there was no damage, and I guess, in a strange way, I kind of imagined I didn't have anyone to mourn, because the baby was so new.

But, I lost my child. I lost my baby.

And in that moment, it was like it suddenly occurred to me, and I just stood there in Peter's bedroom and sobbed. I couldn't stop. The tears just kept flowing. I didn't want to stand in the bedroom, crying.

This was fucked up.

This wasn't fair.

Why did I have to feel the pain right now?

\*\*\*\*

*Peter*

I was angry.

No, I was fucking pissed.

Fuck it, I was angry and pissed off.

Niamh was in our bedroom, which was the first time she'd actually been there, ever. After our wedding night, I'd brought her back to my penthouse apartment, complete with her additional bodyguards, and she had taken residence in the spare fucking bedroom, which irritated me. She didn't have to go there.

We'd been fine. Admittedly, we were just coexisting in the same space, but we were doing fine. One afternoon leading into evening, and suddenly, I've got a sobbing wife in my bedroom.

I slammed my hand against Ivan's door, and I didn't stop until the door opened.

"You better have a good reason for waking my ass up," Ivan said.

I didn't know how he could be asleep. Niamh wasn't quiet. The tears were real and they were killing me to hear. I couldn't sleep or ignore them. I didn't know what the fuck to do, and that was annoying me even more. What did I do with a crying woman?

Growing up, whenever the kids kept us awake for crying, they were often taken and beaten until the tears stopped. Tears were a weakness. I didn't ever remember crying. I knew there had to have been a point in my life when I did cry, but I had no memory of it.

Crying was death.

Crying was pain.

I couldn't afford to do either growing up.

All I wanted to do was live.

"You've broken her," I said. "You've got to go and fix her."

"Broken who?"

"Niamh. She's fucking crying and it's all your fault."

Ivan frowned. "When I left her, she was smiling. If she is crying, it has nothing to do with me, and everything to do with you."

I shook my head. "That is bullshit and you know it. This is your fault and you've got to do something to fix it." There was no way I was taking the blame for this. I couldn't stand it.

"What did you do?" Ivan asked.

"I didn't do anything."

"Have you seen Niamh cry?" Ivan asked after several seconds of silence.

This made me frown. "What?"

"Has it ever occurred to you that Niamh hasn't mourned the loss of her baby? That a lot of bad shit has happened. You can pretend all you want that you don't give a shit, but deep down, one day, you're going to care. Right now, Niamh is feeling that loss, and it is up to you to deal with it. She doesn't need a stranger. She needs a man she loved. You've got to go to her. You've got to fix her. Not me. This is all you."

And I didn't like it.

Ivan stepped back into the bedroom and closed the door, leaving me hanging.

For several seconds, I just stood there, not wanting to return to my room for fear of what was about to happen. I was not used to this kind of emotion. This was not for me.

I closed my eyes, and felt a wave of sickness wash over me. I didn't deal with emotions. I killed. I hunted. I hurt. I caused pain. Niamh didn't need any of those things. I couldn't hunt down or hurt or kill anything. Our baby was already dead.

Even with my eyes closed, I saw Niamh's face. The days we spent together. The smile on her sweet lips when she found something I said funny. She didn't hold back and I couldn't just leave her.

With one foot in front of the other, I didn't think, I just acted. Stepping into my bedroom, I didn't even hesitate, I walked right up to her and then pulled her into my arms. I expected her to fight me, to tell me to get the fuck away from her. Instead, she surprised me by wrapping her arms around me and holding onto me as if I was the last lifeline she had.

I didn't care. I just held her and refused to let go.

She was in pain and I didn't know why but I had to do something to stop it. Anything. The thought of her hurting was more than I could bear.

"I've got you," I said.

"I lost … our baby."

"It's not your fault."

"I wasn't strong enough."

I let her go but only so I could capture her face. "Stop it. I mean it. Fucking stop it. This is not about you being strong enough. There is no one that could take a beating like you took, and be able to get through that without problems. You were pregnant."

"I was sloppy. I shouldn't have stayed in town. I should have left."

"Is that what you wanted? To constantly be on the run and always looking over your shoulder? I don't think you realize this, but your father was never going to stop." I stared into her eyes, willing her to see the reality of the situation.

"Why?" she asked.

"I don't know, your father is an asshole," I said. One I was going to take great pleasure in killing, along with her fucked-up brother. "Come on." I moved her toward the bed, and helped her inside. I didn't leave her, though.

Climbing over her body, I settled in behind her and wrapped my arm around her waist, pulling her in close. I've already moved the blanket to completely cover her. Niamh didn't fight me, and I didn't know if that was a blessing or not. I held onto her, not willing to let her go.

"Did you ever want kids?" Niamh asked.

"No," I said. "I didn't think I was ever going to have children."

"And now?"

"I don't know, Niamh. I guess that is up to you."

"He's given me an out," Niamh said.

This made me frown. "What?"

"Ivan. He said when all of this is over and my father is no longer a threat, I can leave. I don't have to stay. He'll grant me a divorce and we'll both be free."

I held onto Niamh and didn't say a word. The truth was, I didn't like it. I was married to Niamh. She was my wife and Ivan was giving her a choice. No one else got a fucking choice. I hated it when Ivan told me, but it was now even worse hearing it from Niamh, because I couldn't help but wonder, did she want to take it?

Slowly, I felt when Niamh had fallen asleep. I waited several minutes and told myself not to go to Ivan and fuck him up, but I just couldn't let this sit for a moment longer.

I pulled away from Niamh, and waited to make sure I hadn't woken her. I made my way over to the door, opened, closed it, and then went to my spare bedroom. Ivan was already waiting, the door was open, and I stepped inside.

"Niamh okay?" he asked.

"You gave her a fucking choice?" I asked. I wasn't going to lead with that, but I didn't like it.

"In case you didn't know, Niamh is a very rich woman and she can do or be anything she wants. She doesn't need you or me, and yes, I have given her a choice. It's what she deserves."

I was so fucking pissed off, but I didn't comment. I couldn't.

"I want to kill her father," I said.

"I know."

"What do you need from him?"

Ivan's got this look, it's hard to explain, but it's that look that says he's got something planned but he's not going to tell me what it is exactly, and that was even more irritating.

"For fuck's sake, Ivan, what more is it going to take for me to prove to you that I'm not here to make waves?" I was past caring about protocol or showing respect. There were no soldiers around.

Ivan was my friend, at least that was the assumption I had.

"Some things are best left unsaid," Ivan said. "There are plans in place. I need Finn Byrne to be exactly where I need him to be for now."

And once again I was frustrated.

"You know, if you have a problem with me giving Niamh a choice, which you clearly seem to, maybe it would be in your best interest to give her a reason to make the right choice."

"What is that supposed to mean?"

"If you love her, then let her know it."

"I don't do love."

Ivan smiled. "You know, we as men make those excuses all the time, but it's only when we're really tested and we finally lose something or someone we love, that we realize how precious it is."

I stared at Ivan. "Have you lost someone?" I asked.

"Good night, Peter."

And he moved toward the door, which told me that was all I would get tonight.

## Chapter Eighteen

*Niamh*

I was tired when I woke up the following morning, but I was also happy there was no sign of Peter. I didn't know why I suddenly cried last night, but I just couldn't stop it.

It had been years since I last sobbed in that way, and certainly never in front of anyone. I think the last time I had cried like that, had been on my eighteenth birthday. My mom had forgotten, Dad had hit me with his belt, and, well, there had been no cake, no celebration. Just pain and that coldhearted reminder that I was alone in the world.

After going to the bathroom, I fixed a robe around my body and stepped out into the main penthouse, only to come to a pause when I saw Ivan sitting at the dining room table. At first, I was perfectly still.

I'd already seen that I looked a mess in the bathroom. My eyes were still poofy and slightly bloodshot.

"You're still here," I said.

"Good morning to you too."

"I'm sorry." I noticed a mug already in front of him. "Coffee."

"I'm already full. There is breakfast waiting for you in the oven."

"You cook?" I asked.

"Sometimes, but Peter made this for you, and he told me to tell you to eat."

Peter was trying to take care of me. I thought

back to last night—how he walked back into the bedroom and then just wrapped his arms around me, like he didn't want to let me go. I didn't want to let him go, not for a second.

Walking into the kitchen, the scent of coffee was too good to resist. One peek in the oven and it looked like baked oatmeal. I got it out of the oven and scooped some into a bowl, before taking a bite. It was delicious with a hint of sweetness, apple, and cinnamon. A favorite of mine.

Loaded up with breakfast and coffee, I was tempted to stay in the kitchen, but I didn't want Ivan to see me as I attempted to hide.

Stepping back into the main dining room, Ivan was still at the table. He looked so calm, so collected, and underneath that exterior of coolness, a monster was waiting to be unleashed.

"No one knows you were married before, do they?" I asked, knowing I'd already asked this before, but he didn't give me an answer. I didn't think he was ever going to give me one.

"No."

"You don't want them to know?"

"No."

I nodded. "What do I do if Peter asks?"

"Simple, you don't tell him what you know."

"But that is keeping secrets from my husband."

Ivan shrugged. "Will he still be your husband for long?"

I didn't know how to answer that. I took a sip of my coffee and then scooped some of the oatmeal. Like I knew it would be, it was so good. I closed my eyes and savored every bite. "It was good."

He smiled. "Peter's a good cook. He learned to fend for himself. He doesn't like to rely on anyone."

This made me stop. "He doesn't?"

"No, relying on anyone else always got people into trouble. You're aware of some of Peter's past, I assume?"

"Yes, he told me what his father used to do. How he turned it into a game for him."

"Peter saw a lot of people he assumed were his brothers or sisters get killed, when in fact, they were just strangers. Lost souls if you will, that fell through the cracks of the system."

"Is that what you were?" I asked.

Ivan smiled. "No, I wasn't lost, I was nothing more than trash, tossed out because I wasn't what my father wanted. I had a stutter."

"A stutter?"

"Yes."

"And your father kicked you out?"

"Actually, my father sent me off to be killed, but the guy who was sent to destroy me couldn't do it. My only problem was a stutter. Probably the biggest mistake that man ever made, because I was young, and I knew in that moment my father was not going to see the last of me, and he didn't."

"You rose up."

"Yes, I rose up, and I made sure he suffered before I took over and created what you see before you now."

"You're a rich, powerful, and wealthy man."

Ivan nodded.

"But you're not happy," I said.

He tilted his head toward me. "What makes you say that?"

"Because … you don't seem it."

"I am very happy. I have three men who are happily married, having children, and creating an empire."

I took another bite of my oatmeal. "But you're not."

Ivan stared at me. Silence fell between us.

"When I met you in that hospital on the day my mother was getting her stomach pumped, you were the same man you are today. You have the best suits, and you are as dangerous now as you were then. But that day, in that hospital, you died. Your happiness went with it."

"You speak so bluntly with a man you claim to be so dangerous."

"You can hurt me," I said. "I know you can, but after all these years, you didn't forget me. I'm not claiming you love me or anything like that. I made an impression on you that day. How?" The only reason I was in this penthouse suite, protected, and married to one of his Brigadiers was because of what I did.

"I told you back at the hospital. I was a stranger. You weren't looking to help me, or to make yourself feel better. You just behaved like a decent human being, and from where I come from, that is rare. I owe you, Niamh."

I laughed. "You don't owe me anything."

He shrugged. "Yes, I do."

I stared down at my oatmeal. "What was her name?" I asked.

Ivan didn't say a word.

Finally, I looked up. "I'm not going to claim that I understand what you're going through, or went through, because I don't. I lost a baby, and I think last night I suddenly realized what that meant to me, and it scared me. I lost a child, and don't know if it was a boy or a girl … I think it was too early into the pregnancy to know, but you lost someone you loved. You lost a wife, a woman who meant something to you. You're not married now either, so she made that much of an impression on you that you haven't found someone else. Peter doesn't know. No one else knows, only I do. Wouldn't you like to talk about her?" she asked.

I waited.

I didn't even know why I was being nice to Ivan. He sent a man to manipulate me, to get me pregnant.

Finishing my oatmeal and coffee, I got to my feet, about to leave, when Ivan's voice stopped me.

"She was beautiful," Ivan said.

I stopped and turned to look at him. I didn't say a word as he looked at me. There was no sadness or pain, or even guilt. It was like Ivan was completely numb.

"I met her when she was eighteen. I was older than her by ten years," Ivan said.

I knew he was near his forties now, and she was dead five years ago.

"I had already taken back what was rightfully mine. Killed my father, and was putting my Brigadiers in their rightful places. Everything was going exactly the way I wanted. Then, one day, I parked my car next to hers in a parking lot of a mall. I didn't even know why I had gone to the mall. Perhaps to pick something up for the woman I was fucking at the time. When I came out, there she was, yelling at my inconsiderate parking."

There was a smile on his lips and I knew he wasn't with me in that moment, but back in time, when he first met her.

He hadn't said her name, and I wasn't going to push. I couldn't help but wonder what it must be like. He married a woman in secret—the love of his life—and yet, he lost her and he never told anyone.

"Kaitlyn," he said.

"Kaitlyn?" I asked.

"That was her name." This time, he got up, but I felt like he had a lot to say.

"Why haven't you told anyone else?" I asked.

Ivan stopped. "There is no one else to tell."

"You have friends. You have Brigadiers. I know they work for you but their loyalty—"

"No one can ever know about this."

"Why not?"

He didn't answer. He got to his feet and I knew that meant this conversation was terminated, but I just couldn't let it go that easily.

"It won't make her go away," I said. "The pain is not going to stop."

He suddenly stopped and turned to look at me. "Be careful."

It was the first real threat he made toward me.

"What would Kaitlyn want you to do?" I asked, knowing I was already pressing against that precious line.

Ivan took a step toward me, then another. The threat was very much there with every step he took. I didn't know how I stayed still. I just stood there and looked at him, waiting for whatever he was going to do. I was frozen to the spot.

If this had been my father, I knew pain would be coming. My dad never held back. Ivan stepped right up until I could feel his breath across my face.

"I'm doing what Kaitlyn asked me to do and if you value your life, you will never say her name again. Do not make me regret sharing this with you, Niamh, because although I have given you everything, I can take it away."

He took a step back, and this time I watched him go.

\*\*\*\*

# A MONSTER IS COMING

*Peter*

I did not mind the other Brigadiers being in my territory. At least, I didn't think I minded, until they arrived at my office with a request. All three of them. Victor was nowhere to be found. Neither were The Beast or The Butcher. However, Slavik, Andrei, and Ive were in my office with a request.

Their wives wanted to get to know Niamh. She was going to be a fellow wife, and they wanted to get to know her. Draw her into their flock.

"No," I said.

I was not against Niamh having friends, but if what she told me was true, I didn't see her wanting to stay my wife when she could finally make that decision.

All three men looked at me and then smiled. "Oh, you think we're asking your permission?" Slavik asked.

"I don't care what you think you're asking. Don't you men have work to do? Territories to return to that are not mine?" It was getting a little crowded and I still had shit I needed to do.

Like, figure out what Ivan needed from Finn Byrne, so I could get it for him, and then rid myself of that bastard for good. Niamh needed to make her choice. I needed Niamh to make her choice, and picking off little bastards around Byrne, while keeping his oldest son captive, was starting to wear a little thin.

Ivan had a list of men who surrounded Byrne, offered him protection, and over the past couple of weeks, we'd been paying them little visits, after which they were dead, and Finn had one less person to protect him.

It would seem over the past twenty years, Finn Byrne had been adding up a load of favors, and then when Ivan came and took over his territory, pushing back, he had called them all in.

Ivan's territory now didn't all belong to Finn, just a small part of it. I believed a section was mine, and also a tiny part of Ive's. Finn had been building his little empire, while Ivan just got bigger faster.

"We'll be returning very shortly," Andrei said. "For now, our women would like to get to know your wife."

I sat back and looked at all three men. Each one was deadly, and together, to many, they probably looked terrifying, but the truth was, I didn't want to share my wife. Not when my marriage hung in the balance.

Ivan had given each of these men a wife, one they got to keep. Mine had a choice—me or her freedom. I had a feeling she was going to choose her freedom, and I knew on some level I shouldn't care about that, but I did. I didn't like that it even meant anything. I didn't do the whole emotion game.

Niamh was a woman I protected. Then … thought about the baby, my failure.

When The Butcher stormed into my office less than a second later, I'd never been so relieved to see another woman.

"Wow, do you know you guys gossip more than women do?" The Butcher asked.

All three men tensed up.

The Butcher and The Beast were not exactly well received by any of us. Where we all had to pass some kind of test and show our loyalty, the other two had gotten picked out of a hat.

I knew what Ivan was doing.

Even though we knew next to nothing about either The Butcher or The Beast, that didn't mean Ivan was in the same boat. He never shared his information, he just worked with what he had, and that's what made him one step ahead of the game. I intended to keep him that way.

The Butcher smiled. "It's so good to see you boys, looking all grown up." She winked at the room and then her gaze turned to me. "We've got to go."

I didn't take orders from her, not in my territory, but if she could get me out of a fucking dinner, then I was more than happy to go. Grabbing my jacket, I nodded at each of the men, and then left the room.

"Do I even want to know what that was about?" The Butcher asked, as we walked to the elevator that would take us to the underground parking.

"Our wives."

I didn't think she would understand but at her shrug, I was a little shocked.

"Makes sense. They're in town for a little bit, why not have all the Bratva wives get together? They're all close, or at least they try to be, seeing as they're all in the same boat."

"The same boat?" I asked.

"Yeah, wives to Brigadiers. In case you haven't noticed, that is an intense gig. Death threats, acts of violence, weird, stoic men, who they have to kind of decipher whether they're loved. You know, you guys."

"I'm not stoic."

"Well, you're not exactly a bundle of fun and joy, are you?" she asked.

The last thing I wanted was to be having a conversation with this woman about my charming personality.

"Do you think Niamh would like to get to know them?"

"Depends, do you think Niamh should get to know them?"

I didn't want to tell her about her choice. If

Niamh made the choice to leave, then no. The less she knew about the Bratva, the better. If she stayed, then the more she became part of my world, the better.

"I don't know."

I saw The Butcher roll her eyes. "What is your problem?" I asked.

"I don't have a problem, but I wish I could be saved from gossiping men, and all the chitchat that seems to be going on around me." The Butcher stepped forward and pressed the button on the elevator, bringing us to a halt.

"Why?" I asked, tense and ready to grab my gun.

"Have you ever considered taking your head out of your ass, and maybe giving Niamh a reason to not leave?"

"I don't know what the fuck you're talking about." And now, I was bored with this topic.

I went to reach for the elevator "stop" button to restart it, but The Butcher grabbed my arm and then twisted it, attempting to keep me from it. There was no way I was having her take control. I reached for her throat, and at the same time she took mine.

We fought until we were both trapped against the back of the elevator. I didn't squeeze her neck, nor did she mine, but the threat for both of us was there. The Butcher was trained, no doubt about that. But—and this was a big fucking but—so too was I. I didn't imagine many men would come off quite so lightly as I was in this situation.

She didn't look impressed.

"Seeing as we're at a little impasse right now," The Butcher said, "I will make it clear for you, because I happen to like Niamh, and you know what, I don't mind you at all either. I know you're a man who doesn't feel love. You're a killer. Talking to another person who had no choice but to do what you had to survive. Where your first kill came at a young age. I get it, okay? Connecting and all that crap, it isn't exactly easy. But, you clearly have feelings for Niamh, and if you don't, then you need to take another long, hard look in the mirror, because for a guy that has no feelings for a woman, you're not acting like it. Now, let's move back, let go, and get our shit together."

I glared at The Butcher, but I didn't want to be standing in an elevator getting nothing done. We pulled apart and she went to press the button, starting up the elevator once again. Slowly, I stood by her side, and the elevator made its last descent, opening into the parking lot.

Stepping out together, we headed to my car. Several of my men were already prepared in a backup car. They knew the drill, especially with The Butcher in tow.

I climbed behind the wheel while The Butcher took the seat beside me. Turning over the ignition, I didn't wait around and headed out of my underground parking lot, taking the directions she gave me to get where we needed to be.

"Where are we going?"

"Some small casino near the bottom of your city. Run by Ryan Connor. He's our target. Fifty years old, ah, I see, he has an extensive list here of the problems he liked to cause. Trafficking, drugs, guns, he's also dealt in dirty cops."

I knew who Ryan Connor was.

Ivan had told me to leave him alone after his little stunt of faking his own death. I knew other territories had a few problems with criminals wanting to take over. I had a few issues with petty assholes, pimps, one or two drug lords, that were all dead. My biggest issue had been with the law. The men I paid to keep me updated had decided to jump ship when they thought Ivan Volkov had died. They'd gone straight to Ryan Connor. I had no choice but to purge the shit out of the men I'd hired, and then deal with Ryan. I kept him alive, and tended to keep an eye on him, but in the last few months I'd been kind of busy.

I glanced over at The Butcher, who merely sat next to me. Once again, she was dressed in a pair of jeans and a blouse, looking like any random woman on the street.

"When did you make your first kill?" I asked.

If she or The Beast took over Pavlov's original territory, then I was going to have to deal with her or The Beast.

"Why would you like to know?"

"You said you got it, that you know I made my first kill when I was young. I guess you know my story."

"Yeah, I know your dad used you along with a bunch of other kids as entertainment for men who were willing to pay the right price to see a bunch of kids fight for their lives. Sick fucks. I was eight," The Butcher said.

Now, this surprised me.

"I had a less than conventional upbringing. I was so used to death and killing that it doesn't bother me. Kind of like gouging that guy's eyes out. I do what I must to get the job done." She shrugged.

"Who did you have to kill at eight years old?"

"A pedophile. My uncle was kind of a bounty hunter, assassin, and a guy that just liked to cause trouble. I'm not going to give you my history, but I did a lot of good. My uncle put me on the street to lure that bastard. The only problem was, he didn't come in time. He was going to try and touch me, and I don't like to be touched, so my uncle had given me a knife for my eighth birthday, and then we went hunting for the pedophile, and you can guess how that ended."

Yeah, I could.

"And you started at a young age."

"Yep, and don't let The Beast fool you. There are bodies they are never going to find. My body count is higher than his. He just likes to pretend differently."

## Chapter Nineteen

*Niamh*

Dinner was cooking in the oven—a lasagna, which happened to be my favorite—and I'd not had it in so long. I'd been tempted to be stubborn and not make any food. Peter had been bringing food home with him, and that was what we'd eaten, apart from the pizza with Ivan.

Ivan had also called to tell me he wouldn't be making movie night tonight, so I'd been alone. I had watched a movie, but then decided I was going to make dinner. My biggest problem was I didn't want Peter to get the wrong impression. This wasn't me making a choice. This was me saying thank you for last night, for him … just holding me. I knew it didn't mean much to Peter, but it did to me.

With the lasagna finishing up, I decided to set the table for two. I wasn't going to be an asshole over this. Opening the fridge, I took out the bottle of red wine that was supposed to go with beef, at least I hoped so. Didn't people always drink red wine with red meat? I didn't know. Wine and alcohol weren't drinks I ever consumed. I knew Peter enjoyed wine, whiskey, and beer.

With the wine open and breathing, I opted for some water, which I poured and added a few ice cubes.

This was not a date, even though I was tempted to light some candles. I didn't know if Peter was going to arrive on time. There were so many questions I didn't have answers to.

I went back to the sofa, turned on the television, and flicked through the channels trying to find something to watch. All the time aware of the ticking clock as my lasagna got closer to being cooked.

I didn't know if I should call Peter to ask if he was coming home, or just leave it. I was not in the habit of following up on a guy.

Ten minutes till my lasagna was done. I got to my feet and started to make my way toward the kitchen, only to stop when the main door of the penthouse opened.

Peter stepped inside, and I tried to ignore that little fluttering in my chest at the sight of him. I shouldn't feel so happy to see him, and yet that was exactly what I was—happy.

"Peter," I said.

He looked up at me, and that was when I saw the blood on his shirt. I didn't recoil. I didn't run away. Instead, I closed the distance and went straight to him. "What happened?"

"I got hit, that's all," he said.

"You need to go to the hospital."

"No."

"Damn it, Peter, don't be stubborn."

"Trust me, Niamh, this is not the first cut or wound I've gotten. When I say I don't need to pay the hospital a visit, trust me, I don't need to pay the hospital a visit."

Wow, he was grumpy.

"Fine, you don't need to pay the hospital a visit, but I'm going to check your wounds." I helped him to the bathroom.

I wasn't sure if I helped exactly, but I was standing beside him as we made our way across the hallway toward our bedroom. I had not moved any of my clothes or stuff out of the bedroom.

I knew Ivan wasn't coming back tonight, but I also hadn't thought about nighttime. Or maybe I had, and

I didn't want to leave Peter's bed. I wasn't exactly sure what I was thinking or feeling, or if I even knew for sure what I was going to do. For now, I just wanted to take care of Peter.

I got him to sit on the toilet seat, which I had put down. "Sit."

He didn't argue and sat right down.

I saw a bruise already forming beneath his left eye, and I glanced over his body. His knuckles were cut, and he must have punched several hard things for them to look like that.

He opened his shirt and winced as he moved to take it out from his pants. I moved quickly, not wanting to see him in discomfort.

"Here," I said. "Let me help."

I removed his shirt, and then I saw several cuts. All the blood on his shirt wasn't from him. I knew that much.

I went to the cupboard in the corner and grabbed a first aid kit. Spinning around, I couldn't help but stop and look at my husband. He had a heavily inked chest, which I had always found fascinating, but now I saw it even more so. There were two slashes on one side of his body, beneath his breast. I sank down to my knees, and then quickly assessed the damage.

"They're not deep," he said.

"Do I need to ask if the other guy is in worse condition?" I asked, giving a chuckle.

"The other guy is dead."

"I was … uh, just joking."

"I'm not."

I nodded. "I don't know if you should be telling me these kinds of things, you know, the less I know and whatnot."

"I'm not going to keep secrets from my wife,"

Peter said, and the way in which he said it sent a thrill down my spine.

Maybe I was going crazy. Peter and I, our ... we're ... so complicated. I wanted to hate him and yet, I couldn't.

Opening the first-aid kit, I found the nonalcoholic wipes and tore into them to begin cleaning his wound. It wasn't too bad. Once I cleaned some of the blood out of the way, I was able to see it was just a flesh wound. I didn't know if a nurse would prefer to offer stitches.

"Why are you doing this?" Peter asked.

I couldn't help but glance up into his eyes. I loved his blue eyes, and despite the lies or falsehoods between us, his eyes hadn't changed.

"Doing what?"

I reached for an antiseptic cream and applied to the area, as well as to the Band-Aid I'd found. It was a big Band-Aid, with what looked like a pad down the center. Carefully, I placed it over his cut.

"Taking care of me."

"Because you are my husband, and regardless of everything, Peter, I don't want to see you hurt."

I put my hands on his knees and stared up at him.

"I'm not hurt."

"Of course not. You have wounds that are a little concerning, and we're going to need to keep them clean. Promise me you'll go to the hospital or call a doctor to help ... fix you."

"I'll promise, if you give me something in return."

This made me frown. "What? You do know this is not how that is supposed to work. You're supposed to want to get better because you've got a giant cut on your side. That is how it's supposed to work." I was kind of rambling, because, well, I didn't know what Peter wanted, and I was a little afraid of what that could mean.

"I know, but I wouldn't be where I am today if I didn't see an opportunity and take it."

"You see me as an opportunity?" I asked.

"No, I see this as an opportunity."

"Then what do you want?" I knew I was playing with fire right now. I didn't know what Peter could possibly want, and I was a little afraid to find out. But, I also wanted to know.

He stroked my cheek with the backs of his fingers and stared into my eyes. "I want to kiss you," he said.

I didn't think it would be a kiss that he'd want at the moment..

"A kiss?" I asked.

"Yes."

I didn't know what was so important about a kiss, but I nodded. "Fine, I'm in agreement." I wasn't going to say what we were agreeing about. I'd kind of lost track of the conversation. Peter had this affect on me, and it wasn't good.

I got to my feet and at the same time, so did Peter. I reached out, but he was not swaying from side to side or doing anything alarming. He looked sturdy on his feet. Steady, even. I couldn't help but glance toward his lips. It had been a long time since we kissed. I couldn't help but think back to the picnic—feeling his lips on mine, and then only moments later, my life became a nightmare.

I pushed those memories to the back of my mind because they didn't have a place in this moment, not with Peter.

Me and Peter.

Alone.

He cupped my cheek and tilted my head back, staring into my eyes. Neither of us spoke, and then Peter closed the distance between us, only he didn't go straight in for a kiss. No, at first, he pressed his face against my neck, and then I felt him breathe me in as if he couldn't resist. With one deep inhale, he couldn't seem to help himself.

Then, he kissed my neck, at that pulse point right where it always felt so good, and I struggled not to say or do anything. Why did he have to begin by touching me there? Not that I was complaining. One touch and I didn't want him to stop.

My hands were by my sides, and I was trying to keep myself contained, but it was hard, especially as I wanted him to touch me. It felt like a sudden, overwhelming need, and then when I least expected it, Peter took possession of my lips and began to kiss me. Gentle at first, and now I couldn't help but touch him. I went for his waist, and then slowly slid my hands up, going around to his back, and kissing him. I did try to keep distance between us, so I didn't hurt him. It was the last thing I wanted to do.

Peter must have known what I was trying to do, because he wrapped his arms around me, pulling me in close. The kiss deepened. Peter traced my lips, and then slid inside.

I couldn't contain my moan and the truth was, I didn't want to. All I wanted to do was kiss this man. He was driving me crazy.

I wasn't sure how we ended up in the bedroom, but I wasn't going to complain. I didn't fight it. I didn't want to fight it.

Sliding my hands down his body, I grabbed his belt and loosened it. I went from a woman who was hesitant to suddenly feeling like I needed him inside me. I wanted Peter. Those feelings I had were not just cut out of me. They were not beaten out of me. I still loved

Peter.

There was still a lot of pain and betrayal between us, but also understanding. He knew who I was, and yet he didn't back away. I knew he was just following Ivan's orders, but even still, this felt good. I had to forget about the past. Ivan had given me a choice. I wasn't ready to make that choice, not right now. All I wanted to do was put the past behind us, and to feel Peter.

With his pants on the floor, I then suddenly remembered the lasagna in the oven, and I quickly broke the kiss.

"Our lasagna. I need to go and turn off the stove."

Peter sighed. "You know what, I'm not going to let you out of my fucking sight."

I let out a scream as he suddenly hauled me over his shoulder. "Peter, what are you doing?" I asked. "You're injured. You shouldn't be carrying me around. This is insane. Put me down." I couldn't help but laugh as he suddenly carried me out of the bedroom, and into the kitchen. He had to impress me by turning off the oven without having to ask me. Not that I should be surprised, Peter could cook.

I was still hanging off his shoulder. "You're going to hurt yourself."

"And you've lost too much weight."

"Don't! Take me back to the bedroom." I didn't want to talk about my lack of an appetite. I knew I'd lost weight. My pants now required a belt to keep them up. Yep, I had nearly flashed one group of three of my guards, but thankfully I'd felt them falling, and caught them.

I'd started to wear belts with my pants and skirts. The dresses were a little big, but I just buttoned them up to the neck, and again, no problem with flashing anyone anything I didn't want them to see.

I didn't expect Peter to listen, but we're somehow back in the bedroom, and he'd gotten my jeans off, as well as my shirt. He was standing in a pair of black boxer briefs, I in my black lace lingerie. It was one of my favorite sets, even if it was a little bigger than usual.

"I'm going to fuck you, Niamh, and then I'm going to feed you."

I felt a quake in my pussy, and I knew, deep down, there were a lot of women who would tell Peter to go fuck himself, that they would hate him for the rest of their lives, but I was not like most people.

Back in Pickle Quest, I fell in love with him. This was no excuse. He was going to leave with me. Again, no excuse. And we were going to have a baby. Now, I was married to him, and all the lies had been shown. Peter hadn't gotten angry with me. He wasn't even judging me.

Maybe hanging out with Ivan, knowing he had lost the love of his life, had put everything into perspective for me. One thing I couldn't deny—I loved Peter. He was alive, and we were married.

Even though betrayal and lies had brought us together, we were still together. I didn't want to lose him. It was strange the way I was feeling tonight, but I didn't want to let Peter go.

Within seconds, Peter had my lingerie off. The bra was on the floor, but the panties hadn't survived and were in pieces on the floor.

The moment his hands were on me, I failed to care about anything else, and just let myself feel. I put all the bad feelings to the back of my mind, and instead focused on what mattered—just the two of us.

However, as Peter wrapped his arm around me and pulled me close, I felt the fabric of his boxers, and I needed them off. I pushed his hands off me, but immediately sunk down to my knees in front of him. I gripped the edge of his briefs, and then without hesitating, I pushed them down to the floor, releasing his rock-hard cock.

At first, I just stared up into his eyes, aware of his dick close to my face. It had been so long since I had tasted him. I'd asked for him back in Pickle Quest to show me how to please him in the same way he did me when he licked my pussy. He'd not disappointed.

Slowly, he glanced down his body, aware of his wounds, but then I went straight to his cock. The tip was already glistening with his pre-cum, and the foreskin had retracted as his erection had grown. I wrapped my fingers around the length of his dick, and then leaned forward, kissing just the tip.

"Oh, fuck!" He released a growl, almost a grunt, but I didn't stop.

Taking his cock into my mouth, I made sure I didn't use my teeth, and I sunk onto his length until he hit the back of my throat. Pulling back, I created a pace that had me sinking on his length, taking as much of him as I could into my mouth, and then pulling away.

My name spilled from his lips, and he reached out, taking hold of my hair, and then showed me exactly what he wanted me to do to his dick.

I sunk onto his length, tasting the pre-cum as it coated my tongue. I didn't want to stop, but Peter had other ideas as he pulled away, but he didn't leave me for long. He took me off my feet, and then pressed me forward until my legs hit the back of the bed, and then I sunk down.

"My turn," he said.

I cried out as within seconds, his tongue was at my clit. He slid back and forth, circling the hardened bud. I didn't think I was so close to an orgasm, but Peter was a master with his tongue, and with just a few strokes, I was already close to coming. I didn't want him to stop. I felt needy. Desperate. I'd not felt this way before.

And as he took me over the edge, I didn't think I was ever going to feel anything so wonderful again.

Peter wasn't done.

Even before the aftershocks of my release had subsided, he moved us up toward the head of the bed. He reached down between us and slid his thick cock between my slit, bumping against my oversensitive clit. I cried out. The pleasure was next level.

He did this a couple of times, and then he moved down, going between my thighs, and sinking inch by inch, deep inside my cunt.

Peter didn't stop until he was seated deep inside me, and now I looked at him, a little taken aback, but totally filled, as I realized that love hadn't gone away. I didn't hate Peter Orlov. I was still as in love with him as the day he came to town. Even though he was a different man, I still loved him, and I didn't want anything to happen to him.

Not ever.

## Chapter Twenty

*Peter*

I woke up the next day, and I had never been happier seeing my wife still beside me, and knowing last night hadn't been a dream. I'd finally made love to my wife, and no, I hadn't used a condom.

Niamh had a choice. She could have told me to use one, but she didn't. I didn't own them, but with Niamh, I didn't want there to be anything between us. I knew that made me a selfish bastard, but for now I didn't care. She had a choice.

After our first time, I had insisted on feeding her that lasagna. It hadn't overbaked, and it was still warm when we got to it. We'd nearly demolished the entire tray. I didn't want to look away from her. The start of our marriage hadn't exactly gone according to plan. I stared at her.

Slowly, as if I willed her to wake up, she began to open her eyes. I didn't know what to expect when she saw me staring at her, but it certainly wasn't that beautiful smile.

"Morning," she said.

"Good morning."

"How long have you been awake?"

"A little while."

"And you've not snuck off to work?"

"I don't have to."

This made her brows rise, which looked so cute. "You don't?"

"In case you didn't know, I am the boss."

"Ah, you see, I did know that, but I was told there

is no rest for a Brigadier. You've been busy, a lot, and you know, you've come back to me injured, which is never a good thing." She gave this cute little tut, that I found totally adorable. This was fun.

"There is no rest."

Niamh sighed. "Where exactly are you going?"

I looked at Niamh. I didn't know what the other Brigadiers told their wives. Our business was private, but I looked at Niamh.

"Ivan's dealing with all the associates that owe your father a favor."

"My father?"

"Yes. It would seem over the course of Finn Byrne's life, he has acquired quite a few people who are willing to go above and beyond to help him."

"I had no idea."

Someone like Finn didn't get where he was today without making connections. I didn't know why Ivan had such a vendetta against him. Unless he had taken issue to the way Niamh was treated, which I did understand. In Finn beating her, she had lost the baby. Another line for the Volkov Bratva.

Ivan was building an empire—children, families, a future for generations—and when it came to Ivan, I had a gut feeling this was more personal. There was only one other person I knew was close to Ivan growing up, and that was Slavik.

"So, I had some of the other Brigadiers come by yesterday. It would seem their wives would like to meet you. You met them at our wedding. Aurora, Adelaide, and Charlotte."

"I remember them. They stood together, close to their husbands at all times."

"That is how it's meant to be when they're in

another man's territory."

"Oh," Niamh said.

"They're in mine."

Niamh chuckled. "I already figured that out. I filled in the blanks." She smiled at me and then stroked my cheek.

"Would you like to meet them? Get to know them?"

She tilted her head to the side, and looked at me. "Why?"

"I just … I want you to be comfortable here. I know it's not going to be easy for you to make new friends, not being my wife, so those you can make, even long distance, would be important."

"I've never been good at making friends," Niamh said.

"I have a feeling you'll find these ladies are … similar," I said.

"Why?"

I took a deep breath. "Don't take this the wrong way, but Ivan has a tendency to find broken, damaged women, who need … someone."

"Oh," Niamh said.

I already knew what was going through her mind, because with her circumstances and family, she fit the bill quite well.

"I, ugh, I kind of fall into that category as well, huh?"

I didn't even answer that.

"My men, as well as their own guards, will be there. You won't be alone, and I will make sure your men are aware that if you give them a signal, they should bring the meeting to an end."

"A meeting?"

"I was thinking you and the ladies could do lunch

today."

"This is sudden," Niamh said.

"I just want you to try and make some friends." And with our wives out of the way, it meant I could talk to Slavik without any trouble. I knew it was a risk.

I had intended to spend today with Niamh, and to explore our newfound … closeness. I wanted every opportunity to spill my sperm deep inside her so I could get her pregnant again. Also, I did want her to have friends. Aurora, Adelaide, and Charlotte were good people.

And so, four hours later, while Niamh was with the wives, I arranged a different kind of meeting with Slavik. He was in a café enjoying a cup of coffee, when I went to join him.

"You used your wife so that you and I could have a meeting?" Slavik asked. "I will have to warn you, if this is in any way designed to terminate Ivan, then you will be dead within minutes."

"My loyalty lies with Ivan Volkov. I give my life to the Volkov, and that will never change." One of the inks right around my chest is the Volkov brand, the V with the ivy around each one. I had the mark inked around my chest so I would always remember my loyalty, my ties.

"Then, what could you possibly want from this meeting?" Slavik asked.

"What has Finn Byrne done to Ivan Volkov to make him remove every person helping him?"

I couldn't quite connect the dots. Ivan was turning this into a hunt. He had the ability to kill Finn. Not only did he have the man's son, he also had the man's daughter, the woman with all the power of the Byrne name. Ivan hadn't used any of it.

Also, he had The Beast and The Butcher at his

disposal, and their reputations were not false. I had seen The Butcher at work, and I now saw why she was named as such.

Ivan had the power, and yet he was taking out everyone around Finn. Almost playing with him, taunting him. Not that I had an issue with how Ivan was dealing with him. We all dealt with our demons in different ways.

This was personal.

Slavik sat back.

Neither of us spoke.

"As far as I'm aware, Finn Byrne was nothing more than a thorn in Ivan's side, but one he'd pulled out."

"Yeah, well, now I have a feeling the little hole that thorn created is bleeding," I said. "He's taking out all the petty thugs, but only those with any connection to Byrne. Why?"

"Well, that is something you're going to have to ask Ivan."

\*\*\*\*

*Niamh*

I was not good at making friends.

This was when the situation was normal.

We all had men, less than two feet away from us. I noticed Aurora only had one guard, as did Adelaide and Charlotte. All three of the women offered me a smile, as I had three men guarding me.

"It's nice to meet you all," I said.

Again, I was awkward. I didn't know what to say. Where the three women appeared to be quite close, I was not used to embracing.

They hugged and looked so happy to see each other. I noticed that Charlotte flinched during the hugs, but she still gave them back, even though they clearly made her uncomfortable.

"This is strange, isn't it?" Aurora said.

At least, I think it was Aurora.

I pressed my lips together, and gave a kind of smile, but it didn't quite reach my eyes, and I wasn't exactly sure if it was a smile or not.

"Apparently you all wanted to, uh, meet with me, I think that's what Peter said. You didn't have to do that. I know we're not ... like friends or anything. We won't even be close, and..." I stopped because I wasn't sure if I should say I had a choice about a potential divorce. Leaving the Volkov Bratva ... and Peter.

It was hard to even think about right now. Last night had been amazing, and I didn't want to leave, but I didn't know if I could stay married to Peter. He didn't do love and the truth was, all I wanted was love and a family, and to be ... wanted.

Wow, how the fuck had I just realized that now? I mean, I knew I'd always wanted a family. That was no secret, but I didn't know if I could have that with Peter. Did he even want to be a dad?

Pushing those thoughts to the back of my mind, I smiled at the women at the table, more thankful than ever, to have the waiter come to take our drink order. I was tempted to give the signal that would mean my guards got me away from this awkwardness, but I promised Peter I'd try.

"So, I think I should go first, because this is kind of awkward. I'm Aurora Ivanov. I'm married to Slavik, and even though our marriage didn't have the best start, I am in love with my husband, and we have two children, and a third on the way. Oh, I was nearly killed as well, and framed for attempting to kill Ivan, but it wasn't me. It was a woman he and Slavik were close to."

This was news to me, but I looked at the other woman and forced a smile.

"I guess that goes to me, seeing as I was the next woman to be married to a Volkov Brigadier. I'm Adelaide Belov, and my sister was supposed to marry Andrei, only she kind of … well, she was sleeping around, and they needed a virgin, and someone who didn't cause too much trouble, and that was me." She held her hands out with a laugh. "Also, we have one baby, and hopefully we'll have another one soon."

I turned toward Charlotte, but the waiter chose that moment to bring over our drinks. I had gotten a glass of water.

The waiter left and Charlotte smiled.

"I was a giant mistake," Charlotte said. "I was the wrong daughter that was taken in the hope of creating negotiations between my father's MC and Ivan Volkov. The only problem is my dad hated my guts, and often used me as a punching bag. I have many scars to show for it, oh, and I once thought of myself as trash … so, good times."

I was shocked by how honest Charlotte was. She wasn't looking for pity either, she was merely stating facts.

"I'm now married to Ive, and we're expecting our first child. Also, my husband is called Ivan, but seeing as Ivan Volkov is Ivan, my husband is now Ive."

Charlotte lifted her glass, and we all toasted.

"Oh, my sister tried to have me killed," Adelaide said.

They all turned toward me, and I glanced down at my water.

"I'm Naimh Orlov." I stopped because I didn't

quite know how to form into words what I needed to say. The women had been open, and I knew they had more tales to tell. "My husband is Peter Orlov, and I met him in the small town of Pickle Quest, where I thought he was a personal trainer. It turned out he'd been sent with a mission of getting me pregnant, which he did. Only, my father found me because I had run away, and he beat me to the point that I lost the baby. Now, I'm married to Peter, and one day, I'm going to have to make a choice whether I stay married to him, or give him up and get my freedom."

At my statement, all three women looked concerned.

"My vote is she is going to stay," Ivan said, startling us all as he made an appearance at our table.

I hadn't seen him since yesterday morning, and he cancelled last night, which I was happy about as I spent the night with Peter.

He smiled at all four of us, and then kissed Aurora's cheek, Adelaide's, and then Charlotte's, before coming to me. He gave my shoulders a squeeze, and one of the guards was already grabbing a chair for him to sit down. The waiter came over and delivered him a drink.

"You do realize you're intruding on a girls' only event," Charlotte said.

"I know, but I needed to make sure you're all getting on well. You know how I pride myself in choosing the perfect brides for my men." Ivan winked at the table.

This made me laugh.

"Ivan likes to think of himself as a matchmaker," Aurora said.

"No, what Ivan likes to do is collect broken and damaged women, and give them a happy-ever-after," Charlotte said.

I turned to look at Ivan.

Broken and damaged.

I had a feeling none of these women knew of Ivan's past with another woman.

"Is there a reason you pay close attention to broken and damaged?" I asked, sipping at my water, and then knowing I couldn't keep drinking water. All three of these women and now Ivan—I needed an actual drink. I was breaking all my rules, but I signaled the waiter and asked for a glass of something strong. I knew I was making a mistake when I asked for it.

Ivan looked toward me. "I have my reasons."

"Care to share them?" I asked.

"No."

Aurora chuckled. "One thing you will learn, Niamh, Ivan will only tell you his reasons when he's good and ready."

There was an agreement around the table.

The waiter came with the stiff drink, putting it in front of me. I averted my gaze from Ivan's to look at the drink. I'd promised myself I would never drink. After going to the hospital too many times that I lost count to have my mother's stomach pumped, I had vowed to never touch a drop of alcohol.

My life had changed a lot in the past few months. I was married to a man I loved, who didn't love me back. According to Ivan, I was a wealthy woman, and when the threat against me was gone, I'd be able to make the choice to leave.

I found this so difficult. I loved Peter; those feelings hadn't changed. I couldn't just turn them off, even though I wanted to. But, I didn't want to stay with a man who couldn't love me back. That sounded like a nightmare, and not one I wanted to live.

Picking up the glass, I felt all of those years of

abuse claw at me, threatening to get out, and then I ignored them and downed my drink, enjoying the hard, bitter burn as it slid down my throat.

## Chapter Twenty-One

*Peter*

At first, I thought Ivan was joking. Niamh didn't drink. She never touched a drop because of her parents, more importantly her mother. Only, Ivan wasn't joking. My wife had been drinking through lunch, and when I arrived at my penthouse, it was to find Ivan sitting on the sofa, while Niamh held my bottle of expensive whiskey and danced on the wooden coffee table in the living room.

"Peter!" She let out a slurred squeal. "Peter is home. Peter is home!"

I'd never seen her like this and as Ivan got to his feet, I glared at him. "What did you do?"

"That, I don't know. My suggestion is, the next time you want to get Niamh close to the other wives, take her out to dinner, and make it a date with the other men. Something triggered her."

Ivan went to leave and I grabbed his arm. He looked down at where I held him. I wanted to ask him so many questions, but I also couldn't leave Niamh alone.

"We need to talk."

"You're right. I've got a few jobs that need dealing with. I'll call you tomorrow. Although, I think you're going to be taking care of your wife." Ivan smiled at Niamh, who waved back at him.

"Love you, Ivan," she said. "Thank you for bringing me home."

I could still understand her, even if her words were slurred as she spoke.

"I'll let myself out," Ivan said. He took a step

away, but then stopped and turned toward me. "You know, if you don't want her to leave at the end of all this, maybe be honest with her, and while you're at it, be honest with yourself."

And those were Ivan's parting words, before he let himself out of my penthouse.

Niamh was dancing and she got close to the edge, causing me to suddenly rush toward her. She stumbled, about to take a fall, but I caught her, stopping her from hitting the table, and capturing her in my arms.

"Peter, you caught me. You are my hero." She rested her head against my shoulder. "Can I tell you a secret?"

"Yes."

"I think I like beer."

"Beer, or my whiskey?" I asked.

She took a sip of my whiskey and then groaned. "It's so strong, but it makes me feel so good."

"You're not going to feel good in the morning."

"Then, I better keep drinking. It's what my mom did whenever Dad came around, or didn't come around. She always had a reason for drinking or doing drugs. I was always the reason. I disappointed her."

She swayed and I grabbed hold of her hips to keep her steady.

Niamh giggled, and tilted her head to the side. "I can now see why she drank as much as she did."

"Why?"

"Because it made life easier."

"Drinking doesn't make life easier, Niamh. All it does is push the problems down the road."

"But what if I *want* all my problems down the road? So far. So away." She swatted her hands to the side and her face was scrunched up.

"What problems do you want down the road?" I

asked, knowing there was a possibility I wasn't going to like the answer.

She stopped swatting at the air and then placed her hands on my chest. For several seconds, she didn't say a word. Just kept her hands on my chest, waiting.

I'd always been a patient man, but when it came to Niamh and her drunk, I had lost my patience, and now I just wanted answers.

"You," she said. "Choices. They do suck, don't they?" She sighed and then pulled away from me.

I had no choice but to let her go. While I'd grabbed hold of her, I'd also taken my bottle of whiskey from her, which she snagged again, and took a long drink.

She swallowed and then coughed. "So hot!" She wiped at her face. "I mean, this is all your fault."

And here we go—the blaming game. I was used to this. I folded my arms and knew I was going to be the villain in her story. Where she'd point the finger of blame at everything I'd ever done. That I shouldn't exist.

"Why did I have to fall in love with you?"

I wasn't expecting that. No one had ever blamed me for being in love. I didn't believe in love. I stared at her, a little taken aback. I'd expected all manner of insults, and instead she just told me she loved me.

"You see, if I was like my mom, this would be so much easier. That money would be totally spent, and she'd probably rub it in my father's face as well. It would be such an easy decision for her. She'd even sell her only daughter for that kind of wealth, at least if Ivan's to be believed, and I have no reason to assume otherwise. Like you said, he always keeps his word." She stopped and took another drink. "My life was going to be simple. Stay on the run, at least until my father died." She wrinkled her nose. "I don't know if there is a hole in that plan, though, because from what I've been told, my brother is as big a monster as he is." She started to pace, albeit not in a straight line. "But then you came to town, and I had this horrible feeling, but I figured my instincts were just failing me. But they weren't failing me. What I felt was real, but by then it was too late, and *you*…" She stormed up to me. "You had to be so kind and so sweet, and yes, I know you don't do love. So I know you can never love me back, so while I want to be pissed at you for lying, I know I can't. I was just as big a liar as you."

She stepped back and held her fingers out. "I'm still in love with you." A finger went down. "I … like seeing you every single day and that means waking up with you." Another finger went down.

"I love it when you hold me while I sleep. I've been woken up so many times in the past by a belt or my father's fist, that I didn't sleep well for a long time, but I know you can take care of me. That you won't let anything happen to me." Another finger went down.

"You're my husband." The fourth finger went down.

"And one day, I'd love to have your babies and be happy." The thumb closed around her fingers.

"And then, on this hand, the only reason I can see to leave, is to set you free." Her lip quivered.

"You don't have to set me free, Niamh."

"But you don't do love. You're not in love with me, and you don't deserve to live your life like this, with a woman you don't like."

I closed the distance between us. I had no idea if she was going to remember this conversation or not. Strong, good whiskey had that effect on the mind. It was why it was such a good drink to lose yourself in. "I don't hate you. I don't not like you. I do like you, Niamh, and I don't want you to leave. I don't want to grant you a divorce. I'd be very happy if you stayed."

And, Niamh had been drinking for a very long time, and the effects of the alcohol were finally catching up to her. Her eyes drooped and seconds later, I caught her in my arms as she collapsed against me. Tomorrow, she would feel the aftereffects of the whiskey.

\*\*\*\*

*Niamh*

It was official, I was never, never, ever, never, ever, ever, ever, ever drinking again. In fact, I'd like to throw in a few more never-evers. I didn't think I was quite clear enough. I had no idea the toilet seat could become my new best friend, but I did have a sudden feeling to pet the damn thing.

I was going crazy. No doubt about it.

My shame was not just my own, though, nope, to help me along the shame trail, Peter had decided to stay. He'd laid beside me all night, and I hoped he'd been able to get some sleep. I knew from past experience that my mom's snores got louder after a night of heavy drinking.

My mother also had the ability to forget her previous night's escapades. She would often chuckle and gasp at all the right spots, but I must not have drunk enough, because I remembered everything. There was even a point where I jumped onto the wooden coffee table and began to dance. I might have invited Ivan to also let loose. Then of course, there was the truth-on-the-hand thing I told Peter.

I didn't know if he was going to let me forget it or not. I was hoping he would, because I didn't want to have to go through any of that.

He held my hair back as another wave of sickness

washed over me, and this had nothing to do with a baby. Nope, I was throwing up my guts because I decided to wash down lunch with a ton of alcohol.

I was like my mother, even though I promised myself I never would be.

All I wanted to do was burst into tears, finish throwing up, and sink back beneath the covers of the blankets, and hope the ground would finally swallow me whole.

No more vomit was coming, and I moved to allow it to flush away. Peter rubbed at my back, and why did he have to be so sweet, so loving? This was not who he was, and yet he did it anyway.

I wanted to give him his freedom, it was one of the reasons I had started to drink, because having this choice was killing me. I did love Peter. There was no easy way that was going to fade away as if it didn't exist, because it did exist, and I couldn't just get away from that.

"There, are you okay?" Peter asked.

"I think so. I don't think any more is going to come." The entire contents of my stomach felt like they were now in the toilet. I'd already flushed the sick down, and now I glanced inside to make sure it was clean. Getting to my feet, Peter let go of my hair, and I pushed some out of my face.

"You need a shower," he said.

I nodded. And also to brush my teeth.

Peter didn't leave right away. He turned on the shower and checked the water. "I'm going to make you some breakfast. Do you think you can survive the shower without me?"

I nodded. "Yeah, I can figure it out."

This was no joking matter.

He stepped up toward me, put both of his hands

on my arms, and then leaned in and kissed me. I closed my eyes, as I felt his lips brush across my forehead. It felt nice. It felt good. Again, this wasn't helping me to set him free. In this moment, I didn't want to set him free. I wanted to keep him and never let him go.

I stared at him, not sure what to do or say.

He stroked my cheek, and then he spun on his heel and left.

Was there even a chance that he could love me? I didn't want to be one of those women who forced a man to love her. Why did Ivan have to do this to me?

I stripped out of my clothes and quickly stepped beneath the hot spray of water, loving the feel of it as it washed over my skin. Closing my eyes, I allowed it to completely soak me, and tilted my head back. The spray, at first, felt almost biting, but slowly my skin stopped feeling so tender, and I got accustomed to the feel of it.

I opened my eyes, and stared across at the tiled wall. I kept seeing Peter last night. How he took care of me. The way he held my hips and I slid my hands down to touch where he had last night. I couldn't feel his grip, even though I wanted to. So, instead, I took a deep breath and just allowed myself to breathe. That was all I could do.

Would it be so wrong of me to stay with a man who didn't love me?

Pushing those thoughts and that damn choice to the back of my mind, I instead focused on getting washed. Peter was making food, and I didn't want it to spoil or get cold. With my hair washed, I soaped up a sponge and ran it all over my body. Letting the suds rinse off, I turned the shower off, stepped out, and wrapped my body in a towel, as well as my hair.

Next step, brushing my teeth, because my breath smelled so bad. I needed to wash the taste of that whiskey out of my mouth.

Once my teeth were done, I swilled my mouth with some mouthwash, and then I cleaned up my mess and went straight to the bedroom. I still found it hard to call it my bedroom, or *our* bedroom. In my mind, it was still Peter's bedroom, even though my stuff had been moved into the space available, and we'd not really talked about it going back.

So, for now, this was "our bedroom." I didn't know why I loved that title, but I did.

I was totally swaying toward large, oversized sweats, but instead, I grabbed a dress. I was going to make an effort. I wasn't sure if Peter was staying with me, or if he'd find some reason to be as far away from me as possible. Not that I could blame him, because I pretty much sucked last night.

I'd become my mother, only caring about my own needs when it came to forgetting my troubles, and that was never going to happen again. If the uncontrolled vomiting wasn't a sign, then certainly the splitting headache and general bad taste I had in my mouth would help me decide.

Once I had dressed in a light, pastel-blue summer dress with a floral design, I headed out to the delicious smell of bacon and coffee.

Peter was standing at the kitchen stove. He had his business suit on, apart from the main jacket. His shirtsleeves were rolled up, showing off the many tattoos he had.

"What's it like to get a tattoo?" I asked.

I had looked at them many times, but the thought of having a needle stabbing my flesh was just a little more painful that I could bear. Also, where would I have found a tattoo artist willing to ink me? My father had a lot more control on me than I had even realized. It was kind of shocking.

"The same as any tattoo. You know what you want, he or she does it. You pay. That's pretty much it."

"Does it hurt?"

"I have a higher pain threshold, so it didn't bother me, which is why I've got quite a few of them."

"Why did you get them originally?" I asked.

Peter paused and I saw it in the way his elbow seemed to go completely still. He glanced over his shoulder toward me.

"If you must know, it was to hide the scars I'd gotten because of my dad's … games."

He'd told me what his father had done.

I had some scars from the beatings my father had given me. Reminders of what he'd done, and that I had survived.

"Do you think the person you used would be willing to … do me?" I frowned. "I mean, you know, give me a tattoo?" I felt my cheeks heating.

"I can get him to come here if you'd like. You don't have to go to his shop."

I shook my head. "I'm not sure what I want, but I was thinking, you know, ugh, like look through what he can do and see if there's anything I like."

"No problem. Once we're finished here, we'll go and get it done."

"We will?"

"Yeah."

"What about … you know, work? Don't you have work to do?"

"It can wait. I'll spend the day with you." This was a surprise, but it was one I wanted.

I offered him a smile, and then watched as he finished serving breakfast. I looked forward to spending the day with my husband.

## Chapter Twenty-Two

*Peter*

Ivan was nowhere to be found or reached. He was not answering his cell phone, which was probably wise for him, because I was so pissed at him. Ivan had been at lunch yesterday, and rather than cut my wife off, he'd allowed her to keep drinking.

Not only was Ivan gone, but it would seem he'd taken The Beast and The Butcher with him. None of them were answering my calls.

I glanced over at Niamh as we stood in Steve's tattoo parlor. He was a good guy. Solid. It was why I kept coming back to him. He didn't get involved in the Bratva shit, but then Ivan had a guy who put his brand on people. The only ink on my body not done by Steve was the Volkov Bratva mark.

Niamh was nervous. I could tell with the tension in her body as she looked over every design. There were a couple she had loved—a dolphin, a flower, a rose, and even a scary-looking tree. I was impressed. I didn't know why she was doing this, and I didn't comment.

With no answer from Ivan and his little team, I moved close to Niamh and subtly breathed in the scent of her hair. Today, she'd gone for vanilla. Niamh had two different kinds of shampoo—one vanilla, the other lemon, and both made her hair smell so good.

I wasn't going to even think about why I was standing at the tattoo artist's counter, sniffing her hair, or the fact I put my hand on her waist and drew her closer to me. None of this mattered. I was her husband, and that gave me permission to touch her when I wanted, to take care of her, and to just be with her.

"I like this one." She pointed to a dying rose.

"Are you sure?" I asked.

"Yeah, I like it, but I also like the dying tree, but you see, it's not dying, because there are little buds of hope." She looked up toward Steve. "Is it possible to have multiple buds that look like new growth?"

"Yeah, I can do that for you."

"Give us a minute, Steve," I said.

Steve looked at me and then toward Niamh. I wasn't going to offer an explanation.

With Steve gone, I turned toward Niamh. "Why are you doing this?"

"Because this is what I want," she said, pointing to the tree.

"You want a dead tree … where?"

"On the inside of my thigh."

Steve was going to have to touch my wife's thigh, and now I was having a hard time grasping just what that would mean. I wasn't happy about it.

"Why?"

"Because, I have a scar on my thigh, and I've had it since I was twelve, and it's a reminder of the fact my father can come and do whatever the hell he likes."

I knew the scar she was talking about. It was a large red line that hadn't faded in all that time. It looked like a botched stitching job, and I had a feeling her father probably paid a two-bit doctor to fix her. The wound hadn't been cleaned properly, and the skin hadn't knitted together smoothly.

"You've gotten tattoos to cover your scars, I just want one on my thigh, to make … I don't know. I just … it's what I would like. The tree is not dying and with the buds, it's like the tree is finally waking up, coming to life."

And I had a feeling that was how she felt.

I couldn't stop her from getting a tattoo.

"You're sure this is what you want?" I asked.

"Yes, it's what I want."

I wasn't going to stand in her way, but there was no way I was going to let her have this ink without myself present. So, I called Steve out and allowed him to come and get my wife prepared. He did look like he expected me to just do his magical work, but that wasn't happening. Even though I wanted to plunge my knife into his guts, I couldn't bring myself to do it, so I stayed by her side with my hands clenched into fists, and just accepted another man touching my wife. To help me get through, I imagined killing him in many different ways, over and over again.

****

*Niamh*

Steve had advised the necessary cleaning instructions and aftercare. My heart had raced after I got the tattoo, but as it began to scab over within the last couple of days, I wasn't so happy. There was itching and some slight discomfort, but I loved the image, and even through the scab, I could see it.

I'd done it. I had finally gotten some ink over that scar I felt gave my father power. Every time I saw it, it was a reminder of what he'd done. Of how he'd left me after hurting me with his belt. It was only when my mother called him to complain that I'd gotten sick, and I was shivering and not able to do my chores, did he come and have a look. That was when he saw the wound had gotten infected. And then, a doctor had come, stitched it up, and even now, I remembered the scent of alcohol on his breath.

It had now been a few days since I had gotten the tattoo and I was once again in the penthouse suite, nursing my leg. I had ointment to help with the scab cracking, which it did because it was on my thigh. I hadn't thought this one ahead.

Three of my guards were standing a few feet away, and as the penthouse apartment door was opened, they tensed up, only to lower their weapons when they saw Ivan coming through the door. He looked … chipper. I'd not seen him since the lunch and drunken episode.

"You can go," Ivan said, dismissing them, which I knew pissed off Peter. He put them on my protection detail. I always felt guilty, though, because I didn't do a lot that needed protection.

Ivan came toward me, and I'd lifted my dress, still keeping my privacy, and rubbed the ointment into my skin.

"Nice, I take it Steve did this handiwork?" he asked.

"You know Steve."

"Yeah, sure do. I've got my own guy, but Steve's pretty good." He took a seat on the coffee table. "Are you drunk?"

I groaned. "Have you come to gloat?"

"Nope, I've come to make sure you're okay," Ivan said.

"As you can see, I'm fine."

"You've got ink. When I left you, you didn't have ink."

"The day after, I was inspired. I had a scar, and I didn't want to have to look at the stupid thing anymore."

"Taking the power away from your father. I like it."

"I think of it more like keeping the power for myself," I said.

Ivan winked.

"If you're looking for Peter, he's at work." And I didn't quite know where work was for Peter. He hadn't taken me to work, and it wasn't something we discussed. I figured with him being Volkov, the less I knew the better.

"No, I came to see how you were," he said.

"You did?"

He nodded. "I shouldn't have allowed you to drink as much as you did."

I shook my head. "It's not your fault."

"But it is, I wanted you to loosen up."

"Why?"

"Because, you're going to have to make a decision soon regarding your future, and when you do, I want you to make it clearly."

"How is getting me drunk going to help with that?"

"Do you remember everything?" he asked.

"Yes, but I don't see why that is so important."

"Simple, I take it you were blunt with Peter, and he hasn't backed down, has he? He hasn't tried to create any distance between you."

I frowned and stared at Ivan. Normally, I can handle cryptic; it was kind of fun to work it out. With my leg and my embarrassment of drinking too much alcohol, I wasn't exactly in the right frame of mind to be handling cryptic.

"Why don't you just come out and say what you're trying to say, rather than being so cryptic?" I asked. "I get that you're trying to manipulate your own way, and that is fine. I get it. I can imagine you've spent a whole lot of time having to do it this way, but cut out the bullshit with me, please." That could be the irritation or the ink, or the pain. I wasn't exactly sure which it was, but I didn't offend Ivan. He held a big smile, which was a little daunting.

Ivan smiling meant trouble. At least, that was what I thought. I was kind of worried.

"Peter believes he cannot do love. That he cannot feel love, and yet I saw him that day when you were taken by your father."

I didn't want to think of that day. I'd seen him as well, how he ran after the car. He had no care for his own safety, or the danger. If one of the guys had pointed his gun and killed him, I'd never have been able to forgive myself.

Peter had been trying to protect me that day. I know that. It was why I had so many questions as to why he was holding a gun. Didn't expect the answer to be because he was a member of the Volkov Bratva, and not just any member, but a Brigadier.

"I know Peter doesn't like the choice I've given you," Ivan said.

"What are you doing?" I asked.

"I'm helping Peter fill in the blanks. He had one of the worst starts in life. All he has ever had to do was survive, to fight. It's all he knows. He doesn't know what love is like, what it means to have a real family. I mean, fuck me, he doesn't even celebrate his birthday."

At the mention of his birthday, this drew my attention. "His birthday?"

"Yes, he doesn't celebrate it, because he doesn't know how."

This made me frown. "When is it?"

"It wasn't something his father ever celebrated."

"Tell me," I said.

Ivan raised a brow.

I rolled my eyes. "I know what you're trying to do, and yes, it is working, and I am also reading what you're not saying as well."

Ivan smiled. "What am I not saying?"

"That Peter doesn't know what love is, but if I'm able to show him, then maybe there's a chance he might love me back." It was a long shot, and it was crazy.

Ivan chuckled. "I always knew you were pretty special."

I looked at Ivan. "I met you five years ago."

"Your point?"

"Why did you wait so long?" I asked.

He didn't speak and in fact, he looked past my shoulder. "I'm in this for the long game," Ivan said.

"A game?"

"It's what life is, Niamh. It's a game, and also, when you make a certain play, you've got to make sure all your players are lined up and ready. I had to get everything into play, and even you had to be ready for Peter."

I looked at Ivan and frowned. "You weren't ready," I said.

He didn't say a word.

"You were hurting and in pain, and all you wanted to do was end your life," I said.

"Don't think you know me, Niamh. A lot has happened in five years, trust me, I came for you when it was your time."

And with that, he got to his feet, and then gave me a date that was in three weeks' time. "That's Peter's birthday, and he has never gotten a single gift, or card, or cake."

Ivan left, and as he did, my three guards came back through the door.

I didn't get the whole truth from Ivan, but I did

know one thing. His wife may be gone, but the memory of her still lived in him, and that pain was driving him to do what he was doing.

\*\*\*\*

*The Butcher*

"Have you finished playing matchmaker?" I asked as Ivan stepped out into the underground parking lot of Peter's building.

"Not quite."

I stared at Ivan, who had asked me to drop him off. For the past couple of days, he, The Beast, and I had been on a hunt. He'd done the final push on removing the men that surrounded Finn Byrne, and now it was about crumbling the protection detail that had been keeping him safe, and also well-kept. It would seem a lot of people owned Finn a great deal, including a shit ton of money as well.

Had he told Niamh her mother was dead? She'd been one of the first women I'd killed after we'd gotten Niamh to safety. I had expected her to ask me about it, to ask about her mother. Nothing.

I got the sense that mother and daughter were not exactly close. The more I learned about Niamh's life and her family, the more I realized I had a much better upbringing than she had, and I'd been raised around death. Although, I had been trained to be the woman I was today, and I knew that was quite terrifying to most, certainly to some men.

When it came to my job, I was a fucking expert, but then I also wasn't afraid to get dirty. Blood didn't bother me. Pain was a comfort to me. My uncle had trained me well. I was the best at my job, and it also helped that I was able to blend in wherever I needed to go.

Ivan was playing a long game. I'd heard many rumors about him. Some a little more far-fetched than others, but what I had come to realize is there was no one box to tick when it came to Ivan Volkov. He was a crazy, calculating, manipulative, patient monster. He was a full package of trouble. I couldn't help but admire him.

Whatever Finn Byrne had done to this man, Karma was being a right bitch to him. Ivan had his sights set on him, and he wasn't going to let it go. He wouldn't give up. Finn was all but a dead man, and yet Ivan was taunting him.

After I killed Niamh's mother, Ivan had me send the body to Finn, which had been a bit of a problem, but I had done it.

From what I knew, that body had been dumped in a lake. Next, Ivan had given me the order to work on the oldest kids, so I did. One by one, I took them out, and it was quite easy to do, seeing as most of them were fucking bastards. The boys were a law unto themselves. Evil to the core, as were the girls.

Like I said, whatever Finn Byrne had done, he'd royally fucked up in targeting Ivan. It was only a matter of time before Ivan ended this for him once and for all.

## Chapter Twenty-Three

*Niamh*

I didn't need Ivan to tell me how to be nice. Even though I'd not experienced a lot of "nice" growing up, I hadn't lost the ability to be nice myself. Rather than allow Peter and I to drift apart, I decided to do something different. I decided to become his wife.

It sounded strange, but it wasn't. What this entailed was simple. First, I made sure I was awake before him, and I set the coffeepot on, cooked breakfast, and also prepared his lunch. I took care of his laundry, cleaned the penthouse, and did some shopping with my guards. With his birthday three weeks away, I wanted to start preparations now.

I didn't have a clue what to get him as a birthday present, so I'd decided to buy him a wedding ring. Yes, I knew it was corny, but that's what I decided. A wedding ring, because he didn't have one, whereas I did.

In a weird way, I was hoping he would get the message—that I was here to stay. I was not going to step away from our marriage. If Peter didn't want to be set free, then I wasn't going to allow him to be. In my head, it sounded romantic, but on paper, it kind of made me feel like a bitch.

I did love Peter. I wanted to spend the rest of my life with him.

After Ivan had left, I couldn't help but think back to that moment when he chased after the car to protect me, to save me. I didn't know if he acted like that because he was doing his job, or if it was because he did in fact have feelings for me. I wasn't sure, but I wasn't going to dwell on it either. I'd made my decision and this time, I was sticking to it.

My leg had also started to heal, and it had been a few weeks since my tattoo. The scab was almost gone. The right treatment had meant for an easier healing process, at least that's what I liked to tell myself.

So, one evening I'd made seared steaks and potatoes, and I met him at the door. My guards, like always, left, and I helped take Peter's jacket.

Each night, he'd grab me around the waist, pull me in close, and kiss me. We hadn't had sex since the last time, and not with the ink on my leg, that was proving to be a bit of a pain. Now that it was all healed, the last few weeks had been a lot of fun. I'd played the role of wife, but it didn't feel like I was playing. It felt right.

He wrapped those large arms around me, pulled me close, and took possession of my lips. That butterfly flutter in my stomach came back to life, and I closed my eyes, loving the feeling and not wanting it to go away. I loved him and I was done fighting it. I wasn't going to leave him. That was my choice.

Ivan and the Volkov could have everything that was Byrne. I'd never been a Byrne, it was just my last name because my father had insisted on it. All his kids had to have his last name. I guess it was the only decent thing my father had done.

Peter pulled away from me and I couldn't help but lick my lips. "I, uh, I made dinner for you."

I took his hand and led him away, going toward the dining room, where I had already set the table.

"If you'd like to sit and pour yourself something, I'll be back with the food." I turned to leave.

"Do you want me to pour you a glass?" he asked.

"No, I learned my lesson. Me and alcohol are

done." I had promised myself I was never going to end up like my mom and I was sticking to that promise.

I went back to the kitchen, grabbed the oven mitts, took out the two prepared plates, and then I carried them to the table. I placed one in front of Peter, and then I put mine down in my place. I rushed back to the kitchen, took off my mitts, turned off the oven, and returned to the dining room.

Peter had poured me a glass of water, and I picked it up, offering him a smile as I took a large sip. He'd poured himself a glass of whiskey, and trust me, I wasn't even tempted.

I didn't get to lose myself in drink. No, what I got was to be embarrassed and the memory of having no control. I had no idea what to say to Peter. I waited as he picked up his knife and fork, cut through the steak, and took a bite.

He closed his eyes, and when he opened them, he offered me a smile. "Delicious."

"Good. How was your day?" Now I could eat. If he'd not been happy with the food, I wouldn't have minded going and doing something extra. That was what a wife did, right?

"Eventful. Slavik and the others have returned to their territory."

"Yes, their wives did call me, and they left numbers for me to contact them. How does that work?" I asked.

"Simple, you want to talk to someone, you call them. They're your friends now."

"But I barely know them."

"I guess that's what talking is all about."

"Are you and Ivan friends?" I asked.

"Yes."

There was a slight hesitation.

"How do you and Ivan know each other?" Peter asked.

I knew I shouldn't ask questions. I was not going to divulge Ivan's secret. It was not mine to tell. This was not me being more loyal to Ivan than my husband. This was me being a friend. Ivan was my friend. I frowned and sat back.

"What?" Peter asked.

"Do you ever have those moments of revelation when you suddenly realize something?"

"Yes."

"Well, I had one."

"Care to share?"

"Ivan's my friend," I said.

Peter looked at me.

"I know, it's crazy. I, uh, I helped him years ago. I was a stranger to him, and I just wanted to make him feel better, I guess." I shrugged. I did so without knowing who he was, and yet Ivan had never forgotten about me. I'd not forgotten about him, and I'd hoped he found peace, love, and happiness. I now knew he didn't have any of those things, but he had gotten a family.

"Ivan's a hard man to be friends with."

"I understand that, but … he is my friend. I want to look out for him. Help him. He helped me, and so did you," I said.

"I was just doing my job."

"Were you?" I asked. "Would it hurt if I were to let you go?"

This was not what I wanted to talk about. This wasn't supposed to be about the future. I'd made the choice to stay. I loved Peter enough for both of us.

Peter put down his knife and fork, and he pushed out his chair. I felt my heart breaking just a little, but then he stopped and cupped my cheek. He tilted my head back and stared into my eyes.

"You're not leaving," he said.

It didn't quite answer my question and I was about to tell him that, when his lips crashed against mine and silenced all manner of protest.

He felt so good, and this was what I loved. His kisses, his touches, his attention. I felt greedy because I wanted it all, without compromise. Did that make me selfish? Probably.

I didn't know how we managed it, but we left the table and kissed our way into the bedroom. He reached down, grabbed my knee, and lifted it over his hip. Peter broke the kiss, and he pushed the dress I was wearing up toward my hips.

"Tell me, does this still hurt?" He pointed toward my ink and I shook my head.

"No."

"Good." He slid his hand up and then grabbed my ass. "Fuck, I have missed this." He broke the kiss and began to nuzzle my neck, sucking at the pulse. His tongue danced across the column of my neck, and I closed my eyes.

His hands felt everywhere, but in a good way. I didn't want him to stop. He felt so good.

Peter removed the dress from my body, and then tore at my panties and bra. Before too long, I was naked, and he was still fully dressed. I couldn't stop him, though, as he pushed me to the bed, and within seconds his mouth was between my thighs. His tongue stroked my clit, and then sunk down, pushed inside me, and made me ache for him.

He drew back and flicked my clit, gliding back and forth, before sucking my nub between his teeth.

It had been too long since I had last felt him, and I couldn't hold back. I screamed his name as he teased my clit, back and forth, around in a circle. Each stroke designed to send me higher and higher, until he pushed me right across the peak, hurtling me toward that very edge.

I came hard, screaming his name, not wanting it to end.

****

*Peter*

I loved the taste of Niamh's cunt. So ripe and juicy, and I also loved the fact that she belonged to me. She was all mine.

No other man had touched her. I was the only one she had desired.

I didn't want her to fucking leave. I couldn't stand the thought of it. She belonged to me.

Fucking Ivan and his meddling ways. In that moment, I hated him, but I pushed all those thoughts to the side because those thoughts didn't have a place when I was making love and fucking my wife. Niamh was mine. All mine. I wasn't going to let her go easily.

She would not be able to leave if she was carrying my child.

I'd already removed my shirt, and my pants were easy, as well as the boxer briefs I wore. All of them were gone from my body within a matter of seconds, and on the floor. I wanted to lick her cunt and hear my name spill from those precious lips, but I didn't have the patience to wait. I needed to be inside her, and the sooner the better. She was driving me crazy with need, and I just couldn't stop it. I had to have her.

Moving her up the bed, I marveled at her full, ripe tits. In the past few weeks, she'd gained back some of the weight she had lost, and she looked amazing. I didn't want her starving herself.

I settled between her spread thighs, gripped my cock, and ran the tip through her wet slit. She cried out as I nudged her sensitive clit. I stroked over it a few times, and then dipped down, seeking out her entrance and finding her so wet, she turned me on even more.

Slowly, inch by inch, I began to sink inside her, and as I did, I took my sweet time. I wanted this moment to last, but I also loved the feel of her cunt as it swallowed my cock. Sucking me inside her as if she couldn't help but feed on me. When she'd taken all but a few inches, I let go of my dick, took hold of her hands, and pressed them either side of her head, keeping them locked into place.

On that last inch, I slammed balls-deep inside her, loving the sound of her subtle moan. Drawing all the way out of her, I thrust back inside, not allowing her to become accustomed to the feel of my dick, but making her take it all.

My name was like a mantra on her lips. She couldn't seem to help herself.

Niamh thrust up to meet me, and I stared into her eyes as I slowed down, making love to her. It was then I realized there was no other place I wanted to be. Yes, this had started as a job. I followed Ivan's orders because I was loyal to him. He'd saved me, and I knew he'd also saved Niamh. I had a feeling all the men that were loyal to him had been saved by him, or by his actions.

Despite all of that, I wasn't doing this because of Ivan's orders. I was here because I wanted to be here. I was balls-deep inside my wife because I wanted to be. This was not a duty, it was not a loyalty, this was me.

Driving inside her, I felt the first stirrings of my orgasm, and I tried to control myself, but Niamh's pussy was just too good, and I came, spilling my cum deep inside her womb. Even after my orgasm subsided, I didn't pull away. The temptation to hold her and give her all my body weight was strong, but I held back and just looked down at her.

She had this soft smile on her face. "I was hoping this is what dinner would lead to."

"Your leg is all but healed, I don't see a reason to hold back." I dropped a kiss on her nose and then took possession of her lips. I kissed her hard, and heard her soft intake of breath.

"We didn't finish dinner."

"I can eat dinner cold," I said.

She giggled.

I knew she and Ivan had their secret. There was more about their first meeting than she let on, but I also had a feeling this was Ivan's secret, not my wife's. I wasn't angry with her that she didn't share it with me. In fact, I was glad she didn't.

After all she had been through, Niamh was strong. She refused to give away Ivan's secrets, and that meant she held a loyalty within her, one that Ivan could respect. All the men and women of the Volkov Bratva had to be loyal. Ivan was king. And to me, Niamh had proven herself.

Kissing her again, I felt my cock start to fill as arousal took over. I heard her moan and felt the answering pulse of her cunt as she tightened around my cock.

I wanted to get her pregnant.

Pulling out of her, I moved her to her knees, getting her into position, and then I drove deep inside her. From this angle, I knew I was going to get as deep as possible, and I wanted to drive her crazy. Reaching between her thighs, I began to stroke her clit, feeling her cunt tighten around me. She was so sensitive that every little touch set her aflame, which was exactly what I wanted.

"Are you close?" I asked.

"I don't think I can come…" She didn't finish, because I changed the angle but didn't stop touching her clit, and where she didn't think she could finish, I showed her she very much could.

I loved the sounds she made and this time, I drew every bit of pleasure from her, hearing my name fall from her lips.

When she couldn't take any more of my teasing, I stopped, grabbed her hips, and then pounded inside her pussy, driving my cock in harder and deeper, and this time, as I came, I pushed every inch of my cock inside her, and spilled wave upon wave of my cum into her cunt.

I wanted her pregnant.

I wanted to fill her up.

I wanted her to belong to me completely.

## Chapter Twenty-Four

*Niamh*

"So, how did you and Ivan meet?" I asked.

This was kind of a dangerous question, because I was worried he'd start to ask me more questions. I'd been honest with how we'd met. I just hadn't filled in all the blanks of our story.

I was curious about Peter.

"My father was part of the Bratva before Ivan turned up. Before Ivan, the Bratva wasn't exactly thriving. They followed their rules and kept old traditions alive. When it came to my father, though, he had his own set of rules to live by. Ivan found me when I was young. He hadn't even begun to take over the Bratva at this time. He snuck onto my father's land, told me what was happening. Told me the truth of my brothers and sisters, who they were, and where they were coming from."

Peter stopped and reached into the water to take hold of my hands. We'd been lying in the hot water for a short time, and I rested against Peter. His legs were on either side of me, and I had been resting my hands on his thighs.

"So Ivan didn't miraculously take over the Bratva from his father?"

"No, we had to take our time. Little by little, he took land and then pushed out the competition. He built a name for himself, made everyone afraid of him, and when the time came, he told me that to swear my loyalty to him, I had to kill my father and everyone associated with the games he played."

I tilted my head to look back to him. "Was that

hard to do? Kill your father?"

He shook his head. "No, it was one of the easiest kills I ever made. Taking him out, along with the men and women who'd earned money from watching us all suffer. That had been easy."

I settled back into the water, imagining all kinds of horrendous things. It was difficult to even think about. Men and women taking joy in kids being terrified, doing whatever they could to survive. "I couldn't imagine going through that."

"I know. Some of the kids, when they arrived, looked like they had been saved, but me and the others knew the truth, and the nightmare had only just begun."

"How can someone do that?"

"Because there are a lot of sick fucks in this world, babe."

I stopped and smiled. "Babe?" He'd never called me that, and I wasn't going to lie, I did kind of like it.

He cupped my cheek and tilted my head toward him. "You're my babe."

His thumb danced across my bottom lip and I felt that spiraling need for him again. I'd given up on hating this man. From what he'd told me, he had already experienced a lot of hate in his life, and I wasn't going to add to it. Reaching up, I pulled him down, and then his lips were on mine, and everything felt all right in the world, it felt safe.

Slowly, I turned around and then moved to straddle his lap. His cock was already rock-hard, and I sunk my fingers into his hair, as I deepened the kiss. This time, I slid my tongue into his mouth and met mine with his, and he tasted like coffee and whiskey.

He gripped the back of my neck, which I loved, but then he slowly began to slide down. The tips of his fingers created a dance of sensation down the length of my back, until he got to my ass, which he gripped hard.

My mouth opened and I tilted my head back, unable to think of anything, but to feel the pleasure of what he was doing to me. It felt so good and I didn't want him to stop.

I needed him inside me, so I reached down, wrapped my fingers around his long length, and then settled between his thighs. I whimpered as I put the tip of his cock at my core, and I was the one that guided him inside my body, taking him hard and deep.

Peter broke the kiss first, and growled, "Fuck!"

I didn't have the words to join him, but he pulsed inside me. The pleasure already heightened and now even more so. Returning my grip to his shoulders, I opened my eyes and stared into his sharp blue ones. These were the eyes of the man I loved. There was no one else I wanted in the world.

He stopped gripping my ass, and instead returned to my hips. He helped me set up a pace, and I rode his long, thick, hard cock, feeling him thicken and grow with every passing second. I didn't want to stop fucking him.

But all too soon, Peter stopped and held me in place. "I want you to come all over my cock. Touch yourself, Niamh."

He'd asked me to do this before, and as I kept looking into his eyes, I reached between us. When he first asked me to do this, back in Pickle Quest, I'd been so embarrassed to touch myself, but he'd helped me break down so many walls that now I didn't mind. In fact, I stroked my clit and watched him as I did so.

With him inside me, I felt almost too full. I loved it when he did this.

"That's it, baby, touch that sweet clit, make yourself come all over my cock. I want to feel it."

Sinking my teeth into my bottom lip, I tried to

contain my screams.

He let me go long enough to cup my cheek, and for his thumb to pull my lip out from between my teeth.

"You make those sounds, I want to hear them. Now, let me hear them."

I cried out, his name spilling from my lips less than a second later.

He took possession of my mouth, and then his hands were on my hips as my orgasm rushed through me, and he began to fuck me, using me for his own pleasure, and I loved it. I didn't want it to stop.

In that moment, I knew we weren't using protection, and I hoped he got me pregnant.

\*\*\*\*

*Peter*

Today was my birthday, and the day had started out as any other day. Waking up, making love to my wife, which wasn't like any other birthday. This was the first birthday I'd gotten that privilege to do so. Then, it had been a shower, again, one taken with Niamh, which had felt like a birthday gift. After that, coffee, breakfast, and out for the day, where I had to take care of a meddling cop, deal with a few payment inconsistencies, do some actual work of checking over the books. All the while aware of Ivan, The Butcher, and The Beast in my territory with Finn Jr., because they still hadn't handled him.

All I'd wanted was to come home. Niamh had texted me, asking me how long I was going to be. I loved her impatience, and as I arrived at my building, my patience was tested at a whole new level as I saw her guards waiting outside the penthouse. This pissed me off.

I felt my hand twitch for my gun.

As I stepped up to the first man, about to wipe that fucking smile off his face, the door to the penthouse opened and Niamh stuck her head out.

"You're home, that's great. Please don't be upset with any of them, I was the one who told them to wait outside until you arrived home."

Now, I was frowning. I wasn't used to this conspiring, not unless someone was about to kill me.

She held the door open a little wider for me to step through. I was still pissed that the guards had left her alone. While Ivan was playing his little games with Finn Byrne, I wanted her always protected. He'd already taken her from me, and I wasn't going to allow that to happen again.

Stepping through the door, I heard soft music playing. Niamh took my jacket, and then grabbed my hands.

"Now, don't be afraid, okay?" Niamh said.

I didn't fight her as she all but dragged me toward the sitting room, and that was when I was shocked. Across the full-screen television read a banner that said, HAPPY BIRTHDAY, PETER.

On the coffee table was a load of party snacks, and Niamh let me go long enough to put a hat on her head and blow on one of those toys that opened up, making a noise.

"Happy Birthday," she said, throwing her hands in the air.

"You did me a birthday party."

"Yes, and I didn't invite anyone, not because I didn't want to, but you don't strike me as someone who is happy to have a lot of people around you for yourself."

I reached for her, pulling her in close. "This is perfect," I said. I'd never celebrated my birthday.

Until Ivan entered my world, I didn't even know what my birthday was, or when it was. We found all the details on my birth certificate.

After discovering what my father did, how he took unwanted kids to exploit them, I had thought I might be like any other orphaned kid, but the only difference for me was I was good at surviving, which was why he declared me his son.

No, I was Orlov's son. It's why I kept his name. This was my reminder of who he was, and not to be that way.

Niamh smiled. "Well, Bill, Ryan, and Smith, it was their turn to guard me, so I got them to help with the streamers and balloons. I was tempted to go with helium balloons, but they were all out of them, so I bought a packet and we blew them up all afternoon."

"You'd been planning this?"

"Ever since I found out when your birthday was. I know it's not a lot, and I know you could get some party organizer to do something on a bigger scale, but this is what I could do."

I cupped her cheeks and stared into her brown eyes. "This is amazing."

She smiled and it lit up her whole face, and I knew in that moment I couldn't let her go. I was just about to tell her I loved her when suddenly my cell phone began to buzz.

I gritted my teeth. Any other call I'd have ignored, but this was Ivan, and I couldn't. He was in my territory, and I couldn't allow anything to happen to him, because if I did, the other Brigadiers would kill me.

"I've got to take this."

"Don't worry, I'll be waiting," Niamh said.

I didn't want her to be waiting.

"What's up?" I asked.

"Happy Birthday to you too. It's done."

"What's done?" I asked.

"What I needed from Finn Byrne, and now you have less than an hour to come and take care of the problem."

I looked at Niamh. I wanted to be the one to kill Finn Byrne with my own two hands, to also make sure the deed was done. But this was my birthday, Niamh had made me a party.

"Where?"

Ivan gave me the location and I told him I'd be there in twenty minutes. I ended the call and looked toward Niamh.

"It's okay, you'll be back as soon as you can?" she asked.

"Yes."

Niamh walked toward me, ran her hands up my chest, and stepped in close. "Then go."

I didn't want to go, but I vowed when I was given the chance, I was going to take care of Finn Byrne. I banded an arm around her waist, pulled her in close, and slammed my lips down on hers. I was coming back to her.

Leaving our penthouse suite, I made my way downstairs to the underground parking lot, and in that moment, I suddenly realized the moment I killed Finn Byrne, Niamh got to make a choice—one that meant she stayed with me, or the other choice, where she left me and got her freedom.

****

*Ivan*

Everything had fallen into place, just as I knew it

would. Ending the call, I turned toward Finn Byrne who was tied to a chair. He'd attempted to run. He tried to get hold of his last contact, only to have the man screaming and begging for mercy. This was courtesy of The Beast. I'd gotten him to do that final kill.

It had all been leading up to this very moment with Peter's birthday. This was my gift to him.

"What the fuck do you want with me?" Finn asked. "I've done nothing to you."

"That's not entirely accurate. Butcher, are you ready?"

I had set up this warehouse to have the maximum effect and as the light came on, he would see Finn Jr. Every now and then, The Butcher had been paying Finn Jr., a visit, finding out all the things that little prick had been up to. It would seem Finn Jr., was just like his dad, only worse. Where Finn Byrne manipulated, lied, cheated, and stole, Junior simply took and took and took. He'd left a trail of broken men and women. Junior didn't mind raping both men and women. In fact, he got a kick out of the men being held down while he overpowered them. Same with the women, and then he'd taunt them. The cops wouldn't arrest him because of who Daddy Dearest was.

I'd taken care of that as well.

There were quite a few of Junior's victims that hadn't been able to handle what was happening. They had taken their own lives. The remaining ones, well, they had left, running, hiding, doing whatever they could not to be seen.

Then, of course, there were the ones that tried to fight, and those had ended up dead.

The Butcher didn't particularly like Junior. She'd been wanting to kill him for quite some time, and when I told her my plan, she was all for it.

Junior had been stripped down, and was now completely naked. It looked like he'd already pissed and shit himself.

"What the fuck are you doing?" Finn asked. "You leave my son alone."

"Wish I could, but you see, he hunted in my territory, and there must be a price for that. Also, he has to die today," I said.

"Leave him alone. Let him go. He's just a young kid, and he made mistakes."

The Butcher held out her knife, and I just knew what she was going for first, and yes, we didn't hear the sounds. I'd gotten the room soundproofed so all Finn could do was see his son struggling. He tried to fight the binds that held him to the chair, but nothing was going to let him go.

For effect, The Butcher pried open Junior's mouth and shoved his cock inside it. She really did love her work.

Now, I turned toward Finn Byrne. I'd been waiting for this moment for a long time. He shook in his chair, and I looked at the man who had taken everything from me, and the bastard didn't even know what it was.

"You know, I lied to your daughter," I said.

This caught Finn's attention. I waited, allowing his gaze to drift to the torture of his son.

"I told her my wife had died of cancer." This caught Finn's attention. No one knew Ivan Volkov was a married man. I had been happily married as well. Even now, Finn thought he was going to be able to escape, but that wasn't going to happen. None of them were. "But that is not entirely true. You see, my wife was diagnosed with cancer, but we had caught it early, and she was on the way back from the hospital. She'd already called me with the news that the doctor had confirmed she was cancer-free. She'd have to go through all the unnecessary checks."

"What the fuck does this have to do with me? I didn't cause fucking cancer."

"You're right. You didn't, but what you did have control of was a bullet." I pulled out my cell phone, and I had kept the information all these years, and I played the tape. My wife, Kaitlyn, had stopped at a gas station. She had a craving for chocolate candy, and as she'd gotten out of her car, Finn Byrne and Junior drove up, and they opened fire.

It turned out they had an issue with a rising crime lord in the local area that went by O'Neil. Finn wasn't happy with a takeover bid, and the fact O'Neil had some kind of shipment of girls. That day, they had killed O'Neil, and in doing so, they had hit the gas station where my wife had been innocently getting a candy bar.

"You see that woman right there, she's my wife. When Niamh's mother was at the hospital getting her stomach pumped, I was there losing mine, who had just beat fucking cancer." I reached out and grabbed the man's throat. I tightened my grip, watching him choke, struggling to breathe, and he couldn't fight it. All he could do was take what I was forcing him to take.

He was close to passing out, and I let him go. Getting to my feet, I pocketed my cell phone, and then I moved toward The Butcher's tools that she had left for me to play with.

"Now, I am a man of my word, and I promised Peter he could end you, and seeing as I've been playing with you for the past few months, it is only fair, but I've got to make sure you can't talk." I held up a pair of what looked like medieval pliers. "Perfect."

"You're just like your father," Finn said.

I looked at him. "Do you really think I give a

fuck about being compared to him? I know I'm not like him, because I have all of this, and he had nothing. I should warn you that he also took from me, hurt me, and I made sure I made him pay for it. I'm good like that." I didn't have to get my revenge right away. I had learned that plotting, planning, and being prepared was all I needed to get what I wanted.

Finn fought me, but after landing a blow to his head with my fist, it weakened him enough for me to get his tongue in the pliers, and I pulled it out of his mouth, and with a simple swipe of the blade, I removed his tongue. I dropped the tongue onto the floor, and then I moved behind him and watched. The Butcher had been working on Finn Jr.

After what happened to Kaitlyn, and when Cara taunted me with her, I had no choice but to kill my best friend. I didn't know how Cara had learned of Kaitlyn. I'd kept her identity a secret. Not even Slavik knew of her. No one had. Only Niamh, me, and now Finn Byrne, but he wasn't going to survive the night.

The Butcher dealt the killing blow just as Peter Orlov walked through the door.

I always kept my promises, and that day in the hospital, I'd known who Finn Byrne was.

"And your empire," I said, whispering in Finn Byrne's ear. "Will be sold up, given away to good causes." I knew what Niamh would do, of that I had no doubt. She was a rare gem, and those I kept safe, because I had failed my own rare gem.

## Chapter Twenty-Five

*Niamh*

It was getting late and I was getting tired. No, I was exhausted. I should have known Ivan would have something a lot more ... alluring for my husband.

I glanced around the room. My guards had already eaten some of the food. They refused to dance or have a drink. They were all still on duty, and I curled up on the sofa, pulling on a little blanket to help warm me up.

Maybe this had been childish of me, and I'd made a big mistake in trying to make this day special for him. I didn't know.

I rubbed at my temple. What did you get a guy who had everything for his birthday?

At the sound of the door opening, I tensed up and glanced over the back of the sofa, watching as Peter stepped into the main penthouse. He'd changed clothes, and he ordered the guards out. He ran a hand across his face, and then turned toward me.

"You changed?" I asked.

Did this mean he was with a woman? Peter glanced down at this clothes, and then ran fingers through his hair before coming toward me. I was tense. What if he was with another woman? I didn't like it and was angry.

He sat down in front of me, and I waited for him to tell me the truth. "Ivan called me tonight because he needed me to take care of business."

"Okay," I said.

"Niamh, your father is dead," Peter said. "And

your mother died a few months ago."

"What?" I must be the world's worst daughter because I suddenly felt free. "They're gone?"

"Yes."

I hadn't even realized how trapped I'd felt. That feeling was gone. My father was dead and so was my mother. It meant I didn't have to run anymore. I no longer had to be afraid to live, to be myself. I was so happy.

"I'm a terrible person," I said, covering my mouth, because I simply couldn't contain my laughter.

"You're not a terrible person," Peter said.

"Who is happy about their parents being dead?"

"I was."

"I can understand why you were."

"The same as you," Peter said.

I licked my lips because the truth was, it wasn't the same. It wasn't nearly the same. Peter's life had been worse than mine. His father had been a monster. He had to fight to survive to prove he wasn't weak. I took beatings and verbal abuse, and yes, I was afraid to sleep at night because when my father was around, he'd wake me up to take out his anger on me. Mine wasn't the same as Peter's.

"This means you're free to make your own choice, Niamh," Peter said.

"Oh."

"I want you to hear me out first. I don't want you to make any rash decision. I don't want you to … leave. I don't want you to make the choice of freedom. You can, by all means, do that, but I don't want you to leave. I don't want you to disappear or to go. I'm … I know I'm not the ideal kind of guy. I'm not sure what love is. I've never felt it before, but what I do know is that I love waking up next to you in the morning. I love hearing you talk and listening to you sing, even though you're also not very good at singing."

This made me laugh. And I felt tears sting my eyes.

"I … I wanted our baby," Peter said. "I wanted it so much, he or she, I didn't care, and I want babies with you. I want to grow old with you." He glanced behind me. "I want to come home on my birthdays to surprise parties. I don't have the first clue about being a dad, but I know I want my kids to look forward to me coming home. Maybe I'll teach them how to survive, but I'll do it our way."

I loved how he said "our way."

"I'm asking you, Niamh, no, I am *begging* you, to choose me, because I do honestly believe if I know what love is, then I know I love you."

The tears that had been glistening in my eyes started to fall down my cheeks.

"Fuck, I didn't want you to be sad," he said. He reached out and wiped away my tears. "I'm sorry. I'm not good at this."

I pulled the velvet box out from beneath the blanket. "I was going to give you this tonight. It's for your birthday."

He looked at the box.

"Don't worry, it's not a bomb or poison, but look at it."

He took the box from me and opened it up.

"I didn't know what to get a man who had everything, but then I realized you didn't have everything, but you could. You didn't have a woman who loved you, but I do. I don't know love, Peter, but I know how I feel, and I love you. I love you with all my heart, and I want to be your wife. I want to have children with you, I want to grow old with you. I want it all with you. Does that make me greedy?"

"No, it doesn't."

He took the ring out of the box and I watched, terrified in case the ring didn't fit, but it slid right onto his finger. I had guessed at the size. Did this mean Peter and I were destined to be together?

In that moment, it felt so fucking right, and I threw myself into his arms, not wanting to let him go. Not now. Not ever.

He belonged to me, just as I belonged to him.

## Epilogue

*Niamh*
*Five Years Later*

I watched as my husband and our five-year-old son and three-year-old daughter were in his arms by the edge of the pool, and then they jumped inside. I laughed as he pulled them out of the water. He was teaching them to swim, and he promised me he wouldn't just throw them into the water.

Both of our kids had on armbands to help them float to the top. Not that they needed it. Peter wouldn't allow them to drown.

When I'd given Peter that wedding ring five years ago, I had done so not knowing I was already pregnant with our son, Ivan Peter Orlov. Peter had insisted we name our son Ivan. As for our daughter, I knew it was a risk, but I had named her Kaitlyn. In a strange way, if it hadn't been for Kaitlyn, Ivan would have never been in the hospital, and I'd have never met him. I wouldn't have known Peter, and I wouldn't be one happy woman enjoying the sunshine in the backyard.

I was also four months pregnant with our third child.

Peter loved when I was pregnant. We loved having kids.

Our marriage wasn't perfect. There were times we did fight and didn't quite meet eye to eye, but we never broke up. We always came back together and figured out how to make it work.

Ivan had known that I'd not said a word about what I knew about Kaitlyn, and after he learned about my pregnancy, I had the Volkov tattoo wrapped around my wrist. I had wanted it around my ankle, and I knew Ivan had been tempted to give me what I wanted, but all the wives of the Brigadiers who had earned their places held the same ink in the same place. It was ivy surrounding a V. It was a beautiful, delicate design.

With our son and daughter paddling in the water, Peter swam toward me, pulling me into his arms. I laughed as he tickled my armpits before sliding his arms around my waist.

"How are my precious bundles?" he asked.

This made me smile. "I'm feeling like the size of a tank, but I think he or she is okay."

We didn't know the sex of the baby. Peter loved the element of surprise. For a guy who wasn't big on surprises, he loved it when I surprised him and when our babies did.

He kissed my neck as our children gave out a squeal. "Thank you," he said.

"What for?"

"For choosing me."

As if I had a choice. I had fallen in love with Peter when I first met him, and that love had grown. There was no one else I wanted more in my life than Peter Orlov. The love of my life.

****

*Peter*

I should have known peace wouldn't last. Not when Ivan had the rest of the Brigadiers descend on my territory. Slavik, Aurora, Adelaide, Andrei, Charlotte, and Ive, as well as Victor, The Butcher, and The Beast were all invited to my country home to enjoy my barbeque, and the time I intended to spend with my wife and kids.

In our own way, we were one big, happy family. Our kids were all playing in the pool.

Niamh was enjoying the other women's company, and I got to watch her. With pregnancy, she just glowed. I knew through Ivan's pregnancy, we'd both been nervous. I had to coax Niamh out of the penthouse because she'd been so afraid of losing another baby.

Once Ivan was in her arms, though, everything was okay. We'd known it was going to be okay.

I glanced over at The Butcher and The Beast, who were playing with the kids in the pool, and I couldn't help but look toward Ivan, who was also watching them. Victor was also talking with Slavik and Ive.

"Have you made your choice yet?" I asked.

"I will make my choice when I have to."

"You know, you could always get The Butcher and The Beast to come to some arrangement. Maybe marry them off or something." I offered it as a suggestion.

Ivan merely nodded his head, but he didn't say a word.

"Thank you," I said, after a moment's silence.

He turned toward me. "Not just for helping me all those years ago and trusting in me, but also for giving Niamh to me."

Niamh had signed over all the Byrne empire belongings, which included a great deal of money and several properties. She told Ivan to do with it as he saw fit. Last I heard, the money had been invested into the properties, and hostels had been set up for men and women who'd been abused.

"You don't have to thank me. I'm just keeping

my promise that I made long ago to someone."

"Who?" I asked.

Ivan got to his feet and walked away, just as my wife came toward me. I pulled her into my lap, but I looked toward Ivan, and I knew whatever had started with Finn Byrne wasn't over yet. Either way, a monster was coming, and I knew we all had to be prepared for it.

Niamh held onto me, pulling me out of my troubled thoughts. This was Ivan Volkov, and I knew whatever he had planned, I would be by his side, fighting. I was Peter Orlov, Brigadier to Ivan Volkov, and he'd given me everything in this life.

Especially something I didn't know I could have.

He'd shown me that I was capable of love, because I loved my wife, I loved my children, and I would protect them with my life.

### The End

SAM CRESCENT

BESTSELLING BBW ROMANCE
SPICY ROMANCE FOR REAL WOMEN

**EVERNIGHT PUBLISHING ®**

**www.evernightpublishing.com**

www.ingramcontent.com/pod-product-compliance
Lightning Source LLC
Chambersburg PA
CBHW050713180626
46814CB00002B/415